What the Critics are saying...

"Ms. Kelly is also an excellent storyteller--her work is mentally engaging and physically stimulating." ~ *Angela Black, Sensual Romance*

"A Kink In Her Tails is a wonderful mix of stories with a little kink in them and a whole lot of love and romance. Ms. Kelly is a great author with the ability to make her readers feel a wide rage of emotions while reading each of these stories. All her characters are very likable and so down to earth that you feel that you personally know them yourself." ~ *Lisa Lambrecht, In The Library Reviews*

"...A KINK IN HER TAILS is an absorbing read, packed full of spice, sex, a hint of drama, and well-written story, and it's one that will leave the reader panting for more. I highly recommend this anthology for those daring enough to try out something a bit new and off the beaten path. Sahara Kelly has garnered yet another fan in this reader!" ~ *Amy Cunningham, Romance Reviews Today*

A Kink in Her Tails

Sahara Kelly

A KINK IN HER TAILS
An Ellora's Cave Publication, October 2004

Ellora's Cave Publishing, Inc.
1337 Commerce Drive, Suite 13
Stow, Ohio 44224

ISBN #1419951351

ISBN MS Reader (LIT) ISBN #1843605287
Other available formats (no ISBNs are assigned):
Adobe (PDF), Rocketbook (RB), Mobipocket (PRC) & HTML

Edited by Brianna St. James
Cover art by Syneca

Warning:

The following material contains graphic sexual content meant for mature readers. *A Kink In Her Tails* has been rated E–rotic by a minimum of three independent reviewers.

Ellora's Cave Publishing offers three levels of Romantica™ reading entertainment: S (S-ensuous), E (E-rotic), and X (X-treme).

S-*ensuous* love scenes are explicit and leave nothing to the imagination.

E-*rotic* love scenes are explicit, leave nothing to the imagination, and are high in volume per the overall word count. In addition, some E-rated titles might contain fantasy material that some readers find objectionable, such as bondage, submission, same sex encounters, forced seductions, etc. E-rated titles are the most graphic titles we carry; it is common, for instance, for an author to use words such as "fucking", "cock", "pussy", etc., within their work of literature.

X-*treme* titles differ from E-rated titles only in plot premise and storyline execution. Unlike E-rated titles, stories designated with the letter X tend to contain controversial subject matter not for the faint of heart.

Also by Sahara Kelly:

Beating Level Nine

Ellora's Cavemen: Tales from the Temple I

For Research Purposes Only: All Night Video

Guardians of Time: Alana's Magic Lamp

Guardians of Time: Finding the Zero-G Spot

Guardians of Time: Peta and the Wolf

Hansel and Gretty

Irish Enchantment

Knights Elemental

Madam Charlie

Magnus Ravynne and Mistress Swann

Mesmerized

Mystic Visions

Partners in Passion: Eleanor & Justin

Partners in Passion: No Limits with S.L. Carpenter

Persephone's Wings

Sizzle

Tales of the Beau Monde: Inside Lady Miranda

Tales of the Beau Monde: Lying with Louisa

Tales of the Beau Monde: Miss Beatrice's Bottom

Tales of the Beau Monde: Pleasuring Miss Poppy

The Glass Stripper

The Sun God's Woman

They Gypsy Lovers

A KINK IN HER TAILS

Acknowledgements

To all those who shared so generously with me during the writing of this story, my everlasting thanks. I hope you'll find I've treated this lifestyle with respect.

To one staunch friend whose support and encouragement never failed, whose seemingly endless supply of URL's took me to places I'd never dreamed of, and who continually urged me to open my mind to all the possibilities, I thank you. If not for you and Matilda, this book would never have been conceived, let alone written. Thanks, Boss.

And to Jen and Briana—there are no words sufficient to express my profound gratitude for your enthusiasm and support. Bless you both for letting me take a chance.

Apartment 4B

Chapter 1

It was Saturday morning. Nobody abused a doorbell at eight thirty on a Saturday morning. Nobody Eve Bentley knew, anyway.

Brrrriiiiinnnggg.

"Goddammit. I'm coming, I'm coming."

Eve sleepily dragged herself from her warm bed, slipped most of her body into her old chenille robe and tied the belt haphazardly round her waist.

She ran a hand through her spiky brown hair and stifled a yawn as she stumbled to the door before it made that disgustingly intrusive sound one more time.

She eased the door open a crack and tried to focus on whoever was disturbing her slumber so rudely.

"What?" she asked.

"Hello?"

She blinked and opened the door a smidgen more.

Oh lord.

He was delicious. Better than coffee. Her sore eyes relished the sight of him. Six foot-and-then-some of delectably masculine attributes. Shoulders that were just perfect for cuddling up to topped a broad chest and tapered down to a huggable waist. It was a package that cried out to be explored, all while being held close by a pair of muscular arms.

"Sorry to bother you…"

Eve shut her mouth with a snap, realizing her saliva had dried to dust and she couldn't swallow. She also realized she looked like death on a bad hair day and wished she could slam the door, go change, and start again.

Given that changing would involve a facial, a hair appointment and possibly some liposuction, she supposed it wasn't an option.

"I woke you, didn't I?"

Swell. Obviously the man was also an Einstein.

"Um, well, I was just going to...actually..."

"Here."

He thrust a package at her.

"This is so sudden. We hardly know each other." Eve couldn't stop the words from slipping out of her mouth.

His lips twitched. "It was delivered to my door this morning and I took it inside and opened it without realizing it. I am awfully sorry, but you know how it is before you've had coffee."

"Oh, do I ever."

She took the package from him and looked at it.

"It doesn't bite, you know. And I already opened it, so I can guarantee it doesn't explode."

"Yeah."

"So, it would probably be okay if you opened it and looked inside?"

"Think so?"

"Mmm hmm."

Eve looked at him again. Her hormones slapped her upside the head—hard. She could swear she heard her dear departed mother's voice someplace, yelling at her. *Eve, find a nice man, for God's sake. You're not getting any younger.*

"So, uh, did you have your coffee yet? I guess I'm just about to make some."

He tilted his head while he considered her contorted statement.

He grinned. "Hey, I'd love to. Can't do anything on just one cup, can you?"

"No. I mean yeah, I guess so. Or not. Or whatever. Why don't you come on in?"

"Thanks."

"Oh. One question."

"Sure."

"Who the hell are you?"

"Simon Austen. Nice to meet you."

He held out his hand, willing her to take it, wanting to touch the rumpled warmth he felt radiating from this enchanting woman.

"Eve Bentley, Ma..." she bit off the response as she shook his hand.

"Ma...? That would be the sheep Bentleys?"

"Sorry." She chuckled as she led the way into the kitchen. "That would be Eve Bentley, Marketing Design, which is how I usually introduce myself when shaking hands. Force of habit I guess." She glanced down at herself. "I remembered just in time that this wasn't a formal moment."

She made a half-hearted attempt to straighten her robe, which failed miserably, bringing a mental cheer to Simon's libido. From where she'd seated him at her small breakfast bar, he had an excellent view of the curve of her lovely breasts beneath her nightgown as she bent to the coffee machine.

She was delightfully mussed, warmly sleepy, and he was finding it hard to resist the urge to pick her up and carry her back to wherever it was she'd just gotten up from. He'd like to muss her some more.

A lot more.

His pants started to hurt.

"So you live here in the building, Mr. Austen?"

"Please, call me Simon. Yes, been here about two weeks, I guess, but what with trying to unpack and also meet a major deadline for a job, well...I really haven't been anywhere for the last ten days but my desk."

"Deadline?"

Simon had a feeling the question was probably more polite than interested. Damn, how long would it take this woman to wake up? To realize that from the first moment he'd set eyes on her, he'd developed a major case of lust, which was probably showing in his gaze and his pants?

"Yes. I'm an architect."

"Oh. How nice."

What she meant, of course, was oh, how boring. For the fifteen hundredth time in his life he wished he was a bullfighter, or a rodeo rider, or a NASCAR driver. Something that would get women's attention more than an architect.

"Would I know anything you've built?"

"Westgate Mall?"

"Don't shop there."

"How about Treetorn Towers?"

"Too high priced for me. But nice windows."

"Thank you. I picked them out myself."

She glanced up and grinned, doing severe damage to his brain cells. That grin of hers was seriously dangerous. It went all the way down his spine and settled comfortably somewhere over his crotch. He could have sworn it hummed when it got there.

"Cute," she answered.

"Aren't I?"

"No, I didn't mean that. I meant your windows crack."

"No they don't. And if they did, they wouldn't be cute." His rapid quip was out of his mouth before he'd really thought much about it. Something about her seemed to bring out his best lines.

There was a distinct moment of silence, when most everything paused. Even the coffee pot held its breath.

"Talking to you is like talking to a snake. Somehow the conversation winds back on itself and ends up biting its own ass."

"I haven't bitten your ass yet, have I?"

One mobile eyebrow flew up toward her serious bed hair. "You are getting quite fresh."

"No, no. You misunderstand. I'm already fresh. It's you who's slightly wilted. But I expect the coffee will put the starch back in your stem."

She shook her head slowly, and poured a large mug of coffee, adding cream and stirring it.

"May I have one too?"

"Oh sh—Oops." She blushed. She'd almost said shit and she actually blushed. Simon promptly fell in love.

"I guess so. That's why I invited you in, wasn't it?"

"I was hoping you were overcome with serious morning lust and wanted to get me naked in order to slake your wicked desires, but this will have to do, I guess…" He gave her his best impish grin while patting himself on the back for his amazing ability to tell the truth no matter what the circumstances.

"Well, in the absence of any desire slaking, how about I open this?" She waved her hand at the package she'd set down on the countertop.

"Mmm. Do." Simon, who already knew what was inside, restrained his urge to snicker.

She peered at the label. "That's odd. No name and no return address. Just the apartment number, which is a bit smeared I must admit. Are you sure it's not for you?"

"Absolutely."

"Oh well, I guess that could be a "B". And you're in…what, 4D?"

"Yep."

She was spreading the tissue aside as she spoke, delicately parting the folds in a way that Simon, for some reason, was beginning to find rather erotically stimulating.

He'd like to part her folds that way, he mused. She'd be pink, too, like the tissue, rippled and ready for him. But she'd be slippery and shiny and hot, not crackly and...her gasp interrupted his rather charming fantasy.

"Good God. It's a dead critter."

Simon burst out laughing. "No it's not," he huffed, gasping for breath at her horrified expression.

"Eeeeuww."

"Oh for Pete's sake, come on, look closely."

Simon picked up the box and tipped it sideways so that the contents fell out onto the tissue between them.

Eve poked at the mass of fur. "It's too small for a mink coat. And it's real fur so that lets out any of my past boyfriends. Never had one that would spring for the genuine article."

"How about present ones?"

"Don't have any."

Simon mentally cheered.

"It's not moving." Eve stared at the tangle on the tissue.

"No it's not. And it won't until you pick it up."

Eve reached between the furs to find a hard length, swathed in the softest suede leather. "Oh my. This is quite lovely."

Simon watched as she grasped the handle and straightened it out, letting the strands of fur slide into neat rows.

"It's a flogger, isn't it? I've seen some on the Internet." Her eyes were wide as she looked at the intricately braided strips that covered the handle and the clever loopy knots at top and bottom. The soft rabbit fur lashes slid through her fingers like sand.

Simon was finding this whole little scene incredibly arousing. God he was hard. If she didn't stop stroking the fur, he was going to grab the damn thing and demand she stroke him like that, not some inanimate object that couldn't appreciate the delicacy of her touch.

"Yes. Definitely a flogger. And handmade too, by the looks of it. Did you order it from someone locally?"

Eve's gaze flew to Simon. "I didn't *order* this. There must be some mistake." She scrabbled through the wrapping paper to find the label again.

"There's no return address, Eve. You already checked."

"I know, but…damn." She tossed the paper down with a frown. "Who on earth would send me one of these?"

She idly flipped her hand, watching the strands swing and sway.

"That's the question, isn't it?" agreed Simon, watching her expression as it changed from puzzled to contemplative.

The swing of her wrist got a little more deliberate.

Simon's cock got a little more rigid.

"My goodness, it seems to be very well-balanced, doesn't it? Just sways so nicely…"

The strands were swinging hypnotically and rhythmically, and Eve's tongue crept out to moisten her lower lip.

Even though she was in her old bathrobe, hair standing on end, no makeup and completely unaware of him, Simon was about as turned on as he could ever remember being.

She gave an extra swing and brought the lashes down on the counter with a thump.

Simon jumped.

Eve grinned. "Oh my."

Chapter 2

"So what did he do then?" Adele Martin put the finishing touches to Eve's nails and blew gently on them.

"Then he got a very funny look on his face, insisted I have dinner with him tonight, and left."

"What kind of a funny look?"

"Hard to tell. Kind of tight looking. Uncomfortable."

"And you were doing what?"

"I was just playing with the flogger, you know? Swishing it around, slapping it backwards and forwards a bit, slapping it on the counter—oh, I think I may have slapped it on my thigh once."

Adele laughed. "Well, sheesh, poor guy. I'm not surprised he got a tight look on his face. His pants were probably cutting his circulation off in a very delicate place."

Eve stared at her friend.

"Oh come *on*, Adele. I was in my ratty robe. I hadn't brushed my hair. Barely one cup of coffee under my belt, and you think I turned him on? Give me a break here."

"He asked you out, didn't he?"

"Well, yeah."

"And you said…"

"I may have been sleepy, but I wasn't dead. I said yes. What do you think I said?"

"And this is why I'm here doing your nails?"

"Well." Eve looked down at the shiny pink polish Adele was putting away in a small bag. "I suppose. I don't want him to think I'm a total scumbag all the time."

"Good God, Eve. You're a marketing manager. That's so far from scumbag it's absurd to even think like that."

"Yeah, but he hasn't seen me as the *suit*. He's only seen me as the *robe*."

"Which he obviously liked enough to ask out."

"Well, yeah, I guess…"

Adele sighed. "All right. Nails done. What else?"

Eve peeked hopefully at Adele's bag of tricks. "You're the expert, you tell me."

Adele sighed. "Honey, I'm a photographer, not a fashion consultant. You want to look good in black and white, I can help you. For a date? Hey, look at me, I'm not exactly successful in that department. What do I know?"

Eve looked bleak. "I don't know what to wear."

"Did he say anything about where he's taking you?"

"No. Just did I like Indian food. Which, luckily I do."

"Well, there you go. Indian restaurants are basically more on the casual side. So dress more on the casual side."

"And that would be…"

"No pearls." Adele grinned at her friend.

"Duh. Are we talking jeans here?"

"Nope. No jeans. Uh uh. Absolutely not."

"But my ass looks good in jeans."

"Sweetie, I have a feeling Mr. Simon Austen thinks your ass would look better in his bed."

"Really?" Eve's eyes widened. "Now there's a thought."

"Hey. Go for it. How long's it been?"

"Don't ask."

"So you're due for some fun. Go have a little. He sounds nice, check him out, if he's on the up and up, give him a spin."

"Give him a spin? Sheesh, Adele, where do you get these expressions?"

"Well, it sounds better than fuck around with him for a while and see if anything clicks."

Eve sputtered her soda. "Yep. You're right. It does. Not that I expect anything to come of it, of course. But maybe just a bit of fun."

Adele tilted her head as she packed her cosmetics neatly away in her photographer's bag. "Seriously, Eve. Did you like him?"

"Seriously Adele? Yeah. He was really nice. Very easy on the eye, that's for sure, but he seemed like fun, too. He had a good sense of humor, and he made me laugh. Which is quite an accomplishment, at that hour of the morning."

"And all this while you were playing with your flogger."

Eve slid from the chair with a final check of her polish. "Yeah. That whole flogger thing is the weirdest. I never ordered it, that's for sure, and yet here it is…" She eased it out of the box again and showed it to Adele.

Adele took it and gave it a few experimental swings. "Oooh nice, Eve. This is a beauty."

Eve raised an eyebrow as she watched her friend's smooth wrist action. "Adele, is there something you're not telling me?"

"Like what, hon?" Adele was now laying a few lashes down across a helpless sofa pillow with unerring accuracy.

"Like you are doing *that* with a scary amount of skill…"

Adele grinned at Eve. "Well, I may be divorced, but that was after being married for ten years. I was younger. We played."

"Really?"

"Sure."

"Um, Adele?" Eve moved closer to the older woman. "Show me?"

* * * * *

"Not too cold for you, is it?" Simon glanced down at the woman by his side who had snuggled herself into his leather jacket.

"Nope. You're the one who must be freezing, though. Are you sure you don't want…?" She tugged on the collar of his coat.

"I'm fine. I have you if it gets too chilly." He grinned, put an arm around Eve's shoulder and pulled her against him.

She glanced up at him and laughed back. "That Indian food was certainly warming. I loved every mouthful, but my God it's good to breathe something cold." She took a deep appreciative lungful of air, which coincidentally brought Simon's smell deep into her senses.

She drifted on the scent of leather, sandalwood and man.

"So you liked it, huh?"

"Oh yeah." She sighed, lost in her own sensuous little fantasy.

"Um—Eve? I was talking about the Indian food."

"Oh. Yes. Well, so was I. It was fabulous. Especially the tandoori."

Simon grinned again, cuddling her a little tighter to him. "Glad you liked it. God, I haven't walked with a girl like this in years."

"A girl? Oh wow, there's a lovely compliment."

"Yes. A girl. You. Soft, smells nice, small feet, curvy, definitely a girl."

Eve chuckled. "You know damn well what I meant. I haven't been called a girl since I don't remember when. I'm Ms. Bentley in the office and Ma'am everywhere else. I *hate* Ma'am."

"So, to me you're Eve-girl. Eve. Essence of woman. First woman. My woman. I like that."

Eve slowed her steps and looked uncertainly at Simon. "Your woman?"

Simon looked steadily back at her. "Eve, I can't hide the fact that I'm very attracted to you. I have been since I first saw you, rumpled and sleepy, and I can't believe it was only this morning. I feel like we've known each other for a long time."

Eve chewed her lip. "That really sounds kind of hokey, doesn't it? I mean I know people say things like that…"

"Can you deny that you feel an attraction to me?" Simon stopped in the street and reached out for Eve, pulling the lapels of his jacket to bring her close to his chest.

Eve gazed at him. The street lamps reflected from his eyes, dazzling her. She let her mind float and listened, for once, to her heart. "No, Simon. I can't deny it. It's there, and was the minute I opened my door this morning and saw you standing there."

Simon drew in his breath. "Thank God." He bent toward her, pulling her even closer.

"Simon?" Eve's hesitant voice breached the small distance between them as he lowered his lips to hers.

The first touch was electric. A brush of skin on skin, then another, then a firm pressure of silken flesh.

His arms went round her clasping her tight, tighter against him as if he wanted to pull her into his ribcage. His lips parted and the warmth of his tongue ran softly along her mouth. Unable to withstand his touch, Eve welcomed him inside.

He moaned as he invaded her moist depths, tongue flickering this way and that as if trying to learn every little dip and secret in the first five seconds. He tasted spicy and sweet, and she found the combination intoxicating.

Eve slid her hands up over his sweater and around his back, relishing his strength and loving the hardness of him. And speaking of hardness, there was a definite hardness making its presence known around her belly. He grew harder as she kissed him, pressing firmly against her and starting an ache way down between her thighs.

It was Eve's turn to moan as Simon slid one hand down to cup her buttocks and pull her impossibly closer. By lifting her slightly, he nudged his cock into the dip between her thighs and she gasped with the pleasure of it. His tongue plunged back into her mouth, darting back and forth as if it had a life of its own and was determined to thrust as deep as his cock when the time came.

And at that moment, Eve knew the time was here.

This was going to be her "wild" adventure. This was what she'd been waiting for. The one man, the one night, the one fuck that would go down in her personal history as the most incredible experience. When she was old and gray and knitting potholders for the senior center group, she'd be able to look back on this night and smile.

She wasn't looking for permanence, for a mate, for an "I do" or a white silk dress. She didn't know if she'd ever be ready for those things. They implied long-term things like commitment, devotion, trust and love. Things that scared Eve silly.

Right now she didn't want to be scared. She wanted to be fucked.

She pressed her hips against his arousal, rubbing herself wantonly over the distended fabric of his pants. "Come home with me?"

Simon raised his head, eyes sleepy with desire. "I was planning on it."

"No, I don't mean walk me home. I mean when we get there, come into my apartment with me. Don't leave now. Not now that we've found this." She put her hand to his cheek and tugged him back to her hungry lips.

He was more than ready, spinning her so that her back was to the wall of a store. He leaned in on her, pressing as much of his body as he could to hers. "God, Eve," he muttered, running his tongue from her ear to her collarbone.

"I know. I want this so badly. But I have to tell you I don't do this kind of thing."

Simon nibbled her earlobe and thrust his cock against her crotch. "What kind of thing is that, sweetheart?"

"Spend the night with men I don't know."

"You know me." His pants were working magic and she wanted them off him so badly she could scream.

"I don't know you very well. I only know that I want you. I want—this." She slid her hand down between them and gripped his cock through the fabric.

He groaned. "It's all yours, honey. All yours. I don't do this kind of thing either. Hell, I haven't dated in two years."

"I got you beat. It's been almost three since I had a real date."

Simon looked at her. "We're a fine pair, aren't we? What say we make up for it tonight?"

Eve met his look squarely. "Take me home and fuck me, Simon."

"It will be my pleasure, Eve."

She trembled. He held her close for a moment as they listened to their heartbeats pounding against each other.

"I hope you have protection, because I don't," muttered Eve.

Simon chuckled. "Ever the practical one, aren't you, babe? Don't worry. We're walking home, and if memory serves me, there's a drugstore along the way."

Eve blinked. She'd completely forgotten where she was. Damn, he was good. She hoped and prayed he'd be even better in bed.

"Come on. I think it's time we took this someplace more private." Simon grabbed her hand and hurried her down the street, heading to the all-night drugstore.

Eve raised an eyebrow as he grabbed a box of one hundred extra large condoms. "Optimistic?"

"Confident."

"Oh my." Eve swallowed. Visions of endless orgasms danced in her mind and nearly blinded her. Maybe even multiple orgasms, if there was such a thing, which she highly doubted. Perhaps the fuck fairy might grant her wish and show her that yes, Eve, there is a G-spot.

Well, okay, probably best not to push it *too* far.

Eve sighed, realizing she'd be happy just to wake up sore in the morning. That's all she asked. One night of very nice fucking. That wouldn't be too much, would it?

She looked at Simon as he paid for the box of condoms. To her, he looked like a God. Handsome inside and outside, funny, a pleasure to be with, single—oh God.

Eve grabbed his arm as they left the store. "You're not married, are you?"

Simon choked out a laugh. "Bit late to ask that, isn't it?"

"*Simon!*"

"No Eve," he answered, taking pity on her. "I'm absolutely not married. I can't stand guys who hit on other women when they have a wife at home. Or worse, a wife and kids at home. I'm probably not married because I like women too much to settle down with just one. And recently it's been all work all the time—I haven't had time to think much about women or marriage or dating or anything but my career."

Eve nodded and let him pull her back onto the sidewalk. "I hear you. Work can take over one's life, that's for sure."

He hugged her close again as the shadows of the street gave way to the lights in the parking lot of their apartment building. "Well, I promise that for the next few hours I'm not going to be thinking about work. I…" he dropped a kiss on her hair, "…am going to be thinking about you."

"You are?"

"Yep. Thinking about your lips, and your eyes, and a few other body parts." His hand slid to her behind and caressed it.

She sighed.

"Thinking about ways to explore those aforementioned body parts." His tongue flicked her ear.

"Okay. Time to stop or you're going to find out what it's like to get raped in an elevator." Eve hurried Simon through the security doors and up the elevator. She stared fixedly at the floor numbers because she knew if she looked at him she'd be all over him like frosting on a cupcake.

Simon grinned as she nearly dragged him to her apartment door. She heard him stifle his chuckle as she dropped her keys and cursed.

The door finally opened and she dragged him in behind her. "Oh God, Simon. *Now.*"

Chapter 3

Simon obliged.

He was in as much hurry as Eve was to get where they wanted to be. He didn't give her a chance to speak, just turned her as soon as they were in the darkened hallway.

The door slammed shut and he pressed Eve hard against it.

She hissed as his chest leaned into her breasts and he felt her nipples beading against him.

He wanted her so bad he could taste it. And her. His mouth bore down on hers harshly, taking everything she gave, demanding more. And he could feel her response, her passion, as she trembled beneath his assault.

Her hips ground against his cock in a blatant invitation he could not refuse.

"I want you."

Simon wasn't sure if it was his voice or hers. He decided it didn't matter. Their goal was the same. He grabbed her hands and pushed them up and back against the door, pinning her in place.

His lips and tongue challenged hers, teasing, plundering, keeping her on the edge of desire. Her position pushed her breasts at him and he swiftly moved to hold her wrists with only one hand.

The other fell to her shirt and with a swift move he bared her. Raising his gaze upwards until their gazes met, he watched her eyes as he slid his hand into her bra and cupped her breast. Her sherry-colored eyes blazed at his touch and he heard himself moan as his fingers teased and pulled her already-hard nipple.

It was almost too much, but nowhere near enough.

He bit his lip in frustration and quickly flipped the catch on her bra. He released her arms and freed her of her clothing, only to find her hands stripping his shirt off his shoulders.

He was going to lose it. Hurriedly he grabbed her hands again, pushing them even higher and bringing her to her toes.

His head fell and his mouth closed around her breast.

She choked out a sob as he let his tongue rove around the delicate skin, and pulled it taut with his mouth.

"God, Simon," she whispered. "Oh God."

She tasted of sweetness and woman and some powdery fragrance that tickled his nose. He sucked her hard, feeling her heartbeat increase.

"I can't take it," she gasped.

"Yes you can," he muttered, switching his attentions to the other breast, leaving the first glistening and rigid in the cool air.

"I need to touch you."

"No you don't, not if you want this to last." He attacked her softness, biting the nipple tenderly and rolling it between his teeth.

"Dear heavens, Simon, I can't—I really can't—" Her breath hitched and Simon felt her legs tremble.

Astounded, Simon realized she really was on the verge of her orgasm. Without even a second thought, he opened her pants and pulled them down over her hips, taking her underwear with them.

He slid his hand between her thighs, over the softness of her mound and pushed two fingers into the searing heat of her cunt.

His mouth and tongue worked her nipple as his fingers began to move.

He was as hard as he had ever been, yet his attention was focused on this woman who shuddered beneath his fingers. He felt like a maestro playing a perfectly tuned musical instrument that responded to his slightest touch. He knew his chest was against her soft body, he could feel his own pulse throbbing in his cock, but these sensations paled next to what was happening to Eve.

Her body was tensing, her breath coming in irregular gasps, and her juices were soaking his hand. Her nipple was bullet-hard against his tongue, pushing itself further into his mouth and demanding his touch.

He suckled her forcefully, and added a slight curl to his fingers.

Eve went rigid against the door. A strangled scream emerged from her throat and her thighs clamped together around his hand. He felt her cunt squeeze his fingers in fierce contractions as her whole body shook with the force of her orgasm.

He leaned against her and took her tremors into his soul.

"Oh. My. God." Eve's body turned to jelly against him, and he had to hold her entire weight to stop her from sliding bonelessly to the floor.

"Are you okay?" Simon quietly asked the woman panting in his arms.

"No."

"You're breathing."

"Are you sure? I thought I just died and went to heaven."

Simon snickered. Judging it safe to release his hold on her, he let her arms down and gently rubbed her shoulders.

She moved a little and kicked herself free of her pants. "You have too many clothes on, Simon. We have to do something about that."

"In a moment." He was certainly hard enough, and ready enough, but he was finding an unusual pleasure in watching Eve as she recovered from the depths of an intense climax. He wanted to see the heat return to those burning eyes as he brought her to another orgasm in a little while. They had all night. There was no hurry.

His cock, however, although impressed with all this whimsy, was definitely sending a message loud and clear. *Let me out!*

As if reading his mind, Eve's hands moved gently to his fly and she unzipped him, delving into the folds to release his straining erection.

"Oh, my. Nice."

Simon smiled a little painfully. "Thank you. I couldn't have done it without you."

Eve pushed Simon's pants down and knelt to help him free himself from his shoes and socks. His cock waved politely at her, growing even more in an attempt to impress her.

She was clearly impressed.

A soft stroke from base to tip nearly did him in.

"Let's get a little more comfortable. Follow me."

Seeing that Eve had a hand firmly around his cock, Simon saw few, if any, options. And that was just fine by him.

She led him into her living room and stopped in front of a large armchair.

"Sit, Simon," she encouraged, releasing his cock and pushing him down gently.

The rough fabric of the chair grated across his buttocks and the backs of his thighs as Eve knelt between them and spread his legs wider.

Her intentions were obvious, and his heart began to pound savagely, as once again she took him in her hands and gently stroked his length.

This time, however, she licked her lips.

* * * * *

Eve couldn't recall the last time she'd felt such an overwhelming need to taste a man. Actually, she didn't think she ever had.

Oral sex was not something she usually indulged in. Tonight with Simon was very different. She dipped her head and placed a quick butterfly kiss on the head of his cock, just to see what would happen.

On the surface, nothing did. But she sensed his thigh muscles tighten on either side of her body, and noticed his knuckles whitening on the arms of the chair.

She slid her hands up the inside of his thighs, enjoying the roughness of his hair as she pressed against its growth patterns.

"Move closer, Simon," she breathed, digging her fingers into his flesh and pulling, showing him what she wanted him to do.

Obligingly, he slid his buttocks forward on the chair, slumping back against the tufts. His cock thrust upwards from its nest of dark hair and his balls hung full and warm just over the edge of the seat.

Now she could play.

She wasn't sure how to, at first, but then remembered snippets of conversation she'd heard from her girlfriends during their endless gabfests on their favorite subject—sex. Basically, the theory proposed that anything you do to a man with your mouth he'll love. There were no rules.

Eve began by examining Simon's cock with almost clinical interest, feeling the veins that bulged from the smooth surface and the dips and ridges that formed the head. She opened herself to his responses as she touched and smoothed different places, noting his strong reaction to her light contact with a little spot beneath the head.

A small bubble of moisture wept from the tiny hole at the tip of his cock and she touched it gently, working it over the deeply reddened flesh.

She was intent on her task and almost jumped as his hand touched her head.

She glanced up at him, to see his eyes half closed and his cheeks flushed.

"Am I doing something wrong?"

"Oh no, babe. I just wanted to make sure you're real."

Holding his gaze, Eve daringly lowered her body and watched his eyes as she slid her tongue around the top of his cock. He seemed to blank out for a couple of seconds when she first touched him, then his focus intensified until the heat of his gaze burned her skin.

She dropped her head forward and tried something else, sliding her tongue down to the base of his cock and tracing the veins back up to the tip. She flicked that little sensitive spot on the way, and was pleased to note that a definite moan resulted.

One more time she swiped his hardness with her tongue, leaving a trail of warm wetness behind. She loved his taste, musky, clean and male. He smelled of warm nights and strong hands, and a body that was hers to play with all night long.

Taking a deep breath, she pulled him into her mouth and fastened her lips around him.

It was his turn to sob, and she glanced up to see his eyes shut, head tilted back and the cords in his neck standing out. He was beautiful.

Again she sucked on him, letting him slide from her mouth with a little plop and then immediately sucking him back in again, as deep as she could. Her technique could probably use work, but Simon didn't appear to mind.

She decided to add a little something to her skills, and slid a hand beneath the cock she was energetically sucking to find his balls. He flinched as she ran her fingers over the soft sac, now pulsing with his heartbeat and tightening as his arousal grew.

It was a heady feeling, to hold a man's responses in her hand and her mouth, and Eve decided she liked the feeling of power it gave her. She enjoyed knowing that she was reducing this man to a state of limp ecstasy simply with her fingers and her tongue. She allowed his balls to move a little within her cupped hand, and stroked behind them to find what her friends had described as a "magic spot."

Her adventuring fingers brought another groan from Simon and he writhed in the chair.

"Eve, honey, what are you…oh God, please Eve—"

Eve wasn't sure if the "please" was to stop or go on. She decided to go on. Mouth continually sucking and releasing as much of his cock as possible, Eve let her hand rove around his balls to the flesh behind and stroke, flick and press the tender flesh she found there.

Simon's harsh breaths told her of her success.

"I'm going to come, Eve, honey…I can't stop—" Simon gasped out the words as his hands scrabbled to pull away from Eve's unrelenting mouth.

Committed to bringing him to climax, Eve soldiered on, sticking to his cock like a limpet. She wanted to be part of that moment when he lost it, when he gave up his tranquility and surrendered to that base human need to procreate, to spurt his cum into another human being.

She felt his balls tighten against his flesh and his whole cock began to throb as she caressed it with her tongue and lips. Intensifying her efforts, she took him in as deep as she could without gagging and sucked him strongly, letting the sides of her mouth tug on his super-sensitive flesh.

"Eve…" he squawked, trying desperately to pull back.

She wouldn't let him.

On a gasp and a shout, Simon came.

His cock jumped in her mouth, muscles twitching, veins throbbing. She felt the spurt of his cum warm and salty, as he erupted down her throat. It was an amazing moment, and one she had always thought she'd dislike intensely. But as she swallowed his juices, she felt a sense of accomplishment and delight.

She, Eve Bentley, had sucked a guy off. And done a pretty good job of it, too, if his blissful state of inertia was anything to go by.

She regretfully allowed his cock to slip from her lips, giving it a last farewell salute with her tongue.

She sighed and leaned her head against Simon's thigh, while his hand gently stroked her head.

"My God, Eve. What can I say?"

She grinned. "How about something like 'nice job, Eve', or 'that was the best I've ever had'?"

"Eve, that wasn't a *nice* job it was outstanding, and it was so much more than the best I've ever had. Words fail me. It was bliss."

"Oh. That's nice too." A warm feeling stole over Eve as she ran her hand idly up and down Simon's shin. She felt a little tug on her hair.

"Hey, sweetheart. Now we know that I give good door, and you give great chair, can we find out what we can do in bed?"

Chapter 4

They lay together on the bed, chest to breast, heart to heart, cock to pussy. Simon ran his hands up and down Eve's body, learning her curves, discovering the silky feel to her skin and just absorbing her into his mind. Her scent, her sounds, her roundness, all intrigued him and became worthy of his intense study.

"What are you doing?" she asked lazily, as he continued his silent caresses.

"Playing," he answered softly. "Do you mind?"

Eve stretched like a cat. "Oh no. I like it. In fact you'll have to forgive me if I purr…" She leaned in to his touch as he reached for her buttocks and stroked them.

"I'm glad you like it. I've always been a tactile person. You can learn so much from touching someone." Simon ran his hands down her thighs.

"Really? Like what?"

Simon had to smile at that essentially feminine question. He knew the translation was "what are you learning about me?"

"Well, for example, I can tell that you like to walk."

"Hmm."

"Really. This muscle here," he pressed against the back of her thigh. "It's nice and firm. It obviously gets used, and that comes from walking a lot. So you move around, maybe walk for pleasure, you're not a desk person by any means."

His hand moved slowly up, caressing the curve of her bottom and settling comfortably with a cheek cupped in his hand.

"And here, we have a wonderfully womanly curve."

Eve snorted. "Nothing wonderful about it. It's my butt and has more in common with the acreage covered by a third world country than a womanly curve."

Simon squeezed it firmly, making her wriggle. "I don't know what it is that women fear about their backsides, Eve, but you have one of the nicest ones I've ever seen. If you think I want to grab on to a handful of skin and bones, you're way off base."

Eve sighed as he clenched his fingers into her buttock and drew her even closer to his hardness.

"I want to know I'm holding a woman. I want to have my hands full of your body, your flesh. I want to be able to grab onto a real pair of hips and have them ride me, or tug them right where I need them so I can sink into the heat of you all the way to my tonsils…" He slipped his tongue over her ear as he spoke, sensing her shivers.

"And when we play together and you're on your knees waiting for me to fuck you oh so sweetly from behind, I want to look down and see warm and willing buttocks parting for me, trembling for me."

Eve's breath was coming faster now, and he could hear her ragged swallow as she listened to his words.

"Really?" Her question came on a breath expelled in a whoosh as he pulled and squeezed her plump curve.

"Really. Let me show you."

He rolled her onto her stomach and eased her arms onto the pillow above her. Straddling her legs, he let his rapidly hardening cock rest against her as he placed both hands onto her buttocks.

She pressed up into his touch with a little sigh of pleasure and widened her thighs slightly, allowing his cock to fall between them. With a small chuckle she pressed them gently back together, bringing a moan of delight to Simon's throat.

"Oh my," he breathed.

"Oh yeah," she whispered.

Carefully, Simon bent to her body. His tongue, his teeth, his lips, all paid homage to the womanly swellings of her bottom.

He nipped and nibbled, licked and sucked, and even left a few love bites that he immediately soothed with a swipe of his tongue. He played to his heart's content, loving the feel of her flesh between his teeth. The primeval urge to mark what was his flooded him, just as sensation flooded his loins with her movements.

He found himself shifting slightly, rubbing his cock between her thighs as he continued to squeeze and knead her backside. Daringly, he pulled the cheeks apart and used his fingers to spread her own juices over her little ring of tight muscles.

He had to laugh at her little yip of surprise.

"Simon?" she said, half raising her body from the bed, and incidentally brushing his cock at the same time.

He gritted his teeth. "Don't sweat it, Eve. I'm just playing here. And you're learning about your body, aren't you?"

"Mmm," she subsided as his caresses continued, light and teasing and gentle around what he knew was virgin territory. He was incredibly aroused at the thought that his was the first touch to awaken her to new possibilities.

Her scent was strengthening, and he knew she was softening into arousal beneath him. Her cunt was wet and he could almost feel the heat radiating from her as she prepared herself for his possession.

"Simon," she moaned, "Please..." She squirmed beneath him, rubbing her breasts against the bed and incidentally rubbing his cock between her thighs.

He suppressed a groan and gave her cleft a last firm swipe with his moistened fingers.

She gasped.

He rose up onto his knees and helped her roll onto her back.

Rosy and flushed in the light of the single lamp she'd turned on, Eve lay sprawled beneath him, body open, gleaming, and waiting.

Waiting for him.

He reached for the box next to the bed.

* * * * *

Dear God, if he didn't get that wonderful cock inside her within seconds she was going to spontaneously combust.

She swore she could feel her clit poking into the air from beneath its hood of delicate tissue. She swore her breasts were at least three sizes larger than they had been this morning, and her nipples felt like the Rock of Gibraltar.

Yet Simon was just looking at her as he sheathed himself.

And that was probably the most arousing thing of all.

"Simon," she whispered. "Don't keep me waiting much longer, please…"

She hadn't meant to beg, she just couldn't help it. The heat in his eyes as he surveyed her body spread out wantonly in front of him was stoking the furnace that threatened to blow her cunt sky high.

She could almost feel his gaze on her flesh, his breath on her skin, and the drops of moisture from his beautiful cock.

She had never imagined it was possible to want a man as much as she did at this moment.

Her world had gone, disappeared, vanished into a miasma of desire and need and want. Her whole focus was on Simon, his cock, and how soon he was going to thrust it where it belonged—inside her.

She got her answer.

Simon moved. Slowly, but relentlessly, he spread her thighs wide and slipped between them.

Teasingly he grasped his cock and stroked it against her pussy, smearing her juices over them both.

She sobbed. "Do that again and I'm finished." The words burst from her as she fought to quell the spiral that was ripping her thoughts into shreds and destroying her pretense of control. She was left facing a raw truth.

She wanted him to fuck her. Now.

As if reading her emotions from her gaze, Simon stared deeply into her eyes. He raised himself into position.

"Now, Eve-girl. My Eve. Essence of woman. Now."

He thrust into her, hard. All the way. He buried his cock so deep she didn't know where it ended inside her.

Her body screamed with joy and her heart stopped beating for long moments as she adjusted to the exquisite sensation.

He slid out and back in, establishing a rhythm that pounded against her and drove her to the brink again and again.

"Oh yes, God, Simon, yes…"

She grabbed his shoulders and hung on for the ride of her life.

His hips thrust against her, his balls slapped her buttocks. The bed shook with their frantic coupling, and Eve struggled for breath.

Simon lifted one of her legs and pulled it high around him, allowing him even deeper access to her cunt.

She gasped as his thrusts were now directly colliding with her clit and driving her ever higher onto another plane of sensation.

Her breath sobbed from her lungs in time with his pounding possession, and she drove her fingers deep into his flesh as she struggled to prolong the pleasure of her rising orgasm.

But Simon was determined. His thrusts never lessened in ferocity, and his rhythm was unceasing. She was being battered by his body and loving every minute of it.

Her leg tightened against him and she slid the other up to lock her ankles around his waist.

He slipped a hand between their bodies, angling her slightly and allowing him access to her clit.

And as he touched it, her world exploded.

He pressed hard and her muscles responded, tightening, shivering, trembling with an awe-inspiring tension.

He flicked it and thrust at the same time and it was as if boiling water was being poured over her buttocks and breasts.

He pulled it and released it…

And she fell.

Fell into a void of sensation where there was only light and sparkles, shudders and spasms.

Where her body turned into a cauldron of molten lava, existing solely for the purpose of swamping the hard cock buried deep inside her.

Where her mind blanked out, her vision blurred, and she could hear nothing but the pounding of her heart as it struggled to cope with the orgasm that was wreaking havoc on her physical and mental existence.

Where the sensation of clamping down around Simon's cock was all that mattered for the long minutes she spent coming over and over again.

Where the sound of his shout was a vague echo of her own noises, and the feel of him pulsing as he spurting his cum caused yet another round of spasms as her cunt reacted according to its programming. It didn't know anything about condoms or protection. It just wanted to pull that seed up to the fertile meadow of her womb.

For a microsecond, Eve yearned for that too.

As her tremors abated, she wondered briefly what it would be like to have Simon fill her with his hot cum. To have it bathe the gateway to her ovaries and to spend the next hours hoping that life had begun.

The thought vanished as Simon rested his forehead against hers, breathing heavily.

"Holy fucking shit, Eve. My God."

Breathless, Eve panted as he carefully eased to her side.

"It was quite a religious experience, wasn't it?" She tried to grin, but her face muscles were as exhausted as the rest of her.

"Church bells rang from here to Samoa." Simon took care of the condom and snuggled them both down beneath the covers.

She was impressed he had the strength. She was just a puddle of sated lust and she loved it.

He wriggled her into his arms, pressing her head down onto his shoulder and letting her find the right spot to relax into.

She looped one thigh over his legs and slid her hand over his chest, hugging him limply as she settled against him.

Eve sighed.

"Happy?" Simon dropped a soft kiss on top of her head.

"Mooo."

"Pardon?"

"That was Eve, contented cow."

"Got it." His chest rumbled with his laughter and brought a smile to Eve's lips.

"Simon?"

"Mm-hmm?"

"Is it always like that for you?" God, why had she asked that? Eve mentally smacked herself around the ears. She sounded like a romance novel virgin. Blechhh. "Sorry. That was a really stupid question."

She rubbed her blushing cheeks against his chest.

"It wasn't a stupid question, Eve. It was a very appropriate one, given my answer. And that answer is—no. It's not always like that."

He turned slightly and ran a finger over her cheek. "This is going to sound like a stupid line too, but it's never been like that. Not for me."

Eve stilled, watching the shadows on his face, wishing she could see his eyes more clearly. Something told her he was being honest with her. Something else told her this might classify as one hell of a "scary moment."

Honesty like this between two people who scarcely knew each other? There was a concept.

"Oh boy." She breathed slowly, absorbing the shift that had just occurred between them.

"Um, Eve?"

"Yeah?"

"What do we do now?"

She knew exactly what he was asking. Their lovemaking had blown them both away. They were in new territory, someplace where neither of them could have imagined being before this night.

"Well, Simon, actually…I don't know. We could sleep, or maybe fuck some more…" She trailed her hand down his body and circled his resting cock. It pricked up its head to listen as she talked. "We could perhaps run a double blind study of our responses. Screw each other senseless for the rest of the night and see if that one time was a fluke or something."

Simon laughed and hugged her.

"I like your train of thought. Logical, scientific and horny. Quite a combination."

Eve chuckled. "Well, this is a new situation for me. Cuddling with a man who has just turned my world upside down…" Her voice trailed off as she realized the truth of what she'd just said.

And the foolishness of saying it out loud.

She waited for him to start with the "It's getting late and I should leave now" things that usually accompanied a statement like the one she had just stupidly made.

"I'm glad."

His answer ricocheted off her heart and zinged its way around her brain like the rolling sound of thunder.

"You are?"

"Yep. Because I'd hate to be the only one in this bed who is having difficulty coming to terms with the fact that my toes are smiling."

"Wow. That good, huh?"

"Yep again. Like nothing I've ever experienced, Eve. Nothing."

"Oh my." She thought about that. "Me too, Simon. Actually I never really knew that sex could rattle my back teeth like that."

"Not sex, Eve. Not sex. I think that may have been the difference. We didn't have sex."

"We didn't? Sure felt like it to me." Eve bit her lip, realizing how trite she sounded.

"We made love, Eve. Oh sure, we fucked, and we had fantastic sex, but we actually made love. It's different. You know it and I know it."

Eve gave a little sigh and cuddled closer to his wonderful warmth.

"I know, Simon, I know. And it's damn scary."

"So back to my question, what do we do now?"

She closed her eyes and let the steady beat of his pulse soothe her chaotic thoughts. "Well, perhaps we ought to revisit this conversation in about six months or so. In the meantime, let's just have fun, okay?"

"You, Eve-girl, are a coward."

"Yep." She snuffled against him. "So sue me."

Chapter 5

Simon had taken her at her word.

Six months.

They'd spent six of the happiest months Eve could have imagined. They'd dated, and played, and spent enormous amounts of time in bed together.

Their lives were busy, professionally, and they'd agreed to work around their schedules. Neither Simon nor Eve wanted their relationship to jeopardize their careers. Ideally they hoped their days and nights could blend into one long orgy of delight.

Without their realizing it, they'd slipped into each other's lives and nested there. Neither could have explained the need to "touch base" with the other at regular intervals, or the sudden urge to check the other's cell phone now and again. It had grown slowly but surely, leading them ever deeper into their entanglement.

Six months had passed and they had reached a point where it was now becoming clear. They were a couple whether they admitted it or not. They had begun finishing each other's sentences. He knew her dress size, she bought him the socks he liked so much. When they were on sale, of course.

Their apartments were merging, with his shorts at her place and her makeup at his. They survived the "meet the parents" experience, although both confessed it was a nightmare they'd rather not have to go through again.

They became more adventurous, renting the occasional XXX movie and experimenting afterwards. Their physical need for each other deepened. They were two intelligent adults.

They both knew there needed to be more.

They had become a little more edgy with each other, a little harsher in their lovemaking. The neediness was overtaking the rapture.

Eve sensed a very strong protective urge in Simon—he was a traditionalist in so many ways. Whether taking her arm as she crossed the street, or unthinkingly opening a door for her, his was a very masculine nature. He did these things without realizing them; they were part of who he was.

She didn't mind. He wasn't patronizing, arrogant or aggressive. Except, occasionally the latter, in bed. Which was fine. Especially when she got to return the favor and take him any way she wanted.

But Eve wondered if this male-thing of Simon's would become overwhelming if they took their relationship to the next logical level and actually discussed the "m" word. The mere thought of that scared the crap out of her.

Eve was frightened. She admitted it privately to herself the morning before their sixth-month anniversary.

Simon had been away at a conference for the past week and it had been six days since they'd seen each other, emails and hour-long phone calls in the evening not counting, of course. He was due home the following evening.

They divided their time between apartments, usually opting to go to whomever's was cleanest, and tonight it was going to be her place all the way. Neither had gone out of their way to mention the significance of this date, but both knew the deadline was bearing down on them.

Eve's cautious nature was coming to the fore and making her very nervous. She worried about a million and one different things so that she wouldn't have to worry about the one big thing. Did she love Simon enough to marry him?

Would he ask?

Could she spend the rest of her life with him? Would she lose something if they became a married couple?

She'd seen so many of her friends divorce. Too many. She'd seen other women become a shadow of their husbands. Losing their own identity to his. Giving up their jobs to stay at home with the kids, and giving up their own rights to their own lives as a result.

Her worries had led her upstairs to Adele's kitchen, where the two women shared a companionable cup of coffee.

"So you see why I'm scared to death," confessed Eve.

"I do. I also see it's a bit silly of you," said Adele calmly, watching Eve as she fidgeted.

Eve sighed. "Yeah. You'd think I was fifteen instead of twenty-seven." She swirled her cup around. "I do love him, Adele. I really do. But loving someone and then saying well that's enough for us to spend the rest of our lives together…that's a big jump."

"Actually, it's a big leap of faith." Adele smiled at Eve. "Don't forget who you're talking to here. I know what it's like to make that leap, and I know what it's like to fall."

Eve bit her lip, not wanting to cause her friend any discomfort. "I'm sorry, Adele. If this is not a good subject for you…"

"No, no. Don't be silly. Water under the bridge as far as I'm concerned. Maybe my perspective can help a little." She leaned back in her chair, balancing on the two back feet.

"Tell me this, Eve. Do you trust Simon?"

"Well, of course."

"I mean really trust him?"

"With my life."

"How about with your body?"

"Excuse me?" Eve frowned.

"I mean do you trust him enough to relinquish control of your body to him?"

Eve thought for a moment. "You mean like be submissive to him?"

"Yep. You visited those Internet sites we talked about, didn't you?"

Eve grinned, remembering the research she'd surreptitiously done after she'd received her mystery flogger. "Yeah. Interesting stuff."

"It is interesting. And often revealing. You say you love Simon, but don't know if you are able to commit to a lifetime together. You're afraid. Perhaps the issue here isn't so much one of love, but one of trust."

"I'm not sure I understand."

Adele sighed. "I'm not really sure I do, either. I just know that for a good marriage there has to be trust as well as love. Along with respect and all the other nice stuff. You can't know what he's feeling, but you can find out what you're feeling. Find out whether you trust him enough to let him control you."

"You mean like pass him my flogger and say here, beat me if you want to?"

"Not quite." Adele chuckled. "It doesn't work that way. Or it shouldn't."

Eve sighed her relief. "Well, good. I don't believe in handing someone a loaded gun and saying go ahead and shoot me with it."

"But that's just it. You do need to trust Simon enough to hand him a 'loaded gun.' Could you do that?"

Eve's mind whirled. Could she?

Could she hand her body over to him? Completely?

She gazed down into her coffee cup, not seeing the liquid or the china or her hands gripping it firmly.

She saw Simon's eyes. Calm, smiling, loving, on fire with passion, his eyes had never shown her anger or temper. Even when they argued, and they'd had some really amazingly intense arguments, she'd never seen his eyes darken into fury.

She realized at that moment that she did trust him. She trusted him to love her. And THAT was the defining thought.

She looked up from her cup and smiled at Adele.

"Yes. Yes I could give him a loaded gun. I trust him and I do believe, all the way down to my toes, that he loves me and wouldn't ever hurt me."

Adele smiled back. "You're on your way, girl."

"Hmm."

"What?"

"Adele, you remember those Internet websites?" Eve's eyebrow rose in a wicked curve.

"Yes…"

"Would you help me arrange a welcome for Simon tomorrow night? A really interesting one?"

* * * * *

The apartment building was quiet as Simon pulled his suitcase from the elevator and headed for his front door. He wanted desperately to go straight to Eve's and just bury himself in her, putting the last few days of annoying business meetings behind him, but he'd had his instructions.

Yesterday the cryptic emails had begun and his curiosity was now completely aroused, along with something else that had been bumping his shorts whenever he thought about his messages.

The first had been pretty straightforward.

"I'm looking forward to you being home, and I think I'm going to plan a special welcome for you. Would my place be OK? Eve@blackstonegroup.org"

Well, of course. Her place, his place, the back stairwell, anywhere would be just fine. As long as it involved him and Eve, naked. He'd grinned and spent the next couple of hours mildly distracted at contemplating what a "special" welcome might entail.

At lunchtime he'd checked his email.

"I've been thinking long and hard about you. Not difficult seeing as there's much that's long and hard about you that I adore. LOL. Will you do me a favor and go to your place first? Shower, change, then come to me about seven o'clock? The welcome should be ready by then. Eve@blackstonegroup.org"

His anticipation grew as the instructions became a little more specific.

"I've left some new clothes for you at your place that I think you may find pleasing. I certainly wish to please you. In fact, you might say that my desire is to please you. In any way. *Eve@blackstonegroup.org*"

Okay. Now his shorts were tight and his palms were sweating. The last meeting of the day was an ordeal. His focus was shot, his attention wandered, and it was a good thing that this was just a formality to close the contract between his firm and their new client.

Good wishes had been exchanged, dinner invitations politely declined on the grounds of an early flight, and Simon had all but raced back to his hotel room to check his email.

What he found sent his pulse pounding and his hand reaching for the phone.

"Simon, I am aching for your return. My body is lonely and lost without its mate. My breasts are waiting for your hands to cup them and stroke them and my nipples yearn to harden between your fingers."

Simon used the aforementioned fingers to flick a bead of sweat from his brow and undo the zipper on his pants before he inflicted serious damage to himself.

"My pussy is yours, Simon, my darling, my master. It cries for you when you are not here to fill it. It weeps with joy when you honor it with your lips. It shudders with pleasure at the touch of your tongue."

Okay. This was getting decidedly hot.

Simon slipped out of his trousers all together, threw the rest of his clothes onto the bed and enjoyed the rough rasp of the chair against his buttocks as he resumed his seat in front of his laptop.

His hand fell to his cock. He felt a bit self-conscious, like some pimply teenager visiting a porn site, but imagining Eve as she wrote these words to him was turning him on like nothing he could ever remember.

"My pleasure will be to give you pleasure, Simon. Whatever your wants, whatever your needs, I am here to fulfill them. Tomorrow night, I shall give you my body, my heart and my soul. Use them as you will."

Whatever his needs? Simon shivered.

He reached for the phone and dialed her number. It rang four times. Then the machine clicked on. He sighed.

"Sorry – leave a message please. Oh, and if this is Simon, get some rest, honey. I want you to be fit and masterful when you get home."

"Uh…Eve? It's Simon. Uh…okay…I'll see you tomorrow."

Jesus. Masterful? As he hung up his mind flashed on leather, spiked heels and laces.

He tugged on his cock with long firm strokes, eyes closed, fantasizing about the wonderful things he wanted to do with and to Eve. He bypassed the domination scenario and went straight to the heart of things. Her breasts in his hands, her tongue held captive by his, he'd rub himself all over her, imprinting her once again on his brain.

He grasped his cock tighter, just as a chime announced he had mail.

He opened his eyes, keeping his rhythm, and read the next note from Eve.

"Thinking of you is making me so hot, Simon. Thinking of taking you in my mouth and sucking you deep into my throat. I need your touch so badly. I didn't know I'd miss you as badly as I have. I'm thinking of your cock, your big wonderful cock, and wishing it was here sliding inside me right now. I wish your balls were slapping me, I wish your hands were slapping me. I wish...I wish...I have to touch myself, Simon. I have to release my love for you even though you're not here. May I? May I do this, Simon? Give me permission...just email me back one word...yes. I'm here waiting, my clit ready to burst, waiting for you to say yes...I know you've called me, but I can't let myself talk to you. Not yet. Eve@blackstonegroup.org"

Yessssss.

He gasped as his cock leapt within his hand and he came hard, spurting his cum across his belly and onto his chest. His body throbbed and his spine tingled, and his mind blurred with visions of Eve.

He'd taken a few moments to recover and wipe himself off, blushing a little at his unrestrained behavior. He hadn't realized what an effect suggestive email could have.

Or maybe it was the fact that it was from Eve. For him.

With hands that still trembled a little, he opened an email to Eve and typed one word.

Yes.

He hit the send button, and sat back, eyes closed, thinking of Eve and wondering if she was in her little study in front of her computer, or if she'd now go into her bedroom and climb up on her bed.

If she'd play with the little vibrator he'd bought her as a joke.

To his amazement, his cock stirred.

He sighed, realizing that it was getting late. He had an early flight and a long day of traveling ahead of him. Practically, he knew he needed to get to bed. Realistically, he knew a cold shower would probably help.

However, neither activity had cleared thoughts of Eve from his mind, and every minute that had passed bringing him closer to her had seemed like an hour.

Now he was here, outside her door, and debating whether or not to honor her request.

Then he remembered the fun and anticipation he'd had reading her emails. The rush of adrenaline flooded his tired body and he turned away to his own door.

What he found inside spread tidily across his bed raised his eyebrows and sent his pulse racing.

He'd always wanted leather pants.

Chapter 6

Eve ran her eyes over the apartment one last time.

"Do you think it looks all right?"

Adele snickered. "Sweetie, Simon isn't going to be running his finger over your coffee table and checking for dust. He's going to be coming in here for you."

Eve's teeth worried at her lower lip. "It's twenty minutes to seven. I'd better see if I can get into this stuff…" She waved her hand at a small pile of leather that adorned the bottom of her bed.

"Go ahead. Yell if you need help with any of it. I'll light the candles and we'll double check for effect."

Adele moved round the room lighting the several candelabra that Eve had arranged carefully on her bureau and bedside table.

Eve took a deep breath and stepped into her bathroom, closing the door behind her. She was showered, shaved, plucked, moisturized, and perfumed. She couldn't think of anything else she needed to do to herself.

Her favorite women's magazine would have been so proud of her. She could have headlined the article on "101 Things To Do Before You Seduce That Man Of Yours."

Stalling for time, Eve slipped her robe off her shoulders and stood naked in her bathroom, wincing at the unforgiving fluorescent lights. She took a deep breath, knowing that she was only postponing the inevitable.

She slipped into the leather thong. It was snug, but more comfortable than she'd expected, the caress of the cool leather between her buttocks heightened by the feel of the air on her flesh. It was a kick.

Less easy was the collar and she struggled a little with the buckle that latched the piece together. A large ring was attached to the front, and Eve snapped the chain "leash" to it, tossing it over her shoulders and out of the way.

Next she reached for the nipple jewelry.

Adele had talked her into this, and for a couple of seconds Eve's rational mind revolted. What on earth was she thinking of? Nipple jewelry for God's sake. She'd only gotten her ears pierced last year. What would be next? A belly button ring? Tattoos?

Fortunately, this adornment required no bodily piercing, and Eve gently slid two small loops over her nipples and tightened them. A delicate rope of crystal beads swung between her breasts and a short drop fell from each rosy tip.

She gritted her teeth and glanced in the mirror.

She gasped.

It looked fabulous. Her nipples were erect, stimulated by the touch of the cool nylon string. Her breasts were full enough to hold the beads out from her body and allow them to reflect every little ray of light. It was as if a fairy had traced the sway of her breasts with glittering magic dust.

Something inside Eve responded to this rather pagan costume. Her body began to enjoy the feel of the leather thong, and she straightened her spine to admire her matching collar. The beads swung from her breasts catching the light and her hair fell softly around her face.

A tap on the door reminded her of where she was and what she was supposed to be doing.

"How's it going, Eve? You managing all right?"

Eve laughed. "I have no idea. You'd better tell me..." She opened the door and rather shyly peeked out.

Adele smiled. "C'mon, Eve. Nothing new for me. I shot the spread for Fetish Fun and Foreplay, remember?"

Eve blushed as she stepped through the door.

"Hey, cool nipple beads. I like those," said Adele, stepping back and surveying Eve critically. "The thong is really great. Just perfect. You do need these, however. Just to complete the picture."

She was holding out lace topped thigh high hosiery in one hand and a pair of black spiked high heeled shoes in another. "You don't have to walk in 'em, and I'll guarantee you won't have them on for long."

Eve felt the color spread down over her breasts. "Jeez Adele. I feel silly."

"Nonsense. You look fabulous." Adele helped her pull the hose up to her thighs and steadied her as she slipped into the shoes. "Now...the last touch," and Adele whipped something out from her bag.

"Oh God. Handcuffs. Adele, you devil..." breathed Eve.

Adele grinned. "No point in doing all this and leaving off an important part. Here. Give me your wrists. Better still, get up on the bed and let's get you ready."

Eve clambered awkwardly onto the top of her bed. Her heels were distracting, and she could feel her thong slipping around and over her soft folds as she spread her legs and sank down onto her knees.

"Good. Now," Adele stepped back and viewed the scene critically. Eve could almost see her mind calculating exposures and lighting. "Move this here..." She tugged Eve's legs moving them to either side of her body. "You comfortable like that?"

Eve wriggled a bit. "Sure. Not for an hour, mind you, but for a little while."

"Good." Adele fastened the cuffs around each of Eve's wrists, and grabbed the delicate leash chain. She twisted the collar around so that the ring was in front and the buckle in back of Eve's neck.

With a quick click she secured the chain to Eve's wrists, binding her. Eve could move, but her hands were pretty much secured together.

A rush of excitement flooded her as she realized she really would be at Simon's mercy. Maybe there was more to this bondage stuff than she'd realized.

"Cool. I think that should do it. Oh…I'm going to leave Matilda here," and she draped Eve's flogger across the pillows of the bed. Eve had named the toy "Matilda," insisting that it was soft and furry and deserving of an identity. She chatted to it occasionally, stroked its fur as she passed it on a regular basis, and had merely sniffed when Adele asked dryly what she fed it and if it was house-trained.

"It's now ten of seven. I'm out of here."

"Adele?" Eve's voice cracked slightly. "Thanks."

Adele grinned at her and raised her hand to her forehead in a mock salute. "Anything for the cause, Eve. Power to us women. You'll have him drooling and slobbering within three minutes. No question about it. Call me, okay?"

"Sure. And thanks…"

Adele gathered her bag and left the room, the sound of the front door closing as she left echoing around the now-still apartment.

Eve's heart began thumping and she shifted, aware of her nipples as the beads swung from them, tugging them slightly.

It was very arousing, and the whole outfit was serving as a kind of fashion foreplay.

She thought about Simon, coming into her apartment and looking for her. Finding her, dressed like "Fetish Female of the Week," and waiting for him. Would he like it? Would he hate it? Worst of all, would he just collapse with laughter?

Could she survive if he did?

And overriding all these concerns was the worry that he might not understand what she was trying to tell him with her amateur theatrics. That she wanted him to know she trusted him enough to submit to him. That she was allowing herself to be vulnerable before him, giving him something she'd never given anyone else.

Including, she suddenly realized, herself. She'd never allowed herself to be this free, this wild. She had insisted on so much control, in her life, her career, her relationships.

It was an amazingly heady feeling to hand over responsibility for the next few hours to someone else.

She wouldn't have to worry about making sure he was happy because he'd be telling her exactly what he wanted. She hoped.

For once, she could let someone else call the shots. She could relax into the moment and let Simon direct her, touch her, move her, as he wished. All she had to do was enjoy it.

Her mind focused into a moment of rare clarity. Even if this relationship with Simon never went any further, Eve had learned something. Learned that to love someone was so much more than being compatible in bed or liking Indian food.

To love someone was to give them control of yourself, knowing that you'd get even more in return.

Eve breathed deeply, trying to come to terms with her epiphany.

She jumped at a sound and brought her whirling thoughts back to the bedroom.

Simon had arrived.

* * * * *

The sound of Eve's door shutting firmly behind him echoed the thudding of Simon's pulse as he shucked off his jacket and left it on the coat rack. He felt surprisingly hesitant as the air hit his bare chest.

He'd realized that his entire wardrobe for the evening was that one pair of leather pants, no shirt, no underwear, no shoes, nothing else had been left for him.

He'd showered in feverish haste, then dressed slowly, unaccustomed to the feeling of nothing coming between him and his trousers. The lining in the pants had slid coolly over his cock, caressing him and stiffening him.

Like he needed any help.

Given what he wasn't wearing, he couldn't begin to imagine what was waiting for him at Eve's, and his erection was flexing its muscles in preparation for what was to come.

In fact, it could well be into bench-pressing by now.

Stepping into the darkness of Eve's rooms he took a deep breath and inhaled that particular scent that screamed her name to his olfactory system. That wonderful blend of perfume, coffee, furniture polish and English muffins. That certain aroma that crept up his nostrils and down into his heart. The one that said "my woman." And meant it.

Simon was well aware of the date. It was six months, and he'd never forgotten her suggestion.

Tonight was the night, as far as he was concerned.

The night he put their relationship to the test and told her how he felt and what he wanted. Which was quite simple.

He loved her. He wanted to marry her.

And he should have gone to the bathroom before he left his apartment.

The magnitude of what he'd planned ran over him with the force of a large earth moving front-end loader, and he shuddered, pausing on Eve's soft carpet as he realized how his life might well change from this night forward. The urge to disappear into the toilet and lock the door for about two weeks gradually faded as he let thoughts of Eve fill his mind and his heart.

She was in there, in her bedroom, waiting for him. God knows what she'd planned, but whatever it was, he was sure he'd like it.

Probably.

He hoped he wouldn't fail her and shatter her expectations. She'd probably set up some very romantic scene for them both, especially as she made no secret of her love for romance novels, devouring the latest one with unfailing regularity.

If his hands would stop shaking he could probably do a better job of being a leather-clad bare-assed romance hero.

Should he sweep into the room and gather her in his arms? Should he sweep into the room and grab her up and over onto the bed, coming down on top of her with, what was the phrase she'd giggled over, "a deliberate intent to adore her body?"

He already adored her body, so that wouldn't work.

Why hadn't he thought to bring flowers? Dammit.

Simon pushed his hands through his hair and exhaled. This was not helping anything. He was working himself into a state, when all he had to do was go through the bedroom door and take his woman.

Because she was his woman. No matter what she'd planned, what awaited him, she was his woman. He'd just have to convince her of that fact.

Straightening his shoulders, and unsnapping the rivet on his pants as a token gesture toward romance-hero ambience, he crossed the room to her bedroom door.

He pushed it open. "Eve?"

"Here, Simon."

His breath stopped.

She was waiting for him. On her bed. But ohmiGod. She was…she was…she was…

Simon's mental processes stuttered to a halt like a badly tuned Corvair.

His pistons froze, his sparkplugs died and his distributor cap hung there with its mouth wide open.

Eve was resting amidst a bunch of legs, no—wait, there were only two, so they must be hers, but they were wearing those lacy black sheer things that only made her thighs look whiter. Oh God, she had spiky heeled shoes on.

Along with a leather thong. God. A leather thong.

Moving upwards, slowly, Simon's eyes found the cuffs and saw the chain that latched them to her collar.

A slight glitter rising and falling in time with her breath revealed the sparkling beads that ran from one nipple to the other.

Simon's engine coughed back to life.

"Eve, my God…"

His pistons started to find their rhythm and his spark plugs settled down to a tidy firing sequence.

"Eve. You're…you're so beautiful."

It was an understatement to end all understatements, but seeing as Simon's engine was now threatening to rev itself out of his leathers, it was quite an accomplishment that he managed to voice anything at all.

Finally, he dragged his fascinated gaze to her face and forgot everything as he gazed into her eyes.

"Welcome home, Simon," she breathed.

Her heart was shining from her eyes, along with a healthy dose of trepidation. She was as scared as he was.

For some reason this settled Simon's nerves and he felt a smile begin to lick around his lips.

"This is quite something, love. Quite something…"

He moved to the bed and ran his finger down her cheek, hearing her exhale with pleasure.

"You like it?"

"Oh yeah…" His hand slipped down her shoulder and pulled on the chain leash, raising her hands toward him and exposing her breasts fully. The nipple jewelry gleamed and shimmered in the candlelight.

"Oh yeah," he repeated, letting his finger nudge the beads and watching as her nipples tightened even more.

"Simon, I need to say something to you tonight. Something important."

Simon dragged his mind away from her breasts with an effort and attempted to concentrate on what she was saying.

He knew it was important, he just wished she'd remembered he was a male and thus easily distracted. Especially by sparkly things hanging from the most fantastic set of nipples.

Sighing, he eased down on the bed next to her, stroking his hand down her calf and playing with her toes inside the shoe.

"May I take this off while we talk?" He slipped his fingers inside her shoe and gently ran them along the side of her foot.

His grin deepened as he saw her flesh color slightly and her nipples shiver.

"Um, yeah, sure," she muttered.

"Okay." Sensually, he slid the shoe from her foot, making sure his hand covered as much of the revealed flesh as possible. He tugged on her toes through the stocking.

She wriggled a little.

"You were saying?" he prompted, caressing his way back up her calf to her knee.

"Um…yeah. I was saying…ooohhh that feels good."

He'd reached the back of her knee and allowed his fingers to play there, knowing that shortly he'd reach her bare thigh and looking forward to slowly peeling off the hose.

"Simon, hold it a moment. Let me say this before I lose all rational thought…"

Simon paused, biting back a smile. "Go ahead, honey. Tell me."

Eve swallowed and straightened her spine.

"I love you. I know I've said it before, but tonight I need to show you just how much. I've been scared to death of what's happening between us, and consequently I've held back. But now I know that's stupid, and silly, and unnecessary. Tonight, I'm not holding back. Anything. Especially my trust in you."

Simon couldn't breathe, he could only watch her as she spoke so seriously.

"Tonight I am your slave. I am giving you my love, my body, and most of all my trust. Whatever you tell me to do I will do. Whatever you tell me not to do I will not do. Whatever you choose to do to me I will accept gladly and willingly. Tonight, I exist only to please you, because I know that pleasing you will please me twice as much."

She lowered her eyes and then gathered her courage to face him once more.

"Do you understand?"

Chapter 7

Eve wasn't sure about the power of prayer, but this was one moment she wasn't about to risk missing out on it.

She prayed.

Prayed that Simon would understand what she was trying to tell him, and prayed that he would respond in kind.

He was watching her, his hand resting possessively on her thigh, thinking over her words, perhaps, or formulating his response.

He was a careful man. That she knew. And he seldom let an unconsidered word pass his lips. So the silence in the room seemed heightened she waited for his answer.

The candles flickered gently, and time itself could well have been standing still.

Her nipples were aching a little now, her knees were starting to pull, and she wanted nothing more than to touch her body to Simon's. The urge to mate was dampening her thong, making her cunt throb with anticipation and sending a dryness to her throat.

She licked her lips and swallowed.

"You wish only to please me, tonight. Is that right?" His voice sounded rusty and hoarse.

"That's correct."

"Because you trust me."

"Yes."

"And you love me."

"Oh yes."

"And you'll do anything I say?"

"Absolutely." Please God don't let him ask for anything too gross. Eve momentarily regretted some of the more offbeat Internet sites she'd visited.

"So if I told you I wanted your mouth on me?"

"I'd tell you to stand in front of me."

She saw his cock jump at her words and grinned to herself. He'd always been a sucker for her sucking.

"And if I told you I wanted to turn those buttocks of yours rosy with a couple of whacks from Matilda?"

"I'd roll over and ask you where you wanted me."

Simon swallowed some obstruction in his throat.

"And if I told you that you were to marry me?"

"I'd…" Eve stopped short as the meaning of his words made it through to her sexually clogged brain.

"Simon…" she breathed, hardly daring to look at him.

He stood, all gleaming leather and chest. Damn him, he'd even undone the top button of his pants. He knew she loved that, being able to see a little of his abdomen and be teased by the promise of more to come.

"If I tell you that you agree to marry me, right here, right now. Or I turn and walk out of this apartment and your life forever."

"Forever?" she moaned.

"Forever." Simon folded his arms across his chest and stared at her, as if daring her to live up to her promise.

"Then yes. I'll marry you." Eve gulped. "Whenever and wherever you want."

Simon choked out a gasp and reached for her. "Thank God." He pulled her up onto her knees and crushed her adorned breasts to his naked chest.

"Thank God," he groaned, rubbing his body over hers and pulling her hands up and away from them with the chain.

"Oh thank God, Eve," he whispered.

His lips met hers in a kiss that promised eternity together. It was warm and loving and possessive and Eve sank into it with her heart and her soul.

Then it turned sensual.

His lips opened wide, devouring hers and his tongue thrust hungrily into her mouth, asking for no favors, simply demanding what he now knew was his.

She gave it to him. And returned it tenfold.

Their tongues dueled as their mouths separated and met again, eating at each other in their rising need.

Simon's hands slid down to her naked buttocks and he squeezed and pulled and kneaded, slipping fingers beneath the thong and tugging it, making it cut into her pussy and heighten her already growing arousal.

His fingers crept between her thighs, finding her juices running freely. He stroked and the moan she'd been holding back escaped from her throat.

With a wrench, Simon pulled back, a wicked grin on his face.

"Well, now that we've settled that, let's discuss this whole slave-master thing, shall we?"

Eve shivered. "Okay," she answered, her heart pounding. Damn. She was going to marry this man.

Simon pulled her off the bed and stood her up, kicking the other high heel away from her.

He stepped back, surveying her body and bringing a blush to her cheeks. And a few other places.

She knew her nipples were taut from his kisses, and that her honey was leaking down between her thighs. She couldn't begin to imagine the lascivious picture she must present with her collar and cuffed hands, her wet leather thong and the scent of her arousal filling the air around them.

Simon's hands slipped to the waistband of his pants, and then paused.

"Your first task, my woman," he grinned. "Remove my clothing."

Oh boy. He was getting into it now. Eve found herself giggling inside. This could be fun.

She awkwardly brought her cuffed hands to his groin, managing to stroke the long bulge beneath the leather as she did so.

He flinched, and bit his lip.

Hah. Take that. No wait, she was supposed to be the submissive one here. Internally, she sighed. She probably wasn't cut out for a life of bondage and domination. The clothes were cute, but the philosophy kept getting away from her.

Gingerly she undid the rest of the snaps and mumbled her pleasure as his cock exploded from the leather into her waiting hands. She gave it a quick pet before bending to slip his pants down and allow him to step free of them.

"Well done, woman." Simon's face was slightly flushed. "Now." He tipped his head to one side as he surveyed her subservient pose. The one she'd practiced in front of the mirror.

The one that said, "Master, I'm here to do your bidding." She had actually managed to hold it for more than twenty seconds without snickering. He'd better hurry up because they were approaching eighteen seconds, and she didn't think she could go for the record this evening. Not with all that luscious man in front of her.

"On your knees," he said, clearing his throat of some obstruction.

Willingly she knelt before him. She loved his body, and his cock and the scent of man and leather that radiated from him.

"Love me with your mouth, Eve," he whispered. "Please?"

"No need to ask, my master," she answered, flashing him a rapid smile. His indrawn breath was reward enough as she opened her mouth wide and took just the head of his cock into its wet warmth.

She slipped her cuffed hands up and rested the palms on his thighs, allowing the chain that locked them together to lift his balls slightly. She dug her nails into his muscles and slipped her mouth down his cock as far as she could go, sucking him back into her throat further than she'd ever done before.

His gasp and shudder shocked her, and sent a thrill of pleasure through her. Truly, pleasing him was pleasing her. His grunts of delight were turning her on even more, and she knew that her thighs were wet and her breasts on fire for him.

He slipped his hand into her hair and watched her. Their eyes met and a shiver crossed Eve's body. His heart was in his gaze and it was burning. For her.

"Enough, my woman. I don't wish to end this yet," he groaned.

"You lie to your slave, master," she teased. "But I am yours to command."

"To the bed. On your stomach. I wish to remove this garment and survey what is mine…"

Oh yeah. He was really getting into it now, thought Eve with a grin.

She turned obediently and was about to clamber up on it when his hands at her waist stopped her.

"Right there, slave. Bend over the bed for my pleasure." His hand placed a firm and juicy slap on her naked buttock and she jumped, partly from surprise and partly from a flush of arousal.

Well. Wasn't that interesting?

She leaned down, letting her belly and breasts rest on the high bed. Simon eased her cuffed hands above her head and stretched her beneath him.

He was hot, so hot she could feel the waves of arousal radiating from his body.

He pulled back as he settled her the way he wanted her.

"Mmmm. This is excellent, slave. You are truly a perfect specimen."

The bedding muffled her snort.

She felt him bend to her and then jumped as he ran his tongue down her spine to her thong.

His fingers caught at the leather and dragged it roughly from her, lifting her legs and freeing her of the constricting garment. She was left with her thigh high hose.

His hands splayed over her buttocks, pulling them apart, fondling them, squeezing them, and occasionally placing a firm slap on them.

"Do you like that, slave?" he asked.

"Ooooh God," she groaned, writhing with the pleasure of it. Another slap followed.

"You must answer, my woman."

"Yes, master, yes. Oh God, I love it when you do that, it tingles and burns, and ooooh…"

Her answer earned her another firm slap, this time lower and closer to her pussy. She moaned at the warmth and sensitivity that his punishment aroused her.

She yelped as his tongue suddenly licked her stinging buttocks, and his mouth nipped her, marking her, branding her with his teeth.

"God Eve, you make me so…" Simon muttered something unintelligible as she felt his cock touching her hot buttocks.

"Tell me, my master," she urged, moaning and doing her best to open her legs and invite him in.

"You make me want to lose myself in you. I do lose myself in you. It's wonderful," he panted, rubbing himself harder against her and using his cock to smear her moisture all over her.

"Simon, master, please…please…"

Her hands scrabbled against the bed linens as his hands slipped around and found her clit.

"What, slave, what do you want?"

"I want what you want, master. I want to give you pleasure."

"Why?" Simon pulled her clit, making her sob and grind herself against his fingers.

"Because I'm your slave. Because...because...dear God, Simon..." She cried out as his fingers teased her unmercifully.

Simon pulled back slightly and reached for the bedside drawer.

He froze.

"Eve. Where's the box of condoms?" The frantic sound of his voice would have amused Eve if she hadn't been trembling on the brink of her own inner explosion.

"We don't need them anymore, Simon."

* * * * *

"What?" The exclamation erupted from his brain. Simon simply couldn't believe his ears.

"Look," said Eve, writhing her buttocks against him and driving all rational thought clean out of his head. "We've reached a point here where we have made a commitment. I think it's time we made another commitment as well." She stilled for a moment and glanced over her shoulder toward him.

"I knew tonight was going to be special, Simon. It's been six months now. We've both been certified healthy, and when I said I trust you, I mean it. On many different levels. This is one of them."

"God, Eve, I've never..." stumbling over his words, Simon realized how true that was. He'd never, ever, in his entire life, taken a woman without a protective barrier between them. There were some deeds that lust couldn't excuse.

"Neither have I, Simon. I wanted you to be my first. " She gulped. "I'm on the pill, so pregnancy isn't an issue. Not until we want it to be..."

Thoughts and visions whirled chaotically through Simon's brain.

Images of Eve carrying his child. Visions of sinking himself unprotected into her heat and emptying his balls, flooding her with his seed. Creating life.

"Are you sure?" His whisper was no louder than a sigh, but Eve heard him.

"Yesssss," she hissed, pressing back against him again in wanton need.

"I have to see you, Eve. Watch you," he muttered, backing away and roughly flipping her over.

"We can't do this unless we see each other's faces. Watch me, Eve, don't take your eyes off me…"

Simon tugged Eve to the very edge of the bed and pressed between her thighs. The black lace clad limbs rose to clasp his hips, and he leaned forward, running his hands over her breasts and keeping his gaze fixed on hers.

"Now, Eve?"

"Now Simon," she breathed, giving him back look for look.

His cock found her cunt, hot, wet and ready for him.

With a steady movement he slid himself into her body.

They both stilled.

"Oh wow," she crooned, tightening her thighs against him.

"Oh wow indeed," he whispered. "You're so hot against me. Like molten lava, like hot silk, like…oh God Eve."

Words failed him. He could only watch her eyes as he slid out and back in again, amazed at the feel of her flesh welcoming his hard cock, slipping and sliding against it and causing a wonderful friction unlike any he'd ever felt.

Or was it simply that it was Eve? And he was now really touching her? Someplace where no one had touched her before?

His heart swelled and his cock felt like it was a mile long and big around as a telephone pole.

Eve took him all. She pulled him in, time and time again, letting her cunt caress and squeeze him as he thrust deeper and faster into her amazing body. He was awed to find that now he could feel the slightest tremor of her tissues, and all the details of the folds and ridges of her inner landscape.

She moaned as his thrusts started to reach deep within her, and he slid one hand down to find her clit.

A gasp of sheer delight told him he'd found his target.

Pulling and teasing the tender nubbin, Simon proceeded to set Eve on fire in just the way he knew she liked.

There was no more Master and Slave, there was only Simon and Eve and the pleasure of what they did to each other.

Eve's ankles were locked around Simon's buttocks and Simon's cock was thrusting into her body, bringing them both to the brink of joy.

Simon stopped, seconds from exploding.

"I love you, Eve Bentley. Thank you for this…"

Eve blinked, but didn't withdraw her gaze from his. "I love you too, Simon Austen. And if you don't move within five seconds from now, I will kill you."

Simon's grin turned into a grimace of arousal as he plunged deep, deeper into Eve and made her dreams come true.

She screamed as his body pounded against her clit and started a wave of orgasmic pleasure that Simon could feel beginning at her toes and working its way upwards.

The muscle contractions within her were incredible, and Simon pressed even deeper, trying to absorb every single spasm with her as she came.

Her undulations along his cock were harsh and rhythmic and within seconds he felt that wonderful burn in his buttocks as his own orgasm began.

Bucking with its force, he buried himself in Eve, balls crushed against her as they emptied.

His cock leapt into her flesh with the force of his climax, and the feel of his cum spurting around her womb was almost more than he could bear.

"Eve!" His strangled scream was followed by a sob of pleasure as he emptied himself for the first time into a woman.

Into Eve.

* * * * *

She rolled lazily over onto her side and squashed her hands against Simon's chest. His breathing had almost returned to normal, and they were lying limply on the covers, waiting for their heart rates to slow down.

"Um, Master?"

A snort greeted her words.

"Eve, the whole concept of master and slave just got redefined. Do you realize that the slave is essentially the master of the entire show?"

Eve merely grinned. No way was she going to answer that one. "If you'd be kind enough to release my chains, your slave will continue your pleasure this evening."

There was silence for a moment as Simon considered her words. She really wanted to giggle but suppressed it, even though her heart was overflowing with pleasure, and her body overflowing with Simon's cum.

It had been something quite surreal for Eve, that feeling of being bathed by a man's seed. Something fundamental had stirred within her. The knowledge that they could create life. It was heady stuff.

He sighed. "Very well. But keep these handy, will you?" Simon neatly unclipped the hooks that fastened the cuffs together, and removed the leash from her collar.

"Um, honey? Wanna keep the collar on? It really looks cool..." He smiled at her and ran his hand over her breast, tugging at the nipple beads and making her wince a little.

"Yes, master. Whatever you say…" She began to slide off the bed.

"Whoa. Where are you going?"

"Merely to fetch something to tend to your needs, master," she replied diffidently, risking a little glance under her eyelashes at him.

His eyebrow was raised, his eyes questioning and a little grin creased his lips. God she loved him.

"Very well, my woman. Tend me." He lay back with an exaggerated groan.

"Yeah right."

He raised his head.

"Sorry. I mean yes, of course, master." Damn. She really had to watch her dominating tendencies.

Slipping into the bathroom, Eve grabbed the bowl and facecloths she'd readied earlier and returned to the room, standing beside Simon as he sprawled contentedly on the bed.

He jumped as she began to wash him with the cool water and the cloth.

"My goodness, Eve," he laughed. "You do take your duties seriously…"

"Well, you see I read about this in…"

"Don't tell me. One of your romances, right?"

Eve bit her lip. "Not this time. I picked up a book by JB Sims. It's cool. You might like it. It's called 'Seven Scenes, Seven Sins'. I'll let you read it." She carefully washed his cock and gingerly wiped around his balls, making sure to dry him afterwards with a soft towel. "You don't like this?"

"On the contrary, dear slave. It's rather deluxe, actually." He was grinning like the Cheshire Cat, so Eve assumed he was happy with her service.

"Of course, I do insist on returning the favor."

Eve's hands stilled. "You mean…"

"Of course. It will please me to clean you, Eve." He'd worded it perfectly too. She was caught in her own trap.

"Lie down here, there's a good little slave girl."

Okay, do not curl lip. Slaves do not sass their masters.

Eve lay back on the bed.

Simon reached for a clean cloth and dipped it into the water, lathering the soap and working it to fragrant suds.

"Washing my slave woman. Hmm. This is a rare experience for me, you know."

Eve grunted as he began to cleanse her sensitive skin, wiping and tugging a little as he removed their intermingled juices from her flesh.

"Now, mustn't miss this little bit here, let me see…"

The cloth found her clit and delicately circled it, just barely touching it with a light flicker of lather.

She moaned.

"Mmm. Looks clean enough to eat. I wonder…woman and lavender. Interesting combination."

Simon leaned forward and slipped his tongue gently over Eve's clean clit.

She moaned again. "Simon, love…"

"That's master love to you, Eve, slave woman. Your master desires your pleasure now. Be quiet while I take care of it."

Simon pushed the cleaning supplies aside and knelt to his task. His face disappeared between her thighs, and before she knew it, a dull ache of arousal was beginning again deep within her.

"Oh Simon," she breathed.

"Oh Eve," he echoed, letting his breath dust her cunt and ratchet up her sexual tension.

His hands slid up and down her abdomen, playing in and around her navel, and eventually sliding beneath her to raise her to his mouth.

His tongue was an entity to itself.

Teasing, flicking, plunging into her little nooks and crannies, and making her juices run anew.

She'd thought that her climax would be of stunning and enormous magnitude, and she was right.

She had no idea that she could actually manage a second one after that. This was surely a night of new experiences.

Slowly and gradually, Simon used his mouth and his tongue to arouse her, and then he leisurely took his time, bringing her along fast, then letting her ease down a little.

Before too long she was a whimpering pile of lust just waiting for his cock to make her explode.

"Simon…" she moaned. "Please…I want you…"

She struggled to reach his cock that was now lying rigid against her body.

Evading her hungry grasp, Simon neatly flipped her onto her stomach and once again draped her legs off the edge of the bed.

"I really like these stocking things, Eve. Can we keep them?" he muttered, as he opened her thighs wide and stepped between.

"Sure, honey," she gasped. "Anything you say…"

"Good," he sighed, grabbing the head of his cock and slipping it into her folds. "Oh sooo good…"

He slid deep, deep inside her, touching her soul. His cock was hot and hard and filled all her empty spaces.

"Simon," she breathed, arching her back and thrusting against him.

"Yes," he said, stroking her with his hands and his cock. "Yes, Eve. Yes. It's right. Us. This. Forever…" His words faded as his speed increased, and Eve's heart melted as his hands stroked her and petted her and loved her in time with the pounding of his cock.

He slammed against her in a frenzy, driving her into the blankets and touching a spot deep within her that made her want to scream with the pleasure of it.

"OhGodohGodohGod..."

She had no idea who was shouting. It might well be her. But in the next instant it no longer mattered.

For the second time that night, Eve Bentley orgasmed.

For the second time that night, Simon Austen was right there with her, filling her, sharing her climax and offering up one of his own.

Her mind emptied of everything but the feel of Simon's cock spurting its seed within her.

Her heart unfurled the last of its worries and let it evaporate into a huge breathy sigh that echoed around the room.

She was his, and he was hers. It was life, it was destiny, it was nature. It was also wonderful.

With a smile on her face and Simon nearly comatose beside her, Eve slept.

Chapter 8

"So you never did use Matilda?"

Adele smiled across the table at Eve, who was feeling rather like the Cheshire Cat. She couldn't stop grinning.

"Nope. Two days later, Matilda was still in a heap on the floor."

"Two days?"

"Hey, being a slave is serious business. And I had microwave pizza..."

"Eeeeuwww."

"Well, yeah. That wasn't great. So we ended up sending out for Chinese."

"But the end result was the same. True love wins out, the lovers end up married happily ever after." Adele tipped her head and looked at Eve.

"Yep. Pretty much. I have your stuff here, by the way. I'm going to keep the thong and the thigh highs, if it's all right with you?"

"God yeah. I've got plenty. Every time I do a fetish-related shoot I get more merchandise. The thigh highs were a success, were they?"

In spite of herself, Eve blushed. "Um, yeah."

"Cool." Adele managed to keep a straight face.

"So, you gonna have a bit of time free in a couple of weeks? Simon and I are going to have a very quiet little thing, just a few words in front of his friend who's an ordained minister. We're thinking out in the garden, you know?"

"Oh yeah, neat. Need photos?"

"Adele." Eve was caught. She desperately wanted Adele there as a guest, but knew she'd never get any better photos than the ones Adele would take.

"What can I say? You'll take the most magnificent pictures I can imagine, but I don't want you working on this day…"

"It's not work to me, Eve. It's my passion. Let me enjoy the day the best way I know how?"

"Weelll…" Eve tugged on her lower lip, wishing Simon were there to advise her. But he'd gone off for a day long conference, and she was stuck with this tough decision.

She sighed. "All right. I'm going with my gut here, because I don't believe you would have offered if you didn't want to. But I insist you bring a date, and you only shoot photos when you feel like it, okay?"

Adele smiled happily. "Wonderful. My date will be my newest boyfriend…"

"Oh?" Eve pricked up her ears.

"Yep. His name's Nikon, he's 35mm, autofocus, SLR…"

"Adele!" Eve laughed. "Can't you dredge up someone?"

Adele shrugged. "Sweetie, at my age they're all too young or too old. I'm happy with my camera equipment and my good friends…" She reached across the table and gripped Eve's hand with hers.

"Just be happy, Eve. You have a wonderful guy. Enjoy him. Enjoy each other for the rest of your lives."

"Oh we will, Adele. I'm absolutely positive of that."

"Good. Now I'm on my way."

Adele gathered her bag of tricks that Eve had packed for her. "Give Simon a hug from me, and I'll see you guys soon."

"Got a shoot today?" asked Eve, following Adele to the door.

"I hope so. And yeah, it's another fetish one. But Jan hasn't checked in yet, which isn't like her, and Brian is a stickler for being on time…" Adele frowned.

"Oooh. Brian. That's the gorgeous cover-model one, right?" Eve grinned.

"Hey, recently-engaged woman. None of that." Adele mock-punched Eve's shoulder.

"Well, yeah, but Brian." Eve let the awe in her voice hang there. "He's a dish and a half. Not as luscious as Simon, of course, but oooh, those bedroom eyes. I don't know how you keep your hands off him. Especially if you get to put him into some of those leather strappy speedo things…"

Adele laughed. "Honey, I've known Brian for many years, and yeah he's a sweetie. He puts his own strappy things on, however, and he's also years younger than I am. End of story."

Eve stood at the door as Adele left. "Pity. He'd have made a great date for the wedding…"

Her words trailed after Adele, who just shook her head and waved goodbye.

Eve turned and closed the door behind her, a thoughtful look on her face, but then turned her mind to the most important problem besetting her.

What could she do to surprise Simon when he came home tonight?

Apartment 6C

Prologue

Most weekday mornings – Apartment 6C…

6:47am…Laura Stratton-Burns gets out of the shower.

7:00am…Laura finishes make up and leaves bathroom.

7:03am…Adam Burns enters bathroom, picks up towels from floor and hangs them up, fetching a dry one for himself.

7:04am…Adam showers.

7:12am…Adam finishes in the bathroom and goes to bedroom to dress.

7:15am…Laura rushes into bedroom, pecks Adam on cheek and tells him to have a nice day.

7:20am…Laura leaves for her law office.

7:30am…Adam retrieves paper from hall, pours second cup of coffee and sits down in kitchen to review the day's lesson plans for his fourth grade class.

Several nights a week – Apartment 6C…

10:20pm…Adam slips naked into bed next to Laura.

10:21pm…Laura closes her book and turns out the bedside lamp.

10:22pm…Adam places his hand on Laura's thigh.

10:25pm…Laura slides her hands over Adam's buttocks.

10:28pm…Adam removes Laura's nightgown.

10:30pm…Adam reaches for Laura's clit, rubbing it gently as he suckles her breasts.

10:40pm…Adam slides his cock into Laura's body as she spreads her legs wide.

10:45pm…Adam brings Laura to a climax using his cock and his fingers.

10:50pm…Laura shudders and sighs, which Adam knows is her way of coming.

10:51pm…Adam himself lets go and comes with a groan.

10:55pm…Laura and Adam straighten the bedding and the pillows.

10:57pm…Laura retrieves her nightgown.

10:58pm…Adam switches the TV channel to the local news station and sets the timer.

11:00pm…Laura murmurs goodnight to her husband and rolls over, falling asleep almost immediately.

Chapter 1

"Jonathan! Put that down." Adam Burns's voice rang out over the playground and encouraged a rambunctious fourth-grader to rethink his strategy regarding the large stick he'd just picked up.

A chuckle from beside him caught his attention. "Adam, you were made to be a teacher, you know that?"

Carolee Hanson was standing next to him, watching the interplay.

"Why? Because I can make myself heard across the sound of two million children at play?" Adam's eyebrow rose skeptically.

"No. Because you're a born dominator. A natural."

Adam felt a little tingle run up his spine. "Carolee, that is a really bizarre thing to say..."

"No it's not. You've been teaching here for four years. You have the best rapport with the kids of just about any teacher I know. You care about them, you guide them and you use your strength to encourage them to do better. It's a Dom thing."

Adam laughed. "There you go again. Dom...sub, I swear Carolee, your husband must be either the happiest man on the face of this earth or the most confused."

It was polite, it was social, and it didn't reveal a damn thing about what was going on inside Adam Burns. At least he sincerely hoped not.

He thought that while the teacher's room could withstand the slightly risqué conversation of Carolee Hanson and her fascination with fetishes, the knowledge that they had a full-fledged, although non-practicing, Dom in their midst might rattle a few cages.

And it had been many years. Too many years.

His wife didn't even know, for heaven's sake.

His wife. A bitter taste in his mouth soured his thoughts. He loved Laura more than life itself, but he was afraid that something was wrong. Something was slowly stifling their passion and driving them to mundane existences within their marriage.

It was all going wrong and he had no idea how to fix it.

The bell rang ending recess, and Adam followed Carolee back into the building, returning to his classroom and the sight of twenty-five sweaty little faces. Twenty-five little mental sponges, eager to soak up the knowledge he was supposed to impart to them.

Sometimes, he felt wonder at the sight of a child finally grasping a difficult concept and he would go home happy, knowing he was in the right place at the right time.

Other days would be pointless, endless frustration, with kids who were either sick, or irritable, or hot or cold, or just flat not in the mood to learn.

Those were the days he really missed going home and enjoying a good workout with his flogger.

* * * * *

Laura Stratton-Burns smiled coolly at the man on her right as he politely passed her the brochure.

Her navy blue pinstriped suit was crisp, her white silk blouse felt soft against her neck, and she knew she was completely in command of herself and this meeting.

Four of the top lawyers from Stratton-Burns, Howard and Mills were seated at the large conference table, along with two administrative assistants and Laura's own right hand person, Mark Ffitch.

The subject under discussion was the adoption of a brochure to be circulated at the upcoming Metropolitan Legal Conference. Such things were of grave import to the sober souls at S-B, H and M.

Laura did her best not to drift, but she'd been over this matter at least ten times prior to the meeting, had given her formal seal of approval and was only here as a token of her support for the graphics department.

"Well, Laura, it looks like we have a winner here." Saul Edelstein smiled at her.

"I agree, Saul. This should definitely make its mark at the conference, and I'm very pleased at the effort that the entire graphics department has put into it." She made a point to smile at Ellen from the graphics group, noting her pleased blush in response.

Laura knew how important it was to make sure that those who worked for her were praised, petted, rewarded and encouraged. It was what made her such a successful head of the firm at such a young age.

Taking the reins from her father, Laura had held tight and driven S-B, H and M to the top of the legal pile by force of will and a couple of strategically brilliant moves. She was well-known in legal circles, mostly respected in spite of her gender, and, in the parlance of the day, was seen to "have it all."

All except a healthy marriage.

She leaned back and drew a deep breath, letting the soft babble of voices drift past her.

She loved Adam. There was no question in her mind that he was her mate, her man, the "one." He had been since the first time they'd met, so many years ago now, at least seven...maybe eight.

The attraction between them had been instant. They'd been naked and in bed within an hour. And they had stayed there for most of their final post-graduate year.

But life had intruded—as it always does. Careers were begun, posts accepted, marriage and domesticity had followed.

When had it all begun to fall apart? When did the sex become routine, and the love taken for granted? And how could she stop it from sliding any further?

A shiver crossed her flesh as she remembered the last time she'd dropped by Lincoln Elementary to pick up Adam. He'd been very closely chatting to another teacher. A young, female teacher. And she'd even been wearing gingham.

Laura snorted at herself for her foolishness. She trusted Adam with her life. He would never look elsewhere. But lately there had been an unusual expression in his eyes. A wistful look, a distance, which told her that he was drifting someplace she couldn't go.

She was very afraid that something was going wrong. And she didn't know what to do to fix it.

Mark reclaimed her attention by laying his hand on her shoulder. "No sleeping, Your Majesty," he whispered teasingly.

Laura smiled up at him, noting the wicked smile in his baby blue eyes. Mark was her lifeline some days, keeping her sane, making her laugh and generally bringing fresh air into the otherwise stuffy environment of her law firm.

His lifestyle choices had been obvious to her from the moment they met, but a friendship had also been born that day. Laura had never regretted the impulse that made her hire the soft-voiced beautiful man with the too tight corduroys and the faded pink streak in his hair.

Now, Mark was elegantly, if quietly, dressed, having developed an appreciation for fine clothing. His position as Laura's assistant allowed him the luxury of handmade suits, and his long term affair with a designer at the nearby gentleman's clothier guaranteed at least one new suit a month.

He called Laura his "Queen"—in the monarchical sense of the word—and insisted he was nothing but her slave. She had but to wave her hand and he would obey her every command.

In fact, Mark had reached the point where she didn't even have to wave her hand. He could anticipate a good number of her orders, and having Mark guard her door had made Laura's days run more smoothly and her challenges easier to face.

She was deeply indebted to him, liked him a lot, and would have been completely lost without him.

She didn't, however, want him as her slave.

A fact which miffed Mark considerably, and about which he would whine incessantly if given half the chance.

Laura had no idea how he'd react if she did strip his clothes off him and paddle his bottom as he'd laughingly begged her to do on numerous occasions, whether or not he'd done something that required punishment.

She just knew how she'd react, and it was with complete disinterest. There was only one bottom for her, and that was her husband's.

With much fanfare, the meeting adjourned, and Mark gathered Laura's papers together as she shut down her laptop.

"Well. That was a nice hour spent talking about nothing at all," grinned Mark. "Gotta love corporate America."

Laura winced in agreement, thinking of the piles of paperwork that awaited her on her desk.

"Come on, Queenie, let's grab lunch before we hit the salt mines. I found a little sandwich place that makes the best egg salad…"

Laura's mouth watered. "Okay, you're on. But forty-five minutes, Mark. No more. Otherwise we'll be waaay behind with things…"

"Ooh darling," crooned Mark with a sly giggle. "That's just how I like it…waaaaay behind."

Laura choked back a laugh. "You're outrageous. Let's go eat."

* * * * *

As usual, Adam was home first, and he juggled his briefcase, his raincoat, his keys and the mail as he made his way into Apartment 6C.

He'd passed Adele on the way upstairs, she of the multitude of amazing cameras and the interesting packages from unusual P.O. boxes. He'd seen her name on several photo shoots, and they always had a nice word as they passed in the elevator, or, on those days when he was feeling guilty about that lunch room Twinkie, the stairs.

Today it had been the elevator. The hours had dragged past, the rain had finally set in just as it was time for him to leave, and the traffic had immediately clogged up as the road slicked ahead of him.

He dropped his coat in the foyer and took the mail through into the kitchen, kicking off his shoes as he went.

It was Wednesday, Laura's night to hit the gym with her friends, so he knew he'd have a sandwich, some chips and a beer for dinner.

Then he could spend two hours with his secret.

An envelope caught his eye as the usual assortment of bills and junk mail spilled over the kitchen counter.

Hand addressed and from someone he didn't recognize, he warily turned it over looking for a postmark. It was blurred and inconclusive.

Adam opened the letter.

"We regret to inform you of the passing of our beloved Master Granger Fields after a short illness. His memory will be honored by his slaves and his followers at a private ceremony at his Dungeon on..."

Oh God. Master Granger was dead.

Adam sat down with a thump, holding the letter in his hand and staring at it in disbelief.

The man who had taught Adam everything he ever knew about being a Dom had died. The man who had been closer than a father to him, who had understood him better than his own father ever had. The man who had helped him come to terms with himself, and who he'd abandoned once Laura had become part of his life.

He hadn't seen the Master since their wedding. He closed his eyes as he remembered the Master's words. "Adam, you are afraid for the wrong reasons. But you must make the choices here, not me. I am sorry that your skills will go to waste. Don't let your life follow suit."

They'd shaken hands, the Master had kissed Laura's, if he remembered correctly, and they'd parted.

Now he was gone.

It was a bitter pill, and one that saddened Adam to his very soul. He passed on the sandwich and chips and went straight for the beer, twisting off the top and taking a long swallow as he went into the den and sat in front of his monitor.

He left the light off, and the gloom of the evening echoed the gloom of his mood. A few quick keystrokes activated his system and within seconds his secret life appeared on the screen.

"Welcome to Shu Adama's Dwelling. The Ultimate On-Line Resource for D/s Information and Conversation. We understand."

* * * * *

Laura leaned against the wall of the elevator, tired to her very soul. The day had been a long and challenging one, her workout had been an effort, and she'd cut it short for the first time she could ever remember.

Her weariness seemed almost a solid weight resting on her shoulders and driving her downwards, and yet she knew that it was something not easily remedied by a good night's sleep.

Adam would be upstairs now, waiting for her. Working perhaps, or watching a little television. Ready to give her a hug and listen to her as she talked about her day.

He'd be surprised she was home early, but she knew he'd be there for her. He always was. So what was the problem?

She didn't know.

The elevator door pinged open and she was confronted by a couple locked in a rather passionate kiss.

"Ahem."

The bodies sprang apart. It was Eve Bentley and Simon Austen from the fourth floor. They grinned at her.

"Hi guys. I'm going up. Want to wait till it comes back down? If you can find something to keep yourself occupied that is," smiled Laura.

"Hey Laura, how's it going?" Eve sparkled. Laura had heard they were getting married shortly. She felt happy for them, then another wave of depression swamped her.

"Fine, Eve. Good seeing you both." The elevator doors slid shut and Laura rose the last two floors.

Her sneakers made little sound on the carpeted hallway as she reached her door, and she let herself into the apartment with a mixture of relief and exhaustion.

She was struck by how quiet it was. Usually there was plenty of light and the sound of the TV or some music going. Tonight it was hushed and dark.

Adam was home, that was for sure. His shoes were tossed against the wall and his jacket was on the rack.

Quietly, Laura closed the door behind her and dumped her gym bag and clothes.

She went into the kitchen. A pile of unopened mail lay on the counter, with one letter on top. Two empty beer bottles stood next to it.

Curious now, she picked up the paper and read, a frown creasing her brow as she struggled to make sense of the words.

"...Granger Fields..." Oh no, how sad. She remembered him from her wedding, a handsome silver-haired man with a very appealing smile. He'd kissed her hand and made her shiver.

"…his slaves…his Dungeon…" Good lord, was the man some kind of medieval fanatic? Laura turned the letter over, noticing a handwritten paragraph on the back of the formal announcement.

"Adam, the Master has left You something special. It's been a long time, I know, but I beg that You will honor him and us by attending. We have missed Your laughter and the welcome sting of Your hands. Your Loving Pet, Fay."

Laura's skin felt too tight for her body, and her throat closed up. For a moment she thought she was going to pass out.

Adam had "a loving pet?" What the hell did that mean?

She scrambled to make sense of the message and put it into context, her analytical mind tumbling about like a clothes dryer full of socks.

The fluff cycle ended. She needed more information.

Dropping the letter back on the counter, she turned to find Adam with curiosity, anger and some fear battling for prime position in her brain.

To her surprise he was sitting glued to the computer monitor in the darkened study.

His focus was complete and absolute, his fingers were flying over the keyboard and he seemed totally unaware of her presence.

She silently moved closer, blessing the large resolution on the monitor. Within a couple of steps she could read over his shoulder.

"So, Alan, never let your sub feel alone after that experience. She will need your comfort and your love more than ever. Your actions, if you perform them correctly, will send your sub into another place, a state of mind that will be like no other she's ever experienced. It will be frightening, exhilarating and exciting for you both. Watch her, Alan."

Adam paused, reached for his beer, took a swig and bent back to the keyboard.

Laura's eyes were getting bigger and bigger as she read more of his message.

"Watch her skin, her eyes, her muscles. See if she's wet for you, if her nipples are reddening and bunching under their restraints. How about her buttocks? Do your blows leave a glow or a stripe? Does she flinch at them then thrust back for more? Learn all of this Alan, learn to read your sub's silent language. Then you will know what to do for her and with her when you have completed the scene. Whether you should take her in your arms and just hold her or fuck her hard and long. Let her tell you, Alan, because the truth is that there is no 'leader' in this experience."

Laura's belly tightened and her body tensed as she read over Adam's shoulder.

"There is no right or wrong, no 'my way or the highway.' There is only you and her. A couple. One entity functioning for pleasure. And oh my, what pleasure it is."

Laura slowly backed away as Adam began to sign his name and tap the keys which would post his message.

She reached the safety of the kitchen and rocked back on her heels, trying to come to terms with what she'd seen and what she'd read.

She was informed enough to be able to put the information together. The death of a "Master." The plea of a "pet." And Adam's email to someone about how to handle a submissive.

Dear God. Her husband was a Dominant.

Adam sat rigid before his computer. His gut churned and his palms were sweaty.

He'd seen Laura's reflection in the screen. Watched her as she'd read his post.

She knew.

Chapter 2

There was a clatter in the front hallway and the door banged shut.

"Adam? I'm home," called Laura.

Okay. This was how they were going to play it. She was going to pretend that she was unaware of anything unusual. No sign that she'd peeked over his shoulder. No discussion of the fact that he'd been busily advising a new Dom about the intricacies of concluding a scene with his sub.

Adam sighed, unsure of whether to be relieved or saddened. He shrugged.

At this point it was Laura's call, not his.

"You're early," he called back, closing down his connection and killing his browser.

"Yeah. I just couldn't take the last hour of steppers, treadmills and spinning. All intensely arranged to make sure that I work like hell and get absolutely nowhere." She grinned at him as he came into the kitchen and crossed the room to hug her.

"Mmm. You smell sweaty. Nice," he murmured, enjoying the feel of her body. She was warm and firm in all the right places, and he thought now, as he had thought for all the years he'd known her, how well their bodies fit together.

Laura chuckled and hugged him back. "You are the only man who thinks sweat smells good."

"Your sweat, Laura. There's a difference." He released her and went to the kitchen counter. "Want a cup of tea or something?"

"Oh yeah, that sounds like heaven. I'll go get out of this stuff. Back in a sec…"

She disappeared in a whirl of athletic gear, her long dark hair swinging free in its scrunched ponytail. This was Laura the wonder-workout-woman, instead of Ms. Stratton-Burns, corporate lady lawyer.

Adam loved them both, but admitted he had a soft spot for the hot and delightfully sweaty heap of aching muscles who staggered home from the gym twice a week. It was very hard for him to not demand she strip naked for him and let him fuck her blind the minute she walked into the apartment.

But he loved her. And he knew that she was flat out exhausted. It would not have been fair. For the ten thousandth time he buried the notion.

He sighed and made tea.

His thoughts flashed to Master Granger. Was this what he meant when he'd begged Adam not to let his life go to waste? Was he simply allowing himself to slide into a mediocre existence? Was he denying a part of himself out of love for Laura?

Or was it out of fear of losing her? He didn't know.

Laura returned, hair tumbled over her shoulders and wearing her favorite robe. She grabbed her tea and took a long deep swallow.

"God that's good." She closed her eyes in pleasure.

"I got some sad news today," began Adam. "An old friend passed away."

Laura opened her eyes and watched as he passed her the letter.

"Oh Adam, I'm sorry. I remember him. Such a charming man…" She turned the letter over. "Adam? Who's Fay?"

Adam chuckled. "Fay is a Pet. A sweetheart. Someone who loves to be nice to everyone."

"Ah." Laura read on. " It seems that she's missed you."

Adam didn't miss the sharpened tone or the pointed glance that went with that statement.

"I don't know if you remember, but I lived with Master Granger and some of his friends for a couple of years. I think it was my senior year and definitely a couple of years in grad school. Right before we met, actually…"

"Master Granger?"

"Yeah, we all called him that. It seemed to fit…" Adam shrugged, passing off the comment with a casualness that cost him a lot to feign.

"A dungeon, huh? Odd place for a wake?"

"Not for Master Granger," smiled Adam. "He was unique. One of a kind."

"I am sorry, Adam. You'll miss him?"

"I will miss knowing he's there. We lost touch a while ago, but that's not the same as this. Losing touch is one thing, losing that person forever is another."

Adam's eyes filled with an unusually strong emotion. "He was a true friend, Laura. Never judged us, never made us feel uncomfortable about who we were. He answered our questions, cared about us, helped us, listened to us…he was a better father than mine ever was."

"Good lord. He was special to you, wasn't he? I never realized…you never said anything…" Laura stared at Adam in astonishment.

"Well, once you and I were married, the situation changed a lot. We were together and my life with the Master sort of slid into the past. We had a future to look forward to."

"We must go, Adam. Definitely. When is it?" She glanced down at the letter again. "Saturday. Right. We'll be there."

Adam bit his lip. "Are you sure? They are a…a different-thinking group. I wouldn't want you shocked or surprised."

"Adam, they've lost a friend, as have you." Laura reached over and put her hand on Adam's. "Let's go and give them what support we can. You say you lost track of Granger recently. I don't want to have that happen with any of your other friends, okay?"

Adam covered her hand with his. "Thank you, Laura." The words came from his heart. She couldn't know how much it would mean to him to be there on Saturday, nor could she know that he wasn't quite ready to tell her all about his life with Master Granger.

Soon, though, he knew he'd have to. And then…well, only time would tell.

* * * * *

The timer had turned off the television, the news was over and it had to be close to midnight, but Laura knew Adam was still awake. She certainly was.

Her mind was working over the information she'd learned on this rather unusual night.

She stifled a snort when she realized it was Wednesday. Weren't major life-changing events supposed to happen on important days? Not at ten o'clock on a Wednesday night?

Adam was a Dominant. Someone who wanted women to submit to them. Or at least that's what she thought it meant. Damn. There was so much she didn't know. Plan number one was to spend as much time as she could over the next forty-eight hours learning every single thing possible about Adam's past lifestyle.

Her mind wandered. Should she get some leather clothes? Nah. Stupid. If Adam had liked her in leather he would have bought her leather. He enjoyed shopping with her.

But a pair of spiked boots? Oooh. Now that might be fun.

Her gut quickened at the thought of standing before Adam in high shiny black boots with a 4-inch, no make that a 5-inch, spiked heel. And nothing else. She shivered.

Adam turned over facing away from her.

What would it be like, she wondered. How would it be to have a man demand everything from you, even your right to function on a purely physical level?

For once, Mark's fervid ramblings about being spanked made a little more sense. She began to visualize a "scene" where she was bending over the bed and Adam…Adam was going to spank her.

She was astonished to realize her nipples were hardening. She was becoming aroused just by thinking of her nakedness exposed to his gaze. Her cheeks would be bare, and his hand would perhaps caress them before he spanked them. Hard.

She fidgeted, and sighed.

This was not good. Her vibrator was in her bathroom cabinet, behind her feminine supplies. She only used it on Sundays when Adam went off to play golf.

It wasn't Sunday, and far from being on the golf course, Adam was right next to her, lying in bed.

He snuffled into the pillow, reaching up and pulling it into a more comfortable position.

Laura froze, a daring thought in her mind. Could she? Would he let her? Could she tell him something of how she was feeling by her actions?

Tentatively, she reached over beneath the covers and rested her hand on his naked hip.

He stilled beneath her touch.

"Adam?" she whispered. "Can't sleep?" She let her hand slide down over his skin until she brushed his cock. He was hard as granite.

"Me neither." She curled her fingers round him, listening to the sharp intake of his breath as she squeezed him gently.

"Laura," he groaned.

"Sssh, let me touch you." Daringly she slid over next to him, pressing herself down the length of his back and legs. She let her fingers play around his cock and slip lower to caress his balls. "I want to touch you," she said, more to herself than to him.

"Laura, I don't…" stuttered Adam.

"You don't want me to?" She pulled her hand back from his heat.

"God, no." He seized her wrist and slapped her fingers back around his cock just to make his meaning absolutely clear. "I want you to. Please. Go ahead. Just don't do anything you don't want to do, okay?"

"Okay." A small smile played around her mouth as she pressed her breasts into his back and let her fingers do the walking. And the talking.

Adam had known she was awake. He could sense her movements, soft but urgent, next to him. If he didn't know better, he could swear he smelled her arousal. What was she thinking? What was she imagining?

Was she yearning for that purple plastic vibrator she'd tucked behind her feminine supplies?

He'd found it by mistake a year or so ago, and been quite fascinated by the mechanics of it. A small exercise in surveillance—simple to anyone who read James Bond novels with any degree of devotion—produced the information that she used it on Sundays when he was off playing golf.

Well, that was fine. Arousing in some ways. She didn't need to know that he imagined her using it on herself when he was jerking off in the shower. Not that he did that a lot, but there were those mornings…

And now, here she was, playing with his cock and doing things to it with her fingers that he'd only dreamed of.

Was she feeling guilty? Trying to discover if he was going to roll over and spank her? Was she curious all of a sudden because she'd discovered he was a Dom? Or maybe she couldn't sleep either, and just wanted to do this. "This" being the most marvelous hand job. She'd not seemed to be very interested in genital foreplay. Or maybe she had and they'd just lost touch with it. He suddenly remembered how she used to spend quite a bit of time loving him with her hands and her mouth. And that he used to return the favor. With pleasure. When had they stopped?

And why was she rediscovering it now?

Whatever the reason, it felt fabulous.

Her hand slid from the base to the tip of his cock, and she gently stroked beneath the head, finding that little spot that sent shudders up his spine.

Her breasts pressed hotly against his back and he knew his own nipples were hard, not to mention the two bullets that were drilling into his skin from behind.

She grunted and pushed herself upright.

"Adam. It's not enough. I want more..." She pressed him onto his back, pulled her nightgown over her head in one fluid move and settled herself between his legs.

Adam's jaw dropped as she leaned forward and sucked him deep into her mouth.

Then his hips bucked as he fought the urge to thrust into her hot wetness. She was working him hard, letting her teeth graze against his sensitive skin as she pulled back and swirling her tongue wildly as she sucked him back in.

Her hands fondled his balls, almost roughly, and he was writhing with pleasure before he knew it.

His heart began to pound and his mind emptied of everything but the sensation of his rising arousal. His buttocks tightened, and he wanted nothing more than to fuck Laura hard.

No gentle loving, no delicate touches or nibbling kisses. He wanted to pound himself into her. Now. This minute. Maybe even sooner. He wanted her beneath him, on her face, buttocks available and naked for his pleasure.

He damn near howled at the thought.

Too close...she was bringing him too close. At this rate he'd come violently down her throat in seconds.

Using every bit of training he could muster, he pulled his cock out of her mouth and reached for her.

His hands grasped her breasts roughly, abrading the nipples and making them harden even more.

He slid a leg between hers and forced it up against her pussy, rubbing it slightly over her and feeling the moisture that was already flowing.

Good, she was aroused too. He moved quickly, fastening his lips around her breast and suckling her with enthusiasm. She sobbed out a breath as his mouth moved to the other breast, tugging, teasing, biting softly.

His hands filled themselves with her buttocks. He squeezed hard, pulling the soft mounds apart. Stretching her skin and then kneading the flesh. His movements were determined, and he knew where her most vulnerable areas were.

He found the one right inside her thigh and she sobbed again, catching a gasp as his fingers spread her juices around her sensitive folds.

In teeth-clenching agony now, Adam flipped Laura onto her stomach and pulled her onto her hands and knees.

She opened her legs and moaned as one hand felt for her clit and pressed it hard.

Adam grasped his cock and pushed against her cunt, finding the way slippery and welcoming, oiled with her honey and lubricated by the drops of pre-cum his cock was already leaking.

With a harsh grunt, he thrust into her body, deep into her warmth, slapping his balls against her as he buried himself to the hilt.

She cried out even as she began to come around him. He pinched her clit and heard her catch her breath as enormous spasms began to wrench her cunt. She clamped down on him again and again, until the movements pulled him over the edge and into his own orgasm.

With a mighty shout he erupted, jerking against her, shuddering inside her, and filling her with his cum against her womb. It was mind blowing and Adam completely lost touch with reality for long seconds as his balls emptied themselves into his woman.

He sagged limply against her as her legs slid apart and she collapsed onto the bed.

"God, Laura," he mumbled, slipping out of her, all sticky and relaxed and wonderful.

"Mmmm," she muttered.

Ever true to her nature, Laura was sound asleep.

Chapter 3

The next couple of days were filled with work and research. Laura juggled meetings, clients, lunches and phone calls with hours spent reading and surfing the Internet in search of information about the Dom/sub lifestyle.

She desperately needed to get some kind of feel for the psychology behind it, and maybe begin to understand the hidden facets of her husband.

Within an hour of her first "search" command, Mark was panting at her shoulder.

"Here, Queenie, try this one..." he said, leaning over and typing in an address. "This is a great site for the philosophical discussion. They've got some good scene suggestions as well...oooh and look here...a new article by Master Thorsonn..."

Mark had not surprised her with his immediate announcement that he was a slave. As soon as he'd seen her research topic, he'd been right there next to her, guiding her, talking to her, enthusiastically answering her questions.

"I'm a slave, dear. That's someone who is submissive pretty much all the time. Some of us can be slaves 24/7. It's hard sometimes, but it's worth it. Especially if you have the most wonderful Master in the whole world." Mark had rolled his eyes with pleasure.

Laura had met Mark's "Master" at one of their office celebrations. Paul was charming, short, and delightfully intelligent and not at all what one would imagine a "Master" to be. His wit and humor had enlivened an otherwise boring affair for her, and she'd simply thought of him as Mark's significant other.

Now she realized that Mark had quietly waited on Paul and hovered at his side, not through a polite need to ease his introduction to the group, but as part of his devotion to his Master.

Mark showed her his ring, an unusual and simple iron band with a small hoop.

"It's modeled after the one in 'The Story of O'," he said proudly. "It does tell others in the lifestyle that I'm a slave. My Master wears a similar one. They're engraved too..."

With Mark's guidance, Laura learned some of the basics. She was surprised, intrigued and confused.

Which Mark said was perfectly normal.

"But Mark, I don't think I could do this stuff forever. How could I possibly function if I had to ask Adam for permission to go to the bathroom, for chrissake?"

She threw her hands in the air after reading one particularly intense discussion between Doms and subs in Mark's recommended chat room. "There's a whole etiquette to this, and what almost seems to be a quite rigid code of behavior to go along with it."

Mark chuckled. "You're getting hung up on the details, oh Queen of mine. There's absolutely no need for you to go that deep. Unless you find you want to. And that's not likely to happen for several years."

Laura sighed. "This is all so unexpected, Mark. It's like a brick came out of the blue and whacked me up beside the ear."

Mark reached around her shoulders and hugged her. "It's quite all right to feel that way, sweetie. You've had exactly—" he glanced at his watch, "—twenty nine hours to absorb the fact that your husband is a secret Dom."

Laura looked back at the screen, noticing how some names were capitalized, others not. It appeared that even entering a chat room had its prescribed behaviors.

"Look, Laura...don't start worrying about this. You've plunged into a very deep pool and a lot of this stuff..." he waved his hands at the screen, "involves people who have been living and thinking this way for their whole lives."

Mark swung Laura's chair around to face him. "Remember that there are a gazillion different degrees of submission. From the occasional scarf-around-the-headboard, through fun with leather and whips, to kneeling every time your Master enters the room. There's Doms and subs, and Masters and slaves, and everything in between."

Laura couldn't have looked away from Mark if she'd tried. The picture he was painting was elusive but fascinating. She felt more intrigued by the minute and more alive somehow at the thought of what could lie ahead for her and Adam.

"It's most likely that you will become a sexual submissive. God, don't fire me for talking like this, okay?"

Laura's eyes were wide as she shook her head. Speech was beyond her as wild visions traipsed their studded and leathered way through her mind.

"Sexual submissives enjoy the dynamics of a relationship where sexually one partner is submissive to the other. It is simply a matter of adding a different and potentially exciting level of fun to a relationship, and invoking some elements of trust, and vulnerability that can deepen and intensify not only the sex, but the love between two people." Mark pulled his face into a very sober expression. "It ends at the bedroom door."

Laura nodded at his words. "So being a sexual submissive is a private, between couples, kind of thing?"

"Good grief, all this is private and between couples, Laura. We don't go around wearing leather thongs that we flash at a moment's notice. There are subtle hints that others in the lifestyle might pick up on, but you aren't going to find yourself on a leash behind Adam as you pick out frozen foods in the supermarket. If you do, let me know. I want pictures."

Mark couldn't hide his grin. "It really is quite funny. Here you are, queen of all you survey. High powered Priestess of Judicia, ruling a big firm with an iron and velvet fist. There's hubby, dear sweet Adam, enriching the lives of innocent fourth graders with crayfish life cycles and the presidents of the USA. And who turns out to be the Dom?" Mark batted his eyelashes. "Why Adam the Gorgeous, of course."

Laura pressed her hands against her eyes. "I'm soooo glad this situation is providing entertainment for someone," she said dryly.

"Only me, darling. You know my lips are sealed tight." He mimed zipping his mouth to Laura, who sighed again.

"Well, dear Mr. Submissive Zipped Lips, what the heck do I wear to a wake held in a Dungeon? To which I am to be accompanied by my newly-revealed Dom husband, and where it appears I will get to meet his former Pet. Or Pets, plural. I haven't figured that out yet."

"Hmm." Mark rested one elegant hip on the desk and pondered the question. "Well. One thing is for sure."

Laura raised an eyebrow.

"We need to shop."

* * * * *

Adam couldn't believe that they were on their way to Master Granger's wake. The last two days had been somewhat of a blur for him.

Both he and Laura had tiptoed around each other, carefully not mentioning the wild sex that had erupted between them, or the trip to the Dungeon that lay ahead. He was thankful, for once, for Laura's unusual sexual response.

It had taken him a year or so into their relationship to get used to Laura's habit of dropping off to sleep immediately after her orgasms. She'd apologized many times, but said it was just part of the way her body worked. Adam had mentioned it briefly to his doctor during one of his annual physicals, and been reassured that yes, it was quite normal for some women to enter the resolution phase of sexual arousal only to immediately relax so completely that their bodies slept.

He had just taken it as part and parcel of Laura, who she was, how she responded. It didn't change the way he loved her, and God knew it had never affected the sex.

And God knew how long it had been since they'd exploded around each other like they had on Wednesday night.

Adam could sense the tension in Laura, however, as she sat next to him, gazing out of the car window.

She looked amazing.

His jaw had dropped as she came out of the bedroom to collect her bag.

Her hair was down, loose and shining around her shoulders, making her appear more vulnerable than usual. Her black pantsuit was a brilliantly cut exercise in sensuality.

The jacket was simple and understated, double breasted, with modest lapels. She wore it buttoned all the way, with a single strand of pearls at her neck. Adam could see no blouse.

The slim pants hugged her hips and fell to the tops of her ankle boots in a straight line of neatly creased fabric. As she turned, Adam noticed how snugly they caressed her buttocks. Not a line of underwear showed.

He couldn't resist. He reached over and ran his hand over her bottom.

She jumped. "Adam!"

He grinned. "Couldn't help it. I like this suit." He'd felt not a trace of a panty. It was a strong possibility that his conservative lawyer wife was not wearing any underwear. His cock liked the thought. So did he.

"Well, I'm glad. After all, I have to meet Fay and her friends," said Laura, not realizing that her voice reflected her uncertainty.

"Sweetheart, I haven't seen Fay or anyone from the Dungeon in years. And even when they were part of my life, I chose you."

"I know. I'm sorry. I guess all wives go through this when they know they're going to meet ex-girlfriends." She grimaced and let Adam pull her into his arms.

She leaned her softness against him. Damn. He couldn't feel a bra either. Did she have anything on underneath?

Distracted, he had a difficult time following her conversation.

"...how long it will take?"

"Mmm?"

"Adam? I said do you have an idea how long the drive will take?"

"Sorry. My mind was wandering." Underneath your jacket and pants. "About an hour, I should guess."

And his estimate was very close, because slightly over an hour's drive had brought them to the winding gravel driveway of Master Granger's Dungeon.

Laura had been mostly silent next to him as they drove, deep in her own thoughts, as was he.

He remembered his first drive to this place.

He'd been a senior in college, confused, lonely, unable to keep a girlfriend, and a little angry at women in general.

Then he'd met Granger Fields at a seminar on human relationships, and been struck by the older man's humor, intelligence and sympathetic friendship. The result had been an invitation to dinner at the Dungeon, and that had led to Adam moving in and changing his life so completely.

His years there had allowed him to absorb the concepts involved in being a Dom. To achieve success and to become a Trainer.

Fay had been one of his trainees.

It had been very sexual between them, in spite of Master Granger's disapproval. But Fay and Adam were young, healthy and attracted to each other.

It spoke volumes for the Master's trust that he continued to allow Adam to train Fay even though they had crossed the physical boundary and had become sexually intimate.

Adam couldn't help but remember how it was to have Fay beg for his cock.

To have a woman desire him to the point where his every need, his every thought was of prime importance to her. Where her only goal was to please him.

He had cared very deeply for her, and been moved by how much she was prepared to offer him. It wasn't until he met Laura that he realized how little he was giving Fay in return.

With Laura he gave all he had.

He'd eased back and gentled Fay away from him, and she had, in some obscure way, understood. She'd cried, but Master Granger had been there to smooth over the rough moments, and Fay had become the Master's slave, slipping into the role as if she'd been born to it.

Adam had never looked back.

Until now.

Until the gravel crunching beneath the wheels of the car opened the floodgates of his memory, and his eyes filled with tears as he realized that this time there would be no Master waiting to embrace his friend on the porch.

Laura slipped her hand into Adam's. It was cold, and Adam found the shock of her cool touch brought his thoughts back to the present.

"You okay?" she asked, concern for him evident in her gaze.

"Yeah, thanks." He squeezed her hand. "It's just difficult for a moment, realizing he's not here."

Laura moved nearer and slipped her arm around Adam's waist, letting her body lean against him and share his emotions.

He dropped a kiss on her head, understanding her gesture, and together they turned to the porch.

The door opened and a petite woman stepped out, sun shining on her blonde hair.

She lowered her eyes respectfully. "Welcome home, Adam, Sir."

"Hello Fay."

Chapter 4

The house was beautiful, as were the grounds upon which it sat. The French doors from the great room were open, and Laura eased herself away from a conversation to stroll outside. And breathe.

She felt stifled inside, lungs oppressed, crushed, prevented from expanding and taking in the oxygen she so desperately needed.

Everyone had been incredibly charming to her and made her feel welcome, even before Adam had introduced her. She noted that no mention had been made of her profession, her professional name, or anything personal. She was "Laura, my wife."

And for her, right now, that was more than enough.

She had not really known what to expect as they'd followed Fay into the house. But this certainly hadn't been it.

Gracious rooms, elegantly decorated, and tastefully furnished? Where were the stocks? The whips? The odd crosses upon which slaves would be chained and punished?

Instead of a dungeon, she'd found a country estate. She couldn't quite decide whether to be glad or sorry, but she did know she liked it.

Who could fail to like the tall ceilings, the book covered walls, and the mammoth fireplace whose darkened bricks told of many a cozy blaze during long winter nights.

She smiled at herself and chuckled as she realized how stupid so many of her preconceived notions had been.

And yet…

She turned and leaned against the low stone balustrade that ringed the patio. From this vantage point she could see back through the windows into the room she'd just left.

And there it was. A certain something that said this was no ordinary gathering of friends at a wake.

Perhaps it was her heightened awareness of people's reactions to each other. Perhaps it was her research into a lifestyle that she'd previously considered involved only druggies, dropouts and maybe motorcycle gangs or leather lovers.

But her eye was accustomed to dealing with large groups— it was part and parcel of her job. And this group was different. There were tight knots of people, touching, nodding, some with eyes cast down, others with heads held high. But always they were radiating some kind of togetherness. A familiarity with each other that bespoke a certain level of intimacy. There were a few tears now and again as they spoke of Master Granger.

Many hugs and touches were exchanged. They were consoling, loving, affectionate and grieving. It was as if a large extended family had returned to share the pain of loss.

And then there were the others. People like her, circulating, clutching their glasses of wine, smiling, chatting, making polite conversation, but clearly not friends, or even close acquaintances. Not part of the circle.

Laura was fascinated by it, even as she envied Adam his place in the middle of it.

"Interesting lot, aren't they?"

A brash voice interrupted her thoughts, and she turned to see a large man standing beside her, stroking his beard in an effort to look scholarly, she supposed.

"Yes, quite."

"Of course, my slave is in there. I let her mingle with her friends for a while. After all, got to be a caring Master about all this."

His arrogance was only matched by his ignorance, thought Laura. Poor slave, whoever she was.

"But you can bet she'll be wanting my leash back on before too long. Who's your slave?"

Laura considered the question, amused that he'd assumed she was a Domme.

"Have you been with your slave long?" she asked, ignoring his question.

"Oh yes, six months or so now. She's properly trained, I can tell you. Loves the crop, does my gal."

The combination of superiority and pseudo-Englishman attitude was beginning to grate on Laura's nerves.

"Cyril, Jennifer is awaiting you," came a voice from behind Laura.

"Oh…er…very well. Good…thank you…" the big man stuttered and deflated before Laura's eyes. He nodded at her and scurried off, leaving Fay to take his place beside Laura.

She smiled. "Obnoxious son-of-a-bitch, isn't he?"

Laura chuckled. "Yes. I can't imagine what his slave's life must be like."

"Oh he doesn't have a slave." Fay's smile grew. "He is a slave."

Laura's eyes widened as she watched Fay bravely try to suppress her laughter. It was too much. They both gave way and enjoyed the humor of the situation.

"Oh lord," gasped Laura. "I should have known."

"Nah," chuckled Fay. "How could you? You're nobody's slave. Not even Adam's."

Laura stilled. Perhaps this was not the time for diplomacy, political correctness or any kind of pretense.

She looked into Fay's blue eyes and read many emotions there.

"Do you still love him?"

The response was unforced, prompt and honest. "How could I not?"

It wasn't the answer Laura was expecting. But she held her tongue, feeling that there was more to come. She was right.

"He was my trainer, Laura. That is a special position for a man to hold in a slave's life. Through Adam I learned to give freely, and that what I gave would come back to me in love, in caring, in protection, for all my life. I will never be able to find the words to tell you how I feel about the man who gave me all that. It's love and so much more. But..." she tugged on her lower lip, "it's not the sort of love you're talking about."

It was Laura's turn to let her eyes silently ask Fay for an explanation.

The birds sang and the conversations continued around the two women who found themselves locked into a space all their own.

"Has Adam become your Master, Laura?"

"No. We've not...we've never...it was only recently I learned of Adam's interest in all this..." Laura struggled to find the words.

Fay thought for a moment. "And now you know, how do you feel?"

How did she feel? God, how long did they have? Confused, scared, puzzled, all these words flew through her mind, but only one came out.

"Intrigued."

Fay smiled. "Good. When Adam met you, he gave you his heart. He chose not to share this with you, because I think he was scared he'd lose you. He's given up so much for you, Laura. Think about it. A Dom, someone who could be a Master, and he lets it all go for love of one woman. You."

Laura nodded, trying to grasp the magnitude of what Adam had done, the changes he'd made. All for her.

"I'm feeling rather humbled by it."

"As you should," smiled Fay. "But you're here now. It's been, what, five years or so?"

Laura nodded.

"So you know you can trust Adam. That you love Adam."

"More than my life, Fay. He's my other half." And that was the absolute truth.

"Then perhaps it's time to let the relationship grow. Time to let Adam reclaim some of what he once was. And time to find out what you can be. That's the kind of love that Adam deserves. I could never have given him that. I'm not strong enough."

Fay raised her hand and stroked Laura's cheek, letting her hand sift through the hair stirring in the late afternoon breeze.

"Laura, I watched you today. I saw the comfort and ease with which you handled this crowd. You're obviously at home in groups, able to chat on many different levels with different people. You're a professional woman, quite in control of her emotions. But then you look at Adam. And there's something in your eyes..."

She leaned over and dropped the lightest of kisses on Laura's cheek. "Something that makes me believe I'll be calling you 'sister' before long. Open your heart, Laura. Let that hidden part of Adam come inside you and discover what pleasure can really be between two people."

Fay smiled and pulled back, leaving Laura to sort through her muddled thoughts.

She shivered and realized that she'd been alone on the patio for some time and the sun was beginning to set.

Someone had lit the candles inside and their glow encouraged her back inside. Adam met her at the door.

"Sweetheart, you're chilled. Come get a cup of something warm. I'm sorry I neglected you, it's hard not to get involved in some long conversations..."

"Adam, please." She put her hand on his arm, and felt the absurd desire to lower her eyes respectfully. "It's no problem. You have many people to talk to here. I understand."

And she realized suddenly that she did. In this environment, Adam was something new, something dynamic. Not the warm, caring teacher, nor the loving husband, but the vibrant and—yes—dominant Adam Burns. His head was high, his back straight, and he carried himself slightly differently. He accepted the lowered glances and respectful greetings naturally, and without affectation, as if they were his due.

Laura felt something drop away from her mind and found she could watch Adam with a new clarity of vision. How could she have missed it? The air of leadership that encircled him?

Was it just that a fourth grade classroom or a black tie legal banquet were not places to expect such a thing?

Or had she just never looked for it in the first place?

Her mind had no answers, but her heart swelled as she looked at her husband with new eyes.

He was hers. Her man, her husband, and her lover. What else could he be? Could he be her Master? Could they explore this new dimension together? Would he let her try?

Laura took a deep breath. There was only one way to find out.

* * * * *

The long box rested on the back seat of the car as they prepared for the journey home.

Adam had been torn between laughter and tears as he'd opened it.

"Master always intended for you to have this, Adam Sir," said Fay, offering the box. "It was one of his wishes. Please accept it as such."

Adam had smiled, bent forward and kissed her gently on the cheek. "Of course, Fay. I shall always honor the Master's wishes." Then he'd looked inside and laughed.

"My first flogger. I can't believe he kept it all these years." His hand stroked the soft red tails and caressed the worn handle. "It carries many good memories of our times together. I shall treasure it."

He wasn't sure if Laura had any idea of what it was for, but he let it go for the time being, just seeing that it was secure. He hadn't lied when he said he'd treasure it.

Laura reached out and stopped him from starting the engine. "Adam, can we talk for a moment?"

Adam breathed deeply, but released the key. He'd known this was coming. How could he not?

"Sure, sweetheart."

He watched as she nervously nibbled her lower lip. It wasn't often his brilliant corporate wizard of a wife was at a loss for words.

"I have a confession."

Whoa. That was a surprise. "You do?"

"Yeah. Um...the other night, Wednesday night. I came home early."

"Oh." Adam kept the surprise from his voice. He had not expected this.

"And...and I saw your site and the invite to Master Granger's wake. I...I put the pieces together Adam. I realized that you were...that you used to be...that this was..."

"That I am a Dom. Is that what you're trying to say?" He reached over and touched her hand. It turned within his and gripped him, hard.

"Oh yes. Thank you. It is. So I wanted to know about it. And I did a whole bunch of research on it. Mark helped."

Adam smiled, thinking how helpful Mark must have been. He and Mark had read each other as fellow adherents immediately, and bonded. Quietly, and without fuss, they had both known they'd found a friend and someone in whom their secrets would be safe.

And coincidentally, a friend who had often alleviated the major boredom of some of Laura's more agonizingly pompous affairs. "I'm sure Mark was a great help. Do you have questions, Laura? Worries? Concerns? What is it, love?"

Her hands twisted this way and that beneath his.

"Adam, I want...I want..." She raised her eyes to his, almost as if she was scared to mouth the words.

"What do you want, Laura? Tell me, sweetheart," he urged gently, squeezing her hands tight.

Please don't let her say she wants to leave me, he prayed. This was the moment he'd dreaded for so many years. This was why he'd never told her anything about his history with this lifestyle.

She took a deep breath. "I want to be your submissive."

Adam's jaw dropped. "What?"

"You heard me. I want to be your sub."

For a moment Adam's mind refused to function. "I...I..." he stuttered, trying desperately to reconnect the neural passageways that would allow him to speak coherently.

"For a Dom, you're surprisingly speechless," risked Laura, giving him a rather naughty little sideways glance.

The world clicked back into place and Adam felt his lungs fill. "Are you quite sure you understand what that means, Laura?"

"No. No, I'm not sure at all, Adam. And that's why I'm so glad I have you. I love you and trust you, and you've been my other half for five years now. But seeing you here and learning everything I've learned makes me realize that something has been missing between us. Something I didn't know we didn't have has been slowly driving us down into someplace I don't want to be. Does that make any sense?"

Her frown as she tried to express her feelings touched something deep inside Adam. They really were on the same wavelength.

"It does make sense. I've felt it too. But I don't know if the answer is you becoming a sub..."

Laura raised her hand, interrupting him. "Adam, I must make one thing clear. I want to be your sub. I don't believe I can be your slave. If this is not possible, then tell me now. We'll work something else out."

Adam smiled. "I don't think I could ever be your Master, love, so that's not an issue. Neither of us are cut out for the 24/7 lifestyle and all that it entails. That's for others, not us. Not me. And certainly not you. But if I understand you correctly, you would like to be submissive to me...sexually."

Adam felt his cock shiver as she nodded and dropped her eyes.

"Yes please, Adam. Sir." She'd added the respectful title she'd learned by watching Fay and the other pets. His wife was nothing if not observant.

His lips curled and his heart lifted. Perhaps the Master had sent him a special gift, and not just the one in the box behind them.

"Very well, Laura, pet." He felt her tremor as he addressed her in the D/s style. "Let us start with a little experiment, shall we?"

"What, here?" Laura peered through the twilight around her at the other cars. All was silent.

She turned back to Adam with a question on her face. He raised one eyebrow and stared at her expressionlessly. It was a look he'd perfected so many years ago on his subs. He'd only used it occasionally since then, although it had proved effective with little Fred Stubbins who was about to put a frog down Jennifer Moreton's dress during their field trip last month.

Like Fred Stubbins, Laura quailed before "the look."

"Yes, Adam. What do I...what do you want me to do?"

"Undo your jacket and spread it apart. I want to see your breasts."

He heard her indrawn breath and saw her hands move to obey him, yet waiver over her buttons.

"Undo your jacket, Laura."

She obeyed, and his cock high fived itself. Shit. This was Laura. He'd have to be careful or he'd come all over the steering wheel. That was not going to help his image as her all-knowing, all-seeing, all-powerful Dom.

She spread the sides of the jacket carefully, revealing her soft whiteness to his gaze. As he had suspected, she wore no bra. The pearls gleamed in the twilight, resting against her soft swells. The nipples hardened as he looked at them.

He raised his hand and lifted the beads, letting them trickle back against her breasts. Her breathing was ragged.

Time for step two.

"Now, undo your pants and slip them down to your knees. I know you are not wearing underwear. I want you to feel the touch of your buttocks against the car seat."

He heard her gulp, but this time there was no hesitation. She did as he asked, letting her bare bottom ease down onto the soft leather.

Adam felt a bead of sweat form on his upper lip, and he surreptitiously wiped it away.

"Spread your thighs so that I can see your pussy."

"Adam," she moaned, following his instructions. "God, Adam."

The Almighty was being invoked a lot. He was praying too, praying for control. Praying that he wouldn't give in to the urge to bury his face in her darkness, or jerk her onto his lap where he could free his cock and plunge deep inside her. Right this minute.

Wrenching his wayward hormones back into line, Adam nodded approvingly. "Good girl. Now we can go home."

He reached over and turned the key in the ignition.

Chapter 5

Laura couldn't ever remember being this turned on. Every fiber of her being was sexually aroused. She could smell her own scent and feel the slight brush of her own breaths against her naked flesh.

Every truck that passed them on the highway was a potential terror, every SUV that loomed large beside them a cause for fear.

"Don't worry. They can't see you."

Adam seemed to be able to read her thoughts. But then he was used to this, she supposed.

She shifted, feeling the car seat beneath her and allowing the sensation to arouse her even more. A little moan escaped her throat and she shivered.

"Are you cold?" Adam was obviously attuned to her body.

"No, not at all. Thank you. Sir."

Adam glanced over and grinned. "You make an excellent sub, pet. Spread your legs wider."

Damn him. How could she? The pants were tight around her thighs. She wriggled.

"Uh-huh. Keep that jacket open. Think about how you're going to move before you do it."

Laura clenched her teeth and eased her pants further down, while making sure her jacket stayed where it was. There. She'd done it.

"Good girl." Adam casually reached down and cupped her dripping pussy.

She groaned. "God, Adam. Careful…"

He ground his hand into her clit, making her gasp, then pulled it away and put it back on the steering wheel.

"Are you questioning me?" His words were sharp and surprisingly cutting.

"No, no…" she immediately responded. Damn, he was good.

"Good. Keep your legs spread open, pet. We'll be home soon."

And then what? She wanted to ask. How do I get upstairs with my boobs hanging out? Is he going to allow me to dress, or do I have to shuffle up the back elevator with my pants down?

Strangely enough, the thought of such a thing was arousing, and Laura found her body relaxing into its nakedness. She felt light and joyful, ready to follow the slightest instructions from her…her husband? Her Dom? What was he? And what was he becoming?

They pulled into the quiet parking lot behind their apartment building and Adam turned off the engine.

He turned to Laura.

"You will now fasten the middle two buttons of your jacket and the button of your pants. You will leave your fly open for my hands should I decide to touch your pussy. We will take the main elevator to our apartment. If we are joined by others, you will turn to me and press yourself against me, resting your head on my chest. Do you understand?"

His voice was firm, his instructions simple.

She nodded. "Yes. I understand."

They got out of the car and Laura arranged herself as instructed. Adam carried the package and Laura's bag.

Praying for solitude, Laura crossed the brightly lit hall to the elevators, keeping her hands lowered in front of her. She wasn't too worried about her jacket hanging open, but she could feel the brush of cool air on her pussy. It was unnerving to say the least.

The doors slid apart and they got in, but just before they closed, a voice yelled "Adam, hold up…" and a man ran onto the elevator and stood, catching his breath.

It was Jason Burke, the quiet and reclusive owner of the penthouse condominium.

"Thanks," he murmured, nodding politely to Laura.

"My pleasure," answered Adam quietly. His gaze fell on his wife.

Mindful of his instructions, Laura turned slightly and leaned against Adam. To Jason Burke, she would simply be a tired wife taking advantage of her husband's convenient body.

However, said husband was, at that moment, slipping one hand inside her trousers and fondling her cunt.

Roughly he teased her flesh, and finding it slippery he thrust two fingers up into her, bringing a gasp to her throat that she bravely stifled.

The digital numbers chimed as the elevator rose, and within moments the doors to the sixth floor were sliding open.

Laura stumbled slightly as she and Adam moved to step out.

"Good night, Jason," nodded Adam.

"Have a good night, Adam." Jason Burke's eyes met Adam's in a long look and then he smiled at Laura.

"Oh I will. Thanks."

The doors slid slowly closed as Laura watched Jason Burke's face. His nostrils were flaring and he was inhaling. Deeply.

He was scenting her.

God, she'd never be able to look him in the face again.

Blushing, she turned to follow Adam letting him precede her into their apartment.

She realized how quiet it was as the door shut behind them, locking them into their own private space.

"You did well, Laura. Would you like to continue?"

Adam posed the question formally, but Laura noticed a slight shake to his hands as he hung up his jacket.

"Yes please, Adam." She spoke quietly but honestly. She couldn't remember ever having such an extraordinary experience as driving home with her body naked and displayed like that. She was aroused and excited and wanted more.

Much more.

"Very well. The first thing we are going to do is to help you understand that you will be giving me control of your body. Will you please go into the bathroom and remove all your clothing? Remove your makeup as well, and wait for me there."

A shiver of anticipation ran up Laura's spine. Oh boy. This was going to be a night she'd long remember. She just knew it.

She obediently turned and headed for the bathroom.

* * * * *

Adam knew his hands were shaking and was helpless to stop it. The mere thought of having Laura as his sub was sending bolts of electricity through his body, most of which ended up charging his cock to dangerously high levels. He tried desperately to recall his days of training, of quietly dominating a sub and leading her along a new path.

Ah crap. This was Laura. The woman he had loved since the moment he set eyes on her. The woman he knew was his. Rational thought was almost impossible.

But he also knew she was excited, aroused and fascinated by what he was doing to her. She wanted this, at least for tonight, and he loved her more than enough to play along.

Whether she'd understand, whether she'd embrace the concept or enjoy the experience…well these were questions that remained to be answered.

He took several deep breaths and, with some difficulty, reached for that place inside himself that had lain dormant for so long. That place that opened like a flower to admit a submissive, to welcome their gifts of control and power, and that offered love, protection and fulfillment in return. That place that allowed an exchange of something precious, something special.

Would Laura be able to go there too? How would she respond to the shift in dynamics that was about to take place?

He didn't know. But damn, he was looking forward to finding out.

Just the thought of Laura slipping out of her suit in the bathroom and standing naked at the sink, brought a rush of heat to his groin.

Gathering himself yet again, he went into their bedroom and stripped to his skin, hurriedly divesting himself of his clothing and reaching into his closet for his robe. Not the warm fuzzy one this time, but the black silk one with the oriental dragon slithering over his shoulder and down his back.

It had been an impulse purchase that he'd had little chance to wear, but for tonight it seemed to be right. It would be different enough that Laura would be reminded of what was changing between them. And yet not overwhelmingly strange or distracting.

The silk slid across his cock like a caress and he gritted his teeth. He'd love to be able to tell Laura that just the thought of what was to come was turning him on, but this was something he couldn't yet share with her. First, he had to bring her up to somewhere near the same level of arousal.

He knew she was getting there. She'd been hotter than hell under his hand in the car, and the elevator had reeked of her scent.

Jason Burke had known.

Shrewd, aware and very reclusive, Jason Burke and Adam had met and chatted over the hood of Jason's sports car.

Adam had enjoyed the conversation with the older man, but felt no need to pursue an acquaintance. Jason had apparently been in full agreement with Adam's decision, because they smiled, exchanged greetings when they passed, and had shared a pleasant hour over beer at the obligatory tenants Christmas function in the little pub around the corner last year.

Adam felt there was a great deal below the surface of Jason Burke. He wasn't surprised that the man had picked up on Laura's fragrance.

His mind returned to Laura, who was waiting for him. He considered and discarded various possibilities, thoughts now focusing on the evening ahead.

This was a slightly different situation than a simple introductory Dom/sub encounter. This was Laura, his wife. For five years she'd borne his name, and for seven years they'd been lovers.

There was an understood familiarity between them, for each other's bodies each other's minds. They knew each other's strengths, weaknesses and sensitivities. There was an enormous foundation of information for Adam to draw on, much more than he would normally have found in such a situation.

He let his mind dwell on the possibilities for a few moments, knowing that the longer Laura waited, naked, in the bathroom, the greater her level of arousal.

There was nothing better than the sub's mind for beginning the adrenaline rush and exciting the body. He ran through a variety of scenarios, enjoying some, dismissing others.

What did he want to achieve tonight? Where did he want Laura to be at the end of their session? And what level of groundwork would he be able to lay for any future D/s relationship that might develop between them?

Adam sighed. These were important questions, and he would have loved a couple of weeks to work them through thoroughly. He didn't have a couple of weeks.

So, he stuck with his basic tenet. Keep it simple. He opened a drawer and removed two scarves.

His lips curved. He'd be blatantly obvious and yet surprisingly unexpected.

Laura was in for the ride of her life.

* * * * *

While plans were being made for her evening's entertainment, Laura was watching the goose bumps as they paraded, full force, across her naked skin. The light in the bathroom had never seemed so harsh as it did now. She critically observed every dip, bump, mole and curve, wondering if her body would stand the test of being closely observed by Adam.

After all, they'd enjoyed each other for years, but never in quite such clinical surroundings.

Suddenly the fluorescent lights seemed to glare terribly harshly off the white ceramic tiles.

Why the hell did bathrooms have to be so brilliantly lit? It wasn't like you were going to do brain surgery in them, for heaven's sake.

She shivered, crossing her arms and running her hands over her skin to her shoulders in an attempt to warm herself. What was he going to do to her?

She'd read plenty on suggested "scenes," and wondered if Adam would tie her up, or blindfold her. Would he want to wash her in the shower? Is that why she was here?

Would he spank her? Would she like being spanked? She glanced around her. Yes, her hairbrush was within reach. It was a wooden one. Of course, his was too.

There was the oddly shaped bottle of perfume that suddenly looked terribly phallic. Oh God, he wouldn't would he?

He'd probably handcuff her. He'd have to if he wanted to do that.

Laura's mind swirled round and over a million different thoughts, some crystal clear and arousing, some blurry, some downright scary. She began to wonder if she'd done the right thing. Maybe she wasn't cut out to be submissive. Maybe she should just yank his handcuffs away from him and whack his bottom.

She leaned on the sink and closed her eyes. Oh God. Maybe she shouldn't be here at all.

It was too late, however. The door opened and Adam walked in.

But not her Adam. Not the Adam who casually dropped a kiss on her cheek every morning as he tied his tie in front of their bedroom mirror. Not the Adam who made tea for her on those nights when she was too tired to lift a finger.

And not the Adam who softly and gently brought her to climax in their bed.

This Adam was different.

He seemed almost taller in that amazing black silk robe she'd almost forgotten about. His gaze roved her body, his expression hungry. He radiated masculine sensuality as he looked her over, and she found she had lowered her eyes before his without even realizing it.

He was masterful in a subtle sense, his body language letting her know that she was there at his sufferance.

He carried two scarves. Hmm. Okay, she could handle being tied up and blindfolded. She felt her pussy flush with heat and her juices leaving their wetness between her thighs.

He nodded, as if pleased with his inspection.

"Laura, spread your legs wide." His order was quiet but firm. There was no question in her mind. She obeyed.

"Now spread the lips of your pussy with your fingers. I wish to see whether your body is anticipating this evening with pleasure."

He leaned against the laundry hamper, casually running the scarves between his fingers.

Laura blushed, trying to make herself remember that this was Adam her husband. He'd seen her there lots of times before. It was nothing new.

So why was she blushing?

Well, it was bright light. She was deliberately opening herself for his inspection. It was freaky, it was wild and it was making something deep inside her ache with arousal.

She slid her hand down to her mound and spread her fingers, pulling at her delicate folds. He shouldn't have any doubts in his mind how she was reacting, because she could feel her juices dripping onto her thighs.

He clearly didn't, because he nodded. "Very good. Wait here."

Damn the man. She was left holding her own flesh while he went away. Now what? She hoped he wasn't going off to catch a rerun of "Law and Order" while she waited.

He returned, holding a clothes hanger. A wooden clothes hanger.

Her eyes widened and a chill of fear ran up her spine. Mad visions of bruises, antibiotic ointment and excuses about running into a door ran across her brain, leaving cold footprints that chilled her soul.

He held out the clothes hanger. "Pick up your suit and hang it up properly."

She released a breath she didn't know she'd held. Damn him and his neatness urges.

Thankfully moving her hand away from herself, Laura did as she was told and picked up her suit from its pile on the floor. She carefully folded the pants and shook out the jacket, putting both neatly on the hanger.

Silently she glanced at Adam for the next instruction.

He nodded at the hook on the back of the door, and she crossed the room to hang the suit up.

"Now please step into the tub and face me."

Taking a deep breath, Laura stepped over the side of the bath and stood, as instructed, facing Adam.

"Raise your arms above your head."

Cautiously, she raised her arms, watching silently as Adam brought one of the scarves over and proceeded to tie her wrists together. His movements were sure and within seconds she was bound lightly but securely.

He then tugged on the scarf and fastened her to the shower rod.

Whoa. That was a surprise.

Her pose thrust her breasts toward him and she felt even more exposed when he took one of her legs and pulled it toward him.

"Rest this foot on the side of the bath."

She did so, realizing that she was now completely revealed to him, her body his to do with as he would.

Her breathing was unsteady as he ran his hands over her skin.

"You please me greatly, pet," he breathed.

"I'm glad, Adam," she answered, only to see a frown cross his face.

"You will not speak from now on, unless I give you permission. Do you understand? Nod if you understand."

At a bit of a loss, Laura nodded.

Adam reached for the other scarf. "To ensure your obedience, I'm going to gag you."

Laura dragged in a breath as Adam placed the second scarf around her head and between her lips, effectively silencing her. Her eyes widened as he fastened it behind her. She could breathe, but not talk.

Okay. This was getting freaky.

Adam stepped back and surveyed his handiwork, nodding to himself.

"Good. Now there are some rules for tonight which I wish you to follow, and I must make sure you understand."

He opened the cabinet door and pulled out a small bag of bath salts. It was soft and pink and had a little plastic rose on top.

"In D/s play there is a need for something called a "safe word." Did your reading explain this to you?"

Laura raised her eyebrows, not sure how to respond without invoking his ire or breaking a rule.

"You may nod your response for yes, shake your head for no."

Laura nodded.

"Good. Because I have gagged you and removed your ability to speak, we need to institute some other method of your using a safe word, so for tonight, it will be this..." He held up the small bag, showed it to her and then reached up and put it in her tied hand, making sure she had a firm grip on it.

"If, at any time, you wish to stop play, all you have to do is drop that bag. I shall be aware of your movements at all times. Do you understand?"

Laura nodded.

"And do you trust me enough for this to be effective? Do you believe I will stop if you ask me to do so?"

Adam stared into her eyes, making Laura realize how important this question was.

She nodded, and watched as his expression became purely sensual.

"Good. Laura, pet, one of the most important beliefs amongst those of us who follow this lifestyle is something called Safe, Sane and Consensual play. Did you also read about that?"

Laura nodded energetically, having found many references to this most important of all rules for any kind of bondage play.

"I firmly adhere to that principle. That's why you have your safety mechanism tonight, and at other times we shall select a safe word for you, should you desire to continue along this path."

Laura nodded again. God, why didn't he get on with it? Whatever it was he was going to do to her.

She was naked and ready, dammit.

And ooh, look, so was he.

His robe swung as he moved and she glimpsed his cock, rigid and erect.

Suddenly, she relaxed. This was still Adam. Her lover, her husband and soon to be her Dom. She wanted him with every single iota of emotion she had. She loved him beyond words. Nothing he could do to her would be anything other than wonderful.

Probably.

It was that little niggling doubt that sent shivers up her spine.

She watched him cross the room to the bathroom cabinet and rummage inside. He pulled out some powder, some shaving cream and…and…her razor?

Good God.

Chapter 6

Adam was in dire straits. The woman he loved was bound and gagged and revealed in all her beauty before him.

Her body was wet and hungry for his, her eyes were dilating with anticipation and arousal, and his was responding to all these signals with a painful need to mate.

He could not remember feeling this sense of urgency with another sub. Ever.

He took a deep breath and nearly did himself an injury as he grappled for some vestige of mental control. He had to stay in control.

Especially tonight. The pattern that they established tonight would go a long way toward defining their future within this lifestyle. If it was going to work it was up to him. He had to make it good for her, good enough for her to want to pursue it.

Shaking, trembling, stuttering and coming over himself just from looking at her was not the way to go.

He let out the breath slowly, attempting a measure of meditation as he exhaled.

He took the implements over to the bath, and almost lost his control again as he smelled her body, hot for him and awaiting his touch.

He busied himself running water into the sink and shaking the can of shaving cream.

It took a couple of agonizing moments, but finally he felt calm enough to turn to her.

"I am going to shave you, Laura. Shave the hair from one of the parts of your body that you will be surrendering to me. Do you understand?"

Laura nodded at him, eyes wide.

"This will remind you that you belong to me. I wish you to keep this area shaved. Every few days as necessary." He glanced up and she nodded again, signifying her assent.

He took a couple of silent breaths and reached for the shaving cream. "Oh, and Laura? You are forbidden to come unless I give you permission. Is that clear?"

Her eyes were questioning as she absorbed the meaning of his words.

He removed the top of the can and squirted the foam onto his fingers. At least that's what he meant to do.

Of course the damn thing was pointing the wrong way and he squirted a nice dollop of fragrant foam onto his foot. Shit.

He hoped she was distracted enough by his last comment not to notice. This time he managed to get a respectable pile of shaving cream onto his hand. He began to massage her mound.

"You will not come without permission, Laura. I will be the one to allow you to enjoy an orgasm. I shall decide whether the time is right, or whether you should wait longer…"

He rubbed the shaving cream over her pussy, knowing she was already sensitive.

She moaned softly, behind the gag.

"You have my permission to make whatever sounds you wish as I touch you. It pleases me to know that you are enjoying the experience."

His hand rubbed a little harder and she obeyed by giving him a very nice groan.

He reached for the razor, dipping it in the sink.

"Your pussy is going to be quite bald, pet. It will not be able to hide its secrets from me."

He gently stroked the razor across her flesh, taking a swath of dark hair with it. Laura was a neat person by nature, and shaved her bikini line regularly. So it was not an excessively difficult job to render her pussy naked.

Just a very appealing one.

He rinsed the razor and applied more shaving cream, bringing another moan to her lips.

"Remember. You may not come."

He stood upright, rubbing the shaving cream into her flesh. "Your breasts please me, Laura. Offer them to me."

She looked wildly at him, her arms automatically beginning to tug on their bonds.

"Think how I might like them offered, Laura. You're going to be my submissive. It will be for you to think up ways to please me. Your breasts and their lovely nipples please me. How can you offer them to me?"

Laura's flesh colored up nicely and her face flushed. His hands brought fresh moisture from her cunt and he could feel her heat as his words and his touches aroused her even more.

She was obviously considering his words.

Then she leaned toward him, straightening her spine and pushing her breasts out even more.

"Good pet. Excellent," smiled Adam.

He leaned forward and took one breast into his mouth, suckling firmly on the nipple, tugging it with his tongue and gently biting down.

Laura sighed and moaned through her gag, her hips beginning to sway toward his hand.

He released her with a little plop, blowing on her wet nipple and watching as it beaded up even harder.

She thrust forward again, as if begging for him to take her back into his mouth.

He immediately pulled back.

"You forget, Laura. You are here to pleasure me, not the other way around."

A sob broke from Laura's throat as her hips moved.

"Now keep still. I haven't finished yet."

He returned to his grooming efforts, slicking the razor carefully around her mound, and rinsing it often to make sure he was getting all the hair away from her soft flesh. He pushed her legs further apart, removing the stray hairs from her flesh and stroking the softness he found around her cunt.

Finally, he was satisfied.

She was soaked with her own moisture, sighing and moaning as his fingers caressed her labia and brushed softly against her clit now and again.

He'd deliberately avoided too much stimulation of her delicate bud, because he wanted her mind to be as aroused as her body. Only then could he fully help her to understand the nature of her submission to him.

He rinsed away the remaining shave cream and toweled off her skin, pulling back to review his handiwork.

She was naked, bald, her little folds and creases open to his eyes and his touch. Her mound was beautiful, a sight that no man but he had seen. She was his, this was his, to do with as he would.

Unable to restrain himself, he leaned forward and ran his tongue over her newly shorn flesh, feeling her clit hard and aroused and ready for him.

He heard and felt her gasp. Her whole body trembled, and he smiled at himself.

Now for the next phase.

Provided his cock didn't self-destruct first.

* * * * *

Laura's mind was in a whirl of chaos.

Torn between the sensual messages she was receiving from every single nerve-ending on her body and the incredible rush of adrenaline that was pumping through her bloodstream at the thought of what might happen next, she was completely and totally beside herself.

She knew her arms were getting a little stiff, but didn't care. She knew her juices were flowing freely between her thighs, but didn't care about that either.

She felt the air waft against her newly shaved pussy and the resulting shiver made her buttocks clench with arousal.

She couldn't have cared less.

All that mattered was Adam. Where was he, what was he going to do to her? Was he going to let her come?

If he didn't she was damn well going to self-combust all by herself. Look ma, no hands!

Her body was shaking and trembling at a level of arousal that was stunning, composed as it was of such incredible mental stimulation as well as physical pleasure.

She prayed that nobody slammed a door in the apartment building, because that might well set her off.

Hell, a butterfly could fart in the Amazonian rain forest and that would set her off.

She wanted to shout for Adam, to scream for him to come back to her from the bedroom where he'd disappeared. To demand that he set her free and fuck her to within an inch of sanity.

Then she realized what was happening to her.

With a shock, awareness of her position blasted through to her consciousness. She was submitting to Adam. To his every whim, order, gesture, each little thing he'd told her to do, she'd done.

And look where it had gotten her.

Strung up on her own shower rail, with a naked pussy, and closer to the biggest screaming orgasm than she could ever remember being. Her whole existence was focused on Adam and what he would do next.

To bring them both pleasure.

This wasn't about dominating bodies or submitting bodies. It was about the mutual exchange of pleasure, of trust, of love.

Of allowing another the freedom to play and permitting one's body to be the toy.

Of relaxing into the pleasure, knowing that there were no unspoken criteria to meet. She would give Adam pleasure tonight because he wouldn't let it be any other way.

She didn't have to worry if he'd come yet, or if it was okay for him. He'd make sure it was. All she had to do was follow his instructions. And so far, doing that had resulted in a blissfully mind-bending shave coupled with excitingly restrained desire.

Satisfying Adam was going to be the most satisfying thing she'd ever done. For herself.

She gulped, overawed by the depths to this new pattern of behavior that she felt she'd only just glimpsed.

But before reflection could replace arousal, the door opened and Adam returned to the room.

He was carrying the Master's legacy. His very own flogger.

Laura's skin shrank all over her body, making her feel tight and tingly.

Oh God. He was going to smack her with it.

Her mouth went dry as she watched him run the soft red leather tails through his hands.

She was mesmerized, captured by the movement of his fingers, by the swing of the leather and the tumble of the strips as they cascaded up and down according to his movements.

She knew her eyes must be the size of saucers as she raised her face to Adam's.

He answered her question.

"You have only to drop the bag, Laura. Our games will stop right this second."

"Mmmpfff…" she sputtered, shaking her head violently.

God no. Don't stop now. If he stopped now, she'd rip this shower rod out of the wall and strangle him with it. And not a jury in the world would convict her.

Well, not if there was a single woman on it.

Adam's expression softened with pleasure.

"That's my good girl."

He kissed her breasts as he unfastened the scarf that bound her to the shower rod.

She was not free, however, just loosened.

He massaged her shoulders. "Not too sore?"

She shook her head again, closing her eyes in pleasure as he rubbed his hands softly over her body.

She moaned.

He chuckled. "Into the bedroom, Laura. Onto the bed. On your back."

She obeyed without question, anxious to find out what lay ahead.

The room was darkened, with candles here and there, flickering odd shadows on the walls and ceiling.

Adam had dug out an old sheepskin throw from somewhere—she was surprised he still had it—and it was on this that he had her stretch out.

The fur was soft against her buttocks, like a caress.

She moaned again and wriggled her body against the lush sensation of being stroked by a gazillion little hairs.

He knelt by her side and pulled her arms over her head once again, fastening the scarf this time to the headboard.

"All right?" he asked, stroking her face with his hand.

She nodded, loving his touch, needing it so much more than she ever had before.

"You please me very much, Laura, my pet. Your body is a pleasure, has always been a pleasure. But even more so tonight, now that you have chosen to give it to my care."

His eyes roved down her nakedness, and she felt a blush steal over her as he pulled her legs apart, taking his time looking over her naked pussy.

He slid his fingers between her legs.

"You are aroused."

She groaned, nearly choked, and rolled her eyes. Thank you, Captain Obvious. Maybe mental deficiency went along with being a Dom.

A wicked grin curved around Adam's lips for a moment then was gone.

"But you will not come. Not until I give you permission. Do you still understand that?"

Laura nodded again. How, she wondered, was one supposed to hold back an orgasm?

"You will not come, even if I might decide to do...this," He bent to her body and suckled one breast, tugging energetically on the nipple and making it rigid within his hot mouth.

Laura gritted her teeth, trying to ignore the electricity that danced over her clit and up into her cunt.

"...Or this..." His hand caressed her belly, swiping low over her tingling skin and returning up to her nipples in a slow stroke.

Her body burned.

"...Or this..." He lowered his mouth to her clit and sucked gently on the little bud.

She groaned and gnawed on the silk scarf in agony, trying to hold back the tide of her orgasm and having no success.

Her legs trembled and she squirmed, but Adam held her buttocks firmly, suckling and teasing her with his mouth.

It was no good, she couldn't hold it back.

Frantically she jerked her arms, trying to tell him she was going to come whether he liked it or not, damn him.

If he didn't want her to come he should take his teasing, tickling tongue away from her body. And if he did, she'd die. First she'd break his damn neck, then she'd die.

With a muffled scream she came, Adam's tongue thrusting deep inside her, drinking her spasms and squeezing her buttocks hard, pulling her deeper into her personal vortex of sensual bliss.

Her body shattered in a million pieces of light, her mind went off to the South Pacific for lunch, and she convulsed in pleasure for what seemed like an hour or two.

Sighing, she let her muscles relax, swimming back up to the surface of consciousness surrounded by her own personal pink haze of satisfaction.

She opened her eyes and looked down.

Adam was watching her from between her legs.

Oh God. She'd disobeyed.

She'd come.

* * * * *

Adam's soul sang as he watched his mate explode into her orgasm beneath his mouth. He held on tight, squeezing her to him, feeling her contractions as she came, strongly, deeply, and around his tongue.

It was a ride of sheer wonder and Adam rejoiced.

It also put him exactly where he wanted to be for the next phase of their evening. He prayed that his experiment would be a success and that she wouldn't, for once in her adult life, fall asleep right after her climax. If she had sufficient adrenaline pumping through her body, she couldn't possibly drop off into a snooze.

Could she?

To her obvious surprise, the answer was no.

A very wide-awake and worried pair of eyes watched him over the top of her gag, but she still held the little bag clutched between her fingers. She hadn't given him the safe word.

Adam heaved an enormous sigh of relief. It was going to work. It was going to better than work, it was going to erupt into a volcanically huge moment between them.

Pulling his random thoughts together, Adam returned to the moment.

"You came against my instructions, Laura."

She closed her eyes and opened them again, making shaking movements with her head and apologetic noises through her gag.

"I appreciate that you are a beginner in this area. Therefore I shall not punish you harshly."

He suppressed his smile as he saw her sigh with relief.

"But you must realize that when I ask for something, I mean to receive it. You are to consider your orgasm a gift that you will give me when I am ready to accept it. Do you understand?"

Laura nodded frantically.

"I must make you see that these rules are for the benefit of both of us. And you have broken the rules."

Adam eased himself off the bed, stroking his hand down her inner thigh as he did so.

"Therefore, I must administer a little taste of discipline. Just to remind you of your mistake."

Laura's eyes grew even wider as he allowed his robe to slide off his shoulders and drop to the floor.

He was hard, ready, and responding to the look of awe on her face. He held himself taut, remembering his years as a Dom and a Trainer. He kept his expression calm and controlled as he reached for his flogger.

It felt so good in his hand, almost as if it had been made just for him.

He flipped the tails through the air, playing with them, letting them tumble loosely then tugging them into a tight arc.

He wasn't sure if Laura was still breathing, she was frozen, immobile, eyes glued to his hands.

And still she held the little bag.

Adam neared the bed and let a couple of solid thumps fall onto the mattress beside Laura.

She jumped. Good, she was still breathing.

"I am going to turn you onto your stomach now."

Her eyes were telling him a thousand different things as he neared her, that she was nervous, aroused, still pumped full of sexual energy and incredibly excited. There was also a dash of fear thrown in for good measure.

Adam's cock throbbed as he brushed against the soft sheepskin and turned his wife onto her stomach.

He settled her comfortably, checking her bonds and making sure the silk was not too tight around her wrists or her mouth.

He gently placed a little kiss on her cheek as he pushed her hair away from her face. He wanted to watch her expressions.

A little shudder wandered across her skin as Adam eased her legs apart and brushed his hand across her buttocks.

"Laura, it's time."

He saw her tense.

"I will not hurt you. If, at any time, you wish me to stop your punishment, simply drop the bag. Nod if you understand."

Laura nodded.

Adam reached for his flogger and held it tightly.

Laura took a deep breath.

With a swing and a swish, the leathers landed on the flat of her bottom with a resounding thwack.

Laura jumped out of her skin.

Then she moaned.

Adam grinned to himself as he watched the soft pink rise to the surface of her skin. He'd barely touched her, his skill returning to his hand as if it had never left.

But he knew she was so aroused by the emotions she'd experienced this evening that any little touch was going to be magnified a thousand times by her mind and her nerve endings.

He used a light, flicking stroke across the tops of her thighs several times in rapid succession.

She gasped behind her gag and sighed.

He flipped the tails up her spine and dragged them down, teasing her flesh and letting them cascade down over her bottom.

He quickly whipped them away, leaving the impression of a sting on her swollen lips.

She flinched as the leather touched her wet folds.

Once again he allowed a solid sounding thump to land on her buttocks, and followed it up with a couple more strokes, alternating from right to left and back again.

He knew the force behind his lashes was negligible. He could have been throwing a leather jacket down on her butt and she would have felt the same pressure. But her heightened arousal, her mental state and her restraints were pushing her into another level of awareness.

She was groaning now, spreading her legs and wiggling her buttocks. She was asking for more with her body, even though her mind may not have realized it.

Adam knew her flesh would be super-sensitized, receptive to every little current of air and touch that he cared to administer.

To double check, he brushed one leather tail over a pink cheek and watched her face as her eyes clenched shut and her lips bit down on the gag.

She was feeling the heat of his flogger in her backside and also probably now in her clit. The blood would be rushing to her reddening flesh and making all the other parts in the area swell with sensitivity.

He raised his knee onto the bed and pushed her legs apart roughly, knowing that this was not the time for gentleness. That would come later.

He opened her wide.

She moaned as his knees grazed along her inner thigh and she spread herself even more for him, opening herself, leaving herself vulnerable to his pleasure.

Adam's heart contracted. He couldn't possibly love her more than he did at that moment.

She had no clue what was coming, no idea of what to expect, and yet she was sure enough of him to offer him everything.

He felt humbled.

He was determined that she'd remember this night for the rest of their lives, and also that he'd give her another orgasm that would rattle her molars and register as a seismic tremor five states away.

He continued his gentle attack with his flogger, sometimes just letting the tips graze her body, or the sides of her breasts. Other times he'd place a nice thud down across her luscious backside.

Never hurting, always caressing, stopping just short of real pain, Adam used all his latent skill on Laura's body as it lay before him.

Slowly her moans subsided and she became silent, waiting, trembling, breathing raggedly.

Adam knew she was nearing a new level of awareness, her tender skin and screaming nerve endings becoming the focus of her mental processes.

There would be no room for thoughts of the office, her day, her workout or what they'd had for dinner.

Her daily existence would vanish for the time she was lost in her body's new sensations. It was sometimes called "space" or "sub-space," and he had a feeling Laura was nearing it.

He felt a thrill run through him at the thought. The sense of achievement that he could introduce his very own Laura to this new sensation. His mind whirled, his body rushed with pure joy and his cock stood up and applauded.

He remained steady in his movements, letting her experience her body, her thoughts and her feelings. This moment was for her, and her alone.

But eventually, the pressure in his groin became too much for him to ignore any longer. All Dom training aside, this was his wife, his woman, and he wanted her.

Now.

Gently, he began to ease off on his strokes, giving her much more in the way of caresses and less in the way of tingling slaps.

He peppered her bottom with little nipping kisses, licking the warm redness of her cheeks, and slipping his fingers through her moisture and up between them.

She lay still, yet wanting, skin shivering at each of his touches, eyes closed, pulse pounding.

Her scent filled the air and her cunt was soaked, her honey covered his hands and his knees where he had rubbed against her. He inhaled deeply, scenting his woman on a primal level.

Gently he leaned over her and released her bonds, letting her arms drop to the bed and massaging her shoulders.

She winced slightly, but moved under his touch, welcoming it, encouraging it, responding to it.

Adam slipped a hand beneath her belly and encouraged her to rise up onto her knees, presenting her ass to him.

She readily obeyed.

He slid his hands through her moisture again and ran up between her cheeks to her anus, letting his fingertips caress the tight muscles he found there.

She sighed with pleasure, and he could feel her tension relax as he continued his intimate touch. He knew she would have taken him there had he so desired. Or at least tried. But that was not for tonight.

Tonight, her submission and her voyage into new worlds of sensation was nearly complete.

Adam rubbed his cock through her moisture and over her clit, feeling the enormous heat of her as he touched her flesh.

Without a moment's hesitation, he slid inside her and buried himself to the hilt.

It was amazing.

He'd never felt Laura's cunt as fully as he did right now. She was sizzling hot, her channel wet with boiling currents of moisture and rippling with fiery contractions which massaged his cock as he withdrew and plunged back again.

He never wanted this to end.

Laura sighed beneath him, and he slid his hands to her body. One hand found a nipple, hard, encouraging, waiting for his touch.

The other sought out her clit, and gently fondled it, teasing the skin around it, pulling softly beneath it, and making a moan of pleasure erupt from her throat.

He sensed her skin tighten as his caresses brought her back to the brink of orgasm, and he released her breast for a moment as he freed her mouth from the gag.

She sobbed out his name, "Adam…"

Faster and faster Adam thrust, pounding now, letting his balls slap her hot skin and her fiery cunt hold him tight as he moved.

It didn't take long.

Laura tensed throughout the entire length of her body, muscles going rock hard as the ecstasy built.

Adam was right with her. His crescendo was beginning low in his spine, and gathering momentum at such a rate he was becoming as helpless to control it as she had been.

Electric shocks danced across his buttocks and his balls solidified as his orgasm neared.

Laura was sobbing and screaming and pushing herself back against him now, in a frenzy of desire, craving that final push that would send them both over the edge into incandescence.

Adam found her clit, slipped his finger underneath it and pushed up.

The resulting explosion must have registered as a 5.9 on somebody's Richter scale.

Adam was sure her body was going to yank his cock clean off. Her cunt grabbed him and pulsed around him so hard it hurt. He had no choice but to let go.

With a shout of pure joy, Adam erupted into his wife, hot cum spurting deep into her body in an endless geyser of life.

For eternal moments they were joined in that special place reserved for lovers—a place where there was no time, no space, nothing but the flickers of passion behind their eyelids and two bodies mating in a vortex of heart-pounding sensation.

Slowly, agonizingly, it ended.

Adam took a ragged breath. He wondered to himself who had mastered whom that night.

Gently, he eased away from Laura.

She turned over and gave him a tired little smile. "My God. Adam," she whispered.

The bag dropped from her fingers and she fell asleep.

Epilogue

The occasional morning - Apt. 6C…

6:44am…Laura Stratton-Burns takes a shower.

6:45am…Adam Burns enters the shower to join his wife.

6:49am…Laura runs her soapy hands all over her husband's body.

6:50am…Adam begins to shampoo Laura's hair as she lowers herself in front of him.

6:55am…Laura has very clean hair.

6:58am…Adam Burns is a very happy man.

7:02am…Laura Burns gets her turn with the shampoo.

7:15am…The windows rattle in the bathroom. Laura has once again hit high C. Neither stop to pick up the towels.

7:19am…Adam grabs Laura's panties and shakes his head.

7:22am…A rather flushed Laura begins an argument by showing her naked behind to Adam.

7:45am…Laura and Adam stagger out of their bedroom.

8:00am…Laura Stratton-Burns is late for her first meeting of the day, and complains of a pulled muscle. This explains why she spends much of the day fidgeting on her chair.

8:30am…Fred Stubbins pulls on his Mom's hand and points at Mr. Burns who is running across the school quad and smiling. Fred tells his Mom that Mr. Burns is going to be late for homeroom. Again.

Some evenings – Apt. 6C…

9:02pm…Laura Stratton-Burns staggers home after her gym session.

9:04pm...Laura finds Adam waiting for her in the foyer.

9:05pm...Adam strips her naked and presents her with a brand new pair of leather cuffs.

9:07pm...With her hands behind her and Adam's tongue all over her sweaty body, Laura is soundly fucked up against her own front door.

9:15pm...Laura and Adam snuggle on the couch, touching, loving, smiling, and discussing their day.

9:20pm...Laura requests permission to shower.

9:21pm...Adam agrees and allows Laura her shower.

9:22pm...Adam arranges the bedroom according to his wishes. It is now the interrogation room of a WWII barracks. Or it's supposed to be.

9:30pm...Laura enters the bedroom and is arrested as a collaborating spy.

The rest of the evening...Adam attempts to get the truth out of the dangerous spy Laura.

11:15pm...Adam and Laura sleep, cuddled around each other like puppies.

The television was never turned on.

Apartment 7A

Chapter 1

Adele Martin opened the large white envelope carefully, knowing what she'd find inside. An invitation to Eve and Simon's wedding.

She sighed and slipped the elegant card free of its covering.

In spite of the fact it was a small affair, Eve had done the thing right, and managed to send out the requisite tasteful assortment of tissue, small notes, envelopes and other paraphernalia that denoted her forthcoming marriage to the truly delicious Simon Austen.

Adele had promised to shoot the entire thing, mostly because she loved Eve like a sister, but also because having a camera in her hand and a purpose to her afternoon alleviated the knowledge that she was dateless, divorced, and over forty. She avoided sitting at the "odd" tables at affairs like these, by waving her camera around and busily mingling with the guests.

Everybody loved to have their photos taken by Adele.

Adele herself was beginning to hate it.

Eve had teased her about a date, and had made sure that Adele's invitation read "…and guest." She'd even added a personalized postscript. "Remember, you said you'd bring Brian…"

Well, she hadn't said she'd bring Brian. Eve had said she should bring Brian.

And the thought was quite impossible.

Entertaining, but impossible.

Adele relaxed into her favorite chair, a large Papasan bamboo job with a soft and fluffy zebra-striped cushion swamping it. It was a great prop, and also very comfortable.

It was where Adele did some of her best mental photography and also where she sat and allowed herself the occasional fantasy.

About Brian.

And how he would eagerly accept her invitation to accompany her to the wedding. And how he'd tenderly stay with her, letting everyone know she was his date. And how afterwards he'd bring her home, come inside, slam the door behind him and take her up against...

Whoa. Enough of that.

Brian McMillan might be the best looking creature to walk the face of the earth, but he was off limits. He was a youngster.

He was...Adele's brow wrinkled as she tried to do the math...he was eight years younger than she was. That would make him a mere child at thirty-three. She being the very ancient forty-one that she'd become two months ago. And not very happily, either.

Turning forty had been sort of fun, a milestone, a great party, a statement that she "was woman," and could roar with the best of them.

Turning forty-one just sucked.

She sighed, idly looking over Eve's wedding invitation as she tucked her long legs underneath her.

Brian was a doll, though. She wondered if he remembered their first meeting, the night he graduated from college.

She'd been out with friends, and sort of celebrating the ink just drying on her divorce papers. Someone had said let's drop by this party for this guy we know, and the next thing she knew she was knee-deep in beer cans, laughter and a pair of sky blue eyes.

Brian had taken one look at her and made a beeline for her and they'd shared the fun and the booze and the jokes until some unGodly hour in the morning.

Then, in the darkness of the hallway, as she'd been rather fuzzily leaving, he'd touched her.

Followed her downstairs, and taken her arm. God, she could still feel that touch like it was yesterday. He'd pulled her against him.

His body was hard, rock hard even then, his muscles firm and masculine and his cock grinding into her like a lead pipe against her pussy. He smelt of beer and cologne and heat, and he'd pressed himself against her, backing her up to the wall.

She'd been soft and relaxed, a little drunk and a lot tired, full of beer and laughter, and her body had responded in an elemental way. She'd welcomed him.

Without a word he'd kissed her.

Hard and long, his lips had devoured hers, pushing, moving, seeking, finally prying her mouth open and thrusting his tongue inside.

She could *still*, even to this day, feel the tingle that had shot directly through her body to her clit. It was like nothing she'd ever felt, before or since.

Brian's mouth had claimed her, eaten her, sucked something out of her body and replaced it with something new. A feeling that was so unique she'd ended up measuring all other kisses by it, and finding them lacking.

If people hadn't intruded on that moment, Adele was absolutely convinced that Brian would have had her panties down and his cock inside her in no more than two minutes. And she would have helped him shorten that time to a minute thirty.

As it was, they had pulled apart, stunned, and Adele vividly remembered the flush that covered Brian's cheeks as the realization of what they were doing seeped into his beer-soaked brain. She was pretty sure she had colored up rather brightly herself.

Under cover of the noise of the party, Adele had left him, knowing her path lay in a different direction to that of a young college graduate.

It had been six years until she'd seen him again.

A chirp from her cell phone distracted her. "Hello."

"Adele, darling, it's Jan. So sorry, but I have this *weeeee* problem with today's shoot?"

Adele pinched the bridge of her nose in an attempt to keep her temper. "What is it this time, Jan?"

"Well, sweetie, you remember I told you about divine Sam, the scuba instructor? Like he's the most fabulous thing in a wetsuit? And out of it..." She gave her little trademark giggle which was supposed to enchant people but simply set Adele's teeth on edge.

"Well, Adele honey, like he's gonna take me scuba diving with him. To the Caribbean? You know? I mean, isn't this like fabulously wonderful?"

"Jan," said Adele, trying to interrupt the flow of words.

"So, like we have to catch this plane, because the Caribbean is like someplace you gotta fly to? And I have to run and pack, although Sam says all I'll need is the bikini. And maybe not that..." The giggle came again, shut off halfway through by the dial tone.

The bitch had done it again.

Adele was steamingly, violently, spit-nails-through-wood angry.

This time, Jan had *"like"* cooked her goose. Burned her bridges. Bent over and kissed her ass goodbye. It was positively the last time she'd ever pull this shit, because Adele would fire her.

She might have been popular, certainly had the breasts for the job, and yeah the camera loved her. Her flesh was creamy white and she photographed like a renaissance virgin on a sex binge.

Adele didn't care how busty she was, or how many vibrators her photo on the box could sell. She'd had it. Jan's career as an Adele photo model was history.

She managed to stop herself from flinging her cell phone at the wall, but the urge was there.

Now what the hell was she supposed to do? She had a box of "For Couples Only" toys, a deadline that was creeping closer, no female model and Brian due in half an hour.

Oh God. Brian. Her loins heated and she frowned. Not now, she sternly told her hormones. Maybe it was the change beginning. Maybe this rush of pumping energy that waterlogged her underwear at the mere thought of Brian was something to do with the upcoming advent of menopause.

Whatever it was, it was bloody annoying. Especially now when she had a crisis of major proportions on her hand.

She sighed. Life could be fucking difficult at times.

* * * * *

Life, thought Brian McMillan, could be fucking frustrating at times. He was waiting for the elevator to take him to Adele's studio on the seventh floor. She called it her studio, but everyone knew it was her apartment as well.

Hell, he had to walk through her bedroom to get to the bathroom to change for the shoot. He'd never obeyed the urge to stop and pry through her stuff, no matter how much he'd wanted to.

Her room was meticulously neat every single time he'd passed through. The bed was made so tight you could bounce a quarter off it. There was never a sign of nightwear, or robes, and if she had bunny slippers they were so far under the bed they'd probably suffocated. He knew the powdery scent that she loved, and that she had a fascination with watches. There were always two or three neatly aligned on the top of her dresser. Her closet was invariably shut tight, and her hamper empty. He knew her rooms better than his own. He'd probably been in there more often than her current lover.

If she had one.

Brian gritted his teeth. His cock was behaving badly, as it always did when he reached these damned doors.

The fact that he invariably had to wait for the elevator gave his body ample chance to consider what lay ahead, and the thought that he'd be spending the next few hours with the most desirable woman he'd ever run across never failed to rouse the fella from his nap.

One day, he mused, he'd like to arrive at Adele's door without being semi-erect.

He grimaced to himself. Never happen. She was too…too…too something, and damned if he knew what it was.

The doors slid apart on a melodious chime and Brian stepped in, turning as he heard a voice behind him.

"Hold that, will ya?" The smilingly harassed face of Eve Bentley ran in behind him and caught her breath. "Thanks. I don't think I could have stood waiting in line any more today."

Brian smiled at her, recognizing her from his frequent visits.

Her eyes went a bit glassy as he turned the full force of his grin on her.

"My pleasure," he said, knowing his voice sounded sexy, and powerless to change it. Why should he? His voiceover residuals gave him a very nice income thank you.

Eve cleared her throat. "I don't know if Adele told you, but I'm getting married." She smiled back at him.

"Yeah, congrats and all that. She did mention it."

"Oh good. Well, I hope you don't think I'm being pushy or anything, but I really want Adele to come to the wedding and this time to have some fun, rather than spend the entire day calculating her lighting angles, or whatever it is she does."

Brian tilted his head to one side, watching the animated woman in front of him.

"So I mentioned to her that you'd be a great date for her that afternoon. That is if you're not currently…um…if you're free, so to speak..." Eve's color crept up her cheeks as she realized she was, in fact, being horribly pushy.

"She doesn't have a date?" Brian kept his voice level as he asked the question, although how, when his heart was jack hammering the back of his Adam's apple, he had no idea.

"Adele? Nah. Hasn't dated in ages. And I hate for her to come stag, it's so depressing. Having done it myself way too often, I really do understand."

Eve smiled then, and Brian couldn't help grinning back. This was one charming lady, and Brian figured Simon had to be responsible for that gleam in her eye. "Let me see what I can do, Eve. No promises, but thanks for cluing me in."

"Happy to, Brian. Simon and I will be really tickled if you can pull it off. Don't mention this..." She waved her hands as the doors pinged open to her floor.

Brian pantomimed zipping his lips shut.

Eve winked and slipped off the elevator, which resumed its journey upwards.

Hmmm. No date. Not for ages. Well, well. Wasn't that interesting? Brian's lips curved and his mind zinged with possibilities. His cock liked every single one of them, and *this* time he got his wish.

He arrived at Adele Martin's front door without a semi-erect cock.

It was fully erect and raring to go.

Chapter 2

"The Caribbean?" Brian's gorgeous eyes widened at Adele across the small kitchen table as they sat and enjoyed their usual pre-shoot conversation.

He toyed with his bottle of spring water, and Adele knocked back her third soda of the day like there was going to be a worldwide shortage announced any minute.

"Yeah, the Caribbean." Adele waved her hand gloomily at the stuff spread out before them.

It had become a habit for them to sit and look over the day's props, discussing the best way to present them, any requirements from the manufacturer or ad agency that was funding the shoot. Brian had clearly learned a lot about the artistic end of photography, and Adele knew that he continually put it to good use, making her job a hell of a lot easier.

For her part, she'd recognized Brian's innate ability to pick out one or two unusual items and use them in a different way, and she was always ready to listen to his ideas and suggestions.

Except today.

"So, *you* do it instead."

"What?" Adele blinked.

"You do the shoot instead of Jan."

"Excuse me?"

Brian sighed. "You have a remote, a timer and limitless rolls of film. It is Thursday afternoon, and your deadline is less than forty-eight hours away. Correct so far?"

Adele nodded.

"These items are couples-oriented, so you need two people on the cover. Yes?"

Adele nodded again.

"So. Do the math. There are two people here. One is male, one is female. Both are relatively attractive. Both can wear this junk and are familiar with the process of shooting the photos. What's not to understand?"

Adele was stunned speechless.

Her mind blanked out, dropped into a galactic vortex of confusion, from whence one overriding thought emerged microseconds later — get almost naked with Brian? *Oh God yes*!

"I couldn't possibly." And that couldn't possibly be her voice. A teenage boy with serious puberty problems would have sounded better. The squeaky break that robbed her words of their determined nature brought a grin to Brian's mouth. Brian's devastatingly sexy mouth. The one that Adele would pay zillions to have pressed all over her body.

Her hormones began a small line dance.

"Sure you could."

"Brian, I'm not Jan. She's young, stacked, very attractive and sexy. Oh, did I mention young?"

Brian grinned again and picked up the small thong that featured a little tuxedo bow tie.

"Adele, you'd look fabulous in this."

The line dance picked up speed and added a quick dip.

"And this…" Brian added the barely visible black demi bra with the mock white shirtfront.

The line dance was really getting into the swing of things.

Adele turned down her inner music and ignored the frustrated boos of her hormonal chorus line.

"Brian, you're sweet to say so, but I couldn't—"

"Why the hell not? It's not as if we have too many options here, Adele. You want to call these people…uh…" He picked up the literature that came with the products and scanned it for the manufacturer's name. "Here we are, you want to call Bun

Bunnies Inc. and tell them that Adele Martin failed to make the shoot?"

Adele's mouth snapped shut. He'd got her there. She'd never, ever, missed a deadline for a shoot. Blizzards, jammed cameras, broken hearts, just about every disaster you could name, Adele had survived and turned in her photos on time.

"You know anyone else who's free within the next hour? I sure don't…"

Brian was hammering valid points at her from across the table and she shut her eyes against the brilliant blue of his gaze.

"Brian," she interrupted, holding up a hand. "I can't. I'm…I'm not…"

"Not what? A busty blonde? No. You're not."

Adele stood nervously and took her half empty can of soda to the sink. She carefully emptied it out, rinsed it, and tossed it into the recycling bin. She then went to the fridge and took out another can of soda.

Brian chuckled. "What was wrong with that one?" He nodded at the bin.

"Huh?" Adele had no clue what he was talking about and was surprised to find herself with a fresh can of soda in her hand. And a growing need to pee.

"Look. Brian. Bottom line." Adele leaned against the counter and took a breath. "I am not the glamorous sex kitten that the sponsor is going to expect to see on the package of his sex toys. I am…um…" She found the words stuck in her throat.

"You are a very sexy, vibrant, real-life woman, who could sell flip-flops to Eskimos if she put her mind to it." Brian grinned over his water bottle at her.

"What?" Adele restrained the impulse to slap her ears and make sure they were working. Brian thought she was *sexy*?

"You heard me. You have hair that makes a man want to wrap himself in it and get lost for days. Your legs go on for miles, your skin is always glowing, and your mouth, well, the less said about that the better. It probably should come with a government warning."

Adele's mouth gaped. The one that didn't have the government warning.

"What the...the *fuck* are you talking about?"

"C'mere, babe," said Brian, standing up and grabbing Adele's wrist.

He led her into her small studio and stood her in front of the mirrored wall that she used to check various angles of her compositions or as a light reflector for some of her more avant-garde shots.

He made her turn and face the mirror, removing the soda from her hand and standing behind her.

"Now. I want you to forget who we're looking at. You are using your photographer's eyes right now. Kinda like using your listening ears at nursery school."

Nursery school. *Bad* analogy. Children. Youngsters. Youth. Brian. Young. Not possible.

He sure didn't feel like a third grader, however, as he stood oh-so-close behind her.

"First, the height. See how nice and tall you are? Just grazing my ear here. We're well matched height wise, you have to admit."

Adele did her level best to follow his instructions, noting that the top of her head did indeed touch his ear. Especially if she tilted it, just *so*...

"Now, the hair." Brian slipped his fingers up and unclipped her large barrette, which she customarily threw in every morning to hold it out of the way.

Long tresses of dark brown hair tumbled every which way over Brian's hands. Was it her, or did he just lift a handful to his nose and inhale? Nah. Must have been her imagination indulging in a bit of wishful thinking.

"See? Now *that's* sexy. Nothing like long hair to get a man's motor running."

"Really?" God. Was that her voice? That wimpy, breathy little whisper? Kittens meowed louder than that. She coughed.

"Look, Brian…"

"Wait, there's more. Photographer's eyes, remember?" Brian gently tugged on a handful of hair that he just happened to be holding. For a long time actually.

Adele nodded.

"Now. The body."

Adele shut her eyes and opened her mouth to begin her litany of her faults. She was not a fool. She knew her shortcomings, and there were plenty of them. Well, two major ones. Or minor ones, depending on how you looked at it.

Brian was slipping her loose sweater off one shoulder and sliding her bra strap down with it.

"Sex isn't just breasts, Adele," he said, breathing on her bare skin and making every hair on her body stand up.

"It's not?"

"Uh uh. Definitely not. It's in a promise of something special. A hint, a look, a suggestion…you know all this. You photograph it…" He slid her sweater down even further. Adele loved floppy sweaters, and now she knew why. She tried to remind herself to go buy twelve more, but then Brian pushed her hair away from her neck exposing the line of her muscle. She promptly forgot her name, let alone her shopping list.

"Sex is this little bit of skin right here…" He touched her pulse that was pounding out an energetic rhythm of its own.

"And here…" He brushed her shoulder and pulled her hair completely back, away from her ear, her neck, everything. He tossed it over her other shoulder.

"Now. The legs…hmmm." He pondered for a moment then slipped his hands up beneath her tunic.

"Brian, what…"

"Bear with me, Adele. Trust me here, honey. We're working for your photos, remember?"

Good thing he'd reminded her, thought Adele. She'd just caught a glimpse of a piece of chest she'd like to gnaw on for about a week.

Gently, Brian eased Adele's leggings down.

She gasped as his hands brushed her buttocks, and wasn't sure whether she was pleased or sorry that she was a thong wearer. Something brushed them again. Something damp and wet. Like maybe a tongue? No. Couldn't be. And yet…what if…she closed her eyes. Bless the saints, she'd build a shrine to St. Buttfloss. Offerings on a daily basis after this.

"Now," breathed Brian, sounding a little out of breath. He'd pulled her leggings away and lowered her tunic back down. "Just one more thing…" His gaze roved around and then lit up. He moved away and returned within seconds bearing a pair of spiked mules.

"Dear God," breathed Adele, as he touched her bare foot and helped her struggle up onto the slutty shoes.

"Oh yeah," he said, straightening up beside her. "Better?"

She nodded, not trusting her voice at this point.

"Now *them's* what I call legs, lady. The original stairway to heaven."

His grin was pure sex and Adele was so damn hot, she felt she was about to explode. "Look, Adele. See what you can do when you put your mind to it?"

Adele looked.

They were almost of a height thanks to the shoes, and their dark hair mingled together in a soft mass.

Brian's blue eyes gazed brilliantly from his flushed face as he lowered his lips to her shoulder and glanced up under his eyebrows at the mirror. Without thinking, she tilted her head away from him, allowing more of her neck to present itself to his mouth.

"Wait…we need one more thing, I think…" he muttered.

Quick as lightning, he pulled his shirt off.

Adele's breath left her lungs in a whoosh. She knew Brian's chest intimately, having studied it at length through her lens, and her glass. But studying it in two dimensions and having it pressed against her in three were quite different things.

"Breathe, Adele," encouraged Brian.

She'd forgotten how.

* * * * *

He was the biggest hypocrite alive. Here he was encouraging the breathless woman in his arms to fill her lungs, when his were struggling to remember what the hell their primary function was.

Brian's body had never felt as alive as it did right at this moment.

He'd had his share of women, in fact some said that with his looks he had his share and some other people's share as well.

He'd known cataclysmic orgasms in just about every position he could think of. He'd been straight and kinky, vanilla and non-vanilla. He'd had a go at most everything within a physical relationship at one time or another.

But nothing—*nothing*—compared to the feeling he had right at this moment.

Adele was pressed against him from shoulder to shin. Her bare skin was millimeters from his lips, just begging for a touch. His mind was swimming in her special scent, a kind of musky warmth that radiated from every pore on her body. His hands had felt the softness of her buttocks as he'd slid her leggings down.

God, her butt. Firm, round, well shaped, her backside was all woman, the perfect cushion for some of his loving pushing. He'd given in to a strange impulse and lightly run his tongue over her cheek. She'd tasted sweet and tangy and like the finest wines. She'd gone straight to his head, and he couldn't begin to imagine what it would be like to thrust his face deep into her pussy and taste her honey as she released her juices for him.

He wanted to bury his mouth between her legs, breathe in her essence, suck her clit until she screamed for mercy, and then do it all over again. Several times. Many times, actually.

A shudder ran through her body, echoing the one that was running madly around his groin. His black jeans were tight, and he was straining the fabric to within millimeters of its tolerance, not to mention savagely crushing his balls.

"See how sexy you look, love," he breathed, sternly gathering control of himself while encouraging her to lose hers. There was a symmetry to the situation which doubtless he'd appreciate. Some other time.

Her brown eyes were luminous, glowing at the picture they made. Her soft pink sweater had slithered down one side, exposing her even pinker flesh and her shoulder.

Her legs were bare and long, soft and womanly, yet with a well-defined set of muscles that screamed walker or possibly jogger.

Brian doubted she had the time for a daily jog, but knew she was always on the move. These were not the legs of a couch potato.

She leaned on one leg and bent the other at the knee a little in an unconsciously wanton pose.

"Brian, this is okay, I guess…but would it sell a sex toy?"

She was trying too. He could almost see her teeth clenching as she fought for control. Oh yeah, he was getting to her. He'd fulfill a few dreams and get her naked today, or his name wasn't Brian…umm…whatever. She leaned against him even more.

He clamped down hard on his glee.

"Of course, babe. Mind you, you'd have to be wearing less…" He tugged at her tunic. "This is not the costume you'd be wearing for the photo…"

She snorted. "I know that, thank you very much. And that's another problem right there. I don't exactly have over-developed assets, you know."

This, thought Brian joyfully to himself, was almost *too* easy. "Well, now, let's see what we have here…"

He slipped his hands around Adele and gently cupped her breasts, doing his best to ignore her gasp.

"Hmmm…34s I'd say, maybe a B? No wait…" He hefted her breasts in his hands, making sure that he got a good rub in over the nipples he could feel hardening beneath the soft sweater.

She sucked in air and struggled to keep her face from revealing the arousal he knew was shimmering through her.

It matched the one that was playing hell with him.

"Maybe a C…whatever they are, they're perfect."

She snorted. "Maybe for some things, but the cover of a sex toy box probably isn't one of them."

"Good God, Adele, why not? It's not like people are so ecologically aware that they're going to save the packaging and jerk off to it later. That's what girlie mags are for. In fact, this particular type of box is probably the most hastily disposed of wrapping around. Would you want your mom or your roomie to know you had just opened up your 'Vibrating Bunny Plug' or your 'Rabbit Warren Plunge of Ecstasy'? Would you?"

Adele shook her head. "I guess not. Although it's sad in a way. All my hard work and it gets shredded within a minute of delivery." She sighed.

Which did nice things to Brian's libido seeing as he still had two hands full of her breasts as she did so.

"Okay. So it's settled." With a sigh of his own, he released her breasts. He was harder than he could remember being since his teens, he wanted nothing more than to fuck Adele until her eyes rolled back in her head and they both passed out, but she'd not given him one single indication that she'd be willing to endorse that plan.

"You set up the shoot, and I'll go get changed. We'll start with the 'Titillating Tuxedo for Two,' I think."

He turned hurriedly so that she wouldn't see the hard-on distorting his jeans.

She staggered a little on her heels and quickly kicked them off. He caught a glimpse of a wet shine on her inner thigh.

Well all right. She was turned on too. He grinned painfully as he made his way through the kitchen, grabbed the little mini pouch that was to be his costume and headed for Adele's bathroom.

Quickly. He had a date with his hand before he could face her again.

Chapter 3

Adele took refuge in her cameras, trying in vain to find some measure of calm as she went about the business of setting up her shoot.

Her heart was still thumping painfully, and her ears were ringing, a sure sign that she was in serious trouble. She had a major bonfire of lust built up for Brian McMillan, and he was doing every damn thing right to ignite it.

She stopped twiddling a lens cap and wondered why. She'd felt the hardness of his body against hers and the hardness of his cock against her butt. Her almost naked butt.

She'd been within a hair's breadth of reaching behind her, unzipping those damnably tight jeans of his and impaling her ass on the cock she knew would erupt from that fly of his.

God, it would have felt good too. She shivered once again as she remembered how long it had been since she even mentioned that she enjoyed that particular sexual activity, let alone permitted anyone the privilege.

But Brian? Hell, he could do her here and now, right in front of her 105 f/2.5 lens. All he had to do was say the word and she'd be ass up and ready for him and here's the lube.

Dear God. What was happening to her? Where were her scruples about being older than he was? And what the hell would he think if he came back out of that bathroom to see her forty-year-old backside spread for his pleasure?

Okay. Forty-one-year old backside.

She snorted to herself and put the lid on her sexual urges. The hormones that had worked their way back up to a boot scootin' boogie a little while ago were told to go away and behave themselves.

She reminded herself of her age, her dignity, the fact that her breasts sagged, and that Brian was the handsomest man for several hundred square miles or all the contiguous states, whichever came first.

He was simply psyching her up for this damnable shoot. He was a good friend.

He knew how important her career was, and her reputation for never missing a deadline. He was clearly doing everything in his power to help her keep that reputation intact.

The fact that his touch sent a fiery shiver down her body to her clit was in no way his fault, and the fact that she was wet for him and hungry for him was a simple reaction of female hormones for male hormones.

Yeah. Right.

Adele sighed, facing the horrid truth. She lusted. In her heart and her cunt, and all the way to her toenails, she lusted.

She wanted Brian McMillan in the worst way, and the best way, and all the ways in between. She had since he'd kissed her, uncounted years ago. But she was also much older than him. She was the one who would have to be in control of things. Even if, by some remote and heaven-blessed chance, Brian did find her slightly attractive, it was up to her to squash any hint of anything between them.

It would be by far the best for both of them. Brian was young and had a great future ahead of him. She was…not. Her future was set. She'd turned forty. Gravity, wrinkles, menopause and death lay ahead.

She sighed.

Shit, life sucked.

Brian walked into the room. Life suddenly got a whole lot better, and shrunk to the proportions of one very small, very tight, very black, male pouch, sporting a teeny tiny bow tie. It was worn by a very nice, very naked, Brian McMillan.

Who was also wearing *that* smile.

The one that made her undies melt, the one that the camera loved, and the one that women were known to sigh over, cry over and post on their refrigerator doors to remind them that there really *was* something worth giving up chocolate for.

The one that said, yeah baby, I'm yours, and it's gonna be sooooo good between us.

The one that she was going to have to work very hard to resist.

She jumped as she felt something smack her brain. Literally. Something inside her brain had just upped and smacked her and reminded her that she could have this if she wanted. All she had to do was go for it.

Her eyes feasted on the gourmet meal that was Brian, and her body sang the Hallelujah chorus. Slightly off key.

"So, if you're set, why don't you go get changed, and I'll set up the spares?"

He'd just spoken to her in Swahili.

"Huh?" Adele wrenched her mind out from between his legs and stared at him.

His grin got even bigger. "Go get changed. Shoo…" He motioned her off with his hands. His lovely, well shaped hands. Hands that could caress and squeeze and…my God it was getting hot in here.

"I'll set up the spares. Adele." He waved a battery pack in front of her rapidly glazing eyes. "The spares?"

"Oh." She jumped and blushed. "Sorry, yeah. Okay. Um. Why don't I just go and change then."

"Yes. Do that." Brian chuckled to himself as he turned away, giving her a glimpse of his perfect backside.

She couldn't help it. She moaned.

Then she turned and ran.

* * * * *

She'd never know what effort it cost him to walk casually into the room where she was, wearing something that a respectable mosquito would have turned down in embarrassment for a day at the beach.

Brian breathed deeply, filling his lungs as she left the room, scurrying off to change and taking her legs with her.

He'd taken care of his immediate problem as soon as he'd reached her bathroom, and he hadn't needed a girlie mag for it, either. Just the quick flashback onto the feel of her breasts in his hands, and the taste of her luscious buttock beneath his tongue, and he was spurting and coming like a kid.

He'd stifled his cry, biting his lips as the spasms eased.

But the need hadn't gone away with the erection. The need for this woman was still there, and he didn't quite know what to do about it.

As he took a very quick shower and dried off in one of the towels she always left for him, he pondered the question.

Adele was divorced, he knew that. No children, no close family any more. She was a very self-contained woman, independent, intelligent, talented as all get-out with a camera, and well liked by everyone.

He knew she wasn't dating at the moment, and wondered if she did much at all. God knew *he* thought she was gorgeous, but *she* seemed to have a real case of negative body image going on.

Then there was the age thing. He didn't give a shit, but it seemed to worry her.

Brian placed the spare batteries for the remote behind the chair they'd be using during the shoot. Usually they'd go next to the camera, but this time, he wanted everything within reach. If he got up close and real personal with Adele, he was damned if he was going to let a little thing like a dead battery bugger it up.

Somehow he had to convince her that age didn't matter. That the feelings between a man and a woman were what was important, not what page the calendar was turned to.

Brian narrowed his eyes as he realized suddenly how very true that was. Some of his friends were still acting like they were in high school, while others could have been grandparents or seniors for all the life they permitted themselves.

What the hell did chronological age have to do with any of it? It was what was in the mind and the heart, and yes, the cock and pussy, not what was in some mathematician's mind as he devised a system for measuring the passage of the planting seasons.

Adele Martin was a beautiful desirable woman, who rang his chimes with a vengeance.

She had done since that night he'd claimed her in the front hall of his apartment way back when.

Her lips beneath his and her body pressed against him had become one of his most cherished memories. Ever. The special nature of that moment had become even more clear as time passed, because not one other woman had come close to giving him the sensations that Adele had roused in him with her kiss.

When he'd met her again a few years ago, and they'd begun their professional association, he'd thought his comfort level with her was because she was an "old friend." That he could relax before the camera and let his feelings out without being self-conscious about it.

Now, however, he faced the truth.

He'd been seducing this woman in the only way he knew how for the past several years.

He'd let his body talk to her through her camera. He'd let his smile woo her and encourage her to tell him her secrets. He'd let their brief but regular meetings act in lieu of dates, skipping the awkwardness of dinner, and sliding right into knowing where her bathroom was and what was in her fridge.

He wanted Adele Martin.

And she had looked at him a few moments ago like she could grab a spoon and eat him whole.

Just the thought of those words stirred his annoyingly responsive cock back to life, and that was not good.

Not good, because Mr. Eveready was wearing the penile equivalent of an itsy bitsy teensy weensy whatever, and if he decided to show off by growing up a bit, he'd be blatantly obvious to all and sundry. Meaning Adele.

He wasn't sure if he could subtly seduce her while sporting a hard-on the size of Long Island that was barely covered by a scrap of black silk. Of course, it would be an impressively formal hard-on—it did have its own bow tie.

Brian rolled his eyes and tried to re-establish control over his lower body. If he wanted Adele, and that was "*really*" wanted her, then he'd better come up with a damn good plan.

Today was a great start. He had the next couple of hours with her, up close and personal. And he'd make sure they got *very* up close and *very* personal.

Then he'd persuade her to take him to Eve's wedding as her date. That meant coming back here afterwards. That meant that he stood a damn good chance of finally getting where he wanted to be.

Which was between Adele's long, lovely legs. Her long, lovely, *naked* legs.

And he was planning on staying there for a long time. A real long time. Perhaps, he mused, forever.

* * * * *

Good God, there must have been a mistake.

Adele Martin's mind repeated the litany over and over again as she searched through the packaging for something else to cover her nakedness.

She had a tiny black thong, complete with little white shirtfront and a couple of fake rhinestone studs beneath its bow tie. She had a white collar, also with little bowtie that fastened like a choker around her neck.

She had a complex strip of fabric, which was supposed to be the top.

The top to *what* she couldn't imagine. Small enough to stuff into a thimble with room to spare, a doll would have felt underdressed in it.

She snapped it behind her and fastened the thin strap to the collar. Her breasts rested nicely on the tiny boned platforms and she even managed a little cleavage. What she didn't manage was any covering for her nipples at all.

They just sat there. Quite comfortably, all things considered.

Adele rummaged once more through all the plastic bags, hoping against hope that she'd missed something, anything, that would hide her breasts just a tiny bit more. How could she possibly face Brian, let alone run a series of poses with him, looking like this?

Her nipples screwed up tight as they pondered the same question. Good lord, not now.

Racking her brains, Adele shook her hair over her chest. Better. Not perfect, but better.

For the last few years Adele had been convinced that her hair and her breasts were engaged in friendly competition. Determined to grow her hair long for once in her life, she'd set her breasts as her goal.

Her breasts had thumbed their metaphorical noses at her and proceeded to sag faster than her hair grew. She wondered if a time would come when she'd be able to sit down and her breasts would rest on her knees only to be covered by a nice length of hair.

She sighed.

It was better than nothing, however, and to be fair, the thick tresses did hide her nipples. As long as she didn't do anything silly like breathing or moving.

She heard Brian whistling and knew she had to go out there and face him. Damn, Jan did this sort of thing all the time. If she could do it, then Adele certainly should be able to manage one afternoon.

Of course, Jan had the body of a Goddess and the mind of an amoeba, but still...Adele should be able to handle it.

Taking one last look at the woman in the mirror, Adele tried hard to put on her "photographer's eyes."

The legs would do. Long and slender, muscled in the right places, and they'd look even longer with those slut shoes.

The belly was softening a little, and that might be a problem since the camera notoriously added poundage where it wasn't wanted.

Fortunately Adele was a believer in shaving, so she didn't have to rush in and denude her mound, leaving little red shaving bumps for the camera to pick up on.

Nope, she was bald, beautiful, and loving the feel of the silk against her bare flesh. Whoa. Stop that. Photographer's eyes, remember?

She had good torso length, which would help in the poses, and was relatively limber. Her skin tone was adequate and could be improved by proper lighting. Her breasts...well...not awe-inspiring. She was going to have to make something else the focus of this layout.

Something like Brian.

Who was now tapping on her door. "Hey Adele, c'mon babe, we're ready. Don't be shy. After Jan, believe me, I've seen it all."

But not on me, you haven't, thought Adele.

Taking a deep breath and reminding herself that it was all business, just business, Adele opened the door.

Brian glanced over her outfit and turned away, efficiently pointing out where the cameras were, the lights he'd turned on, and generally chattering about the shoot.

Adele was torn.

Half of her was relaxing as he treated the whole thing as a professional shoot.

The other half was screaming. *Hey, you. Nearly naked woman here. Breasts on display. Can we get a "nice tits" or something?*

Her heart thumped and her skin broke out in a sweat as she followed Brian's gorgeous buns into the studio.

Her pride came to her rescue.

Dammit. If that was how he was going to play it, then she could do it too.

"Perhaps we'll run through a few of your poses first, Brian," she said, moving to the camera and adjusting the lens.

"Let's do half a dozen or so with you and the product package against the curtain backdrop, then we'll toss in the chair and try a few couples shots. Okay by you?"

Brian nodded and reached over for the plastic wrapped product.

He turned and faced Adele and the camera as she adjusted the focus yet again and checked for shadows.

She unthinkingly tossed her hair back over her shoulder as she bent to the eyepiece.

In front of her fascinated gaze, Brian's tuxedo distorted and swelled.

Well, well, well.

Chapter 4

This was a problem. And one he couldn't control. If she hadn't flashed her damn nipples at him he might have been able to manage it, but now, his goose was cooked. Spitted, plucked, roasted and sticking out from between his legs holding a large sign saying "turned-on guy here."

"Umm...Brian?"

He sighed. "Yeah, I know, babe. What can I say? Nipples are my thing, you know? And I have to say that you've got two of the best I've seen."

"Really?" Her eyes widened at him over the camera in surprise.

"Hell, yes, really. I'm sorry about the...uh...equipment here..."

Adele managed some kind of smile, although it wasn't her usual relaxed chuckle.

"Never mind. Let's try some of the couples poses and we'll work around it."

Oh sure. Bring those damn nipples nearer, why don't you. Let's see exactly what kind of tension this slingshot I'm wearing can take before the elastic snaps and shoots my balls across the room.

Brian's thoughts rattled pell-mell around his brain as he watched Adele slide into her high-heeled shoes and walk across the studio to his side.

His hormones moaned their approval of her body, her legs, her hair, her armpits, and her ancestors. There wasn't one thing he didn't approve of on this lady.

And now she was going to plaster herself up against him and take pictures.

Life was really funny sometimes, and one day when his nuts weren't screaming for release he'd sit down and appreciate the irony.

"Let's try something here. I have a…problem…a slight difficulty, with my belly."

Brian dropped his gaze, wondering if there was a scar or something he'd missed.

Nope. Just soft, curved, white skin that cried out for a good loving with his tongue.

Ouch. The elastic begin to make inroads into his flesh. "What problem?"

"Well, it's going to look huge in the photos. Doesn't take much of a bulge there to really throw the lines of the body off. Remember Jan when she had water bloat?"

Brian winced as he recalled Jan's hissy fits every month if she put on so much as a pound, and her conviction that she consequently looked four months pregnant and Adele should *do* something about it. Immediately.

He shook his head. "Babe, that is one prodigiously fine tummy. Do not throw a Jan on me, please."

Adele chuckled a little easier. "Nope. No Jan. But what I'd like is a little more coverage if we can work it so that you're in front of me perhaps."

Her eyes were focusing more and more on the image reflected from the mirror behind the camera and less and less on her near nudity.

Brian relaxed a little, and let his mind wander over the possibilities.

He knew he wanted his hands on her. *Really* badly. Hmm…

"Okay, how about this…you stand here." He placed her in front of the curtain and turned her slightly sideways. The bra and thong and collar were all quite visible, but just to make sure, he brushed her hair back off her shoulder.

Awwww hell. Bad idea.

The tuxedo reached inspiring proportions.

Hurriedly, Brian squatted down next to her, and splayed his hand across her belly, leaning his head into her hip.

"Now, my hand is covering most of your stomach." And indeed it was, the warmth of her flesh searing into his palm. "And the contrast between our skins is a nice counterpoint to the outfits, wouldn't you say?"

Adele narrowed her eyes, shifting both Brian and herself slightly, until she got it the way she wanted it.

"Better. I'm going to hold your hair, like this." She grabbed a handful of hair and tugged gently, pulling Brian's head back and forcing him to look up into her face.

"Good. That's good. Hold it now while I run a few shots."

Brian gazed up into her brown eyes as the clicking of the remote control in her hand activated the camera.

The strobe-like flashes turned her face into an impressive visual display of lines and angles and curves, full lips beckoning and eyes promising so much more than she knew.

His hand pressed into her belly a little, feeling a flutter inside her, a heat, a rising of desire that she couldn't hide.

He drew a breath and scented her arousal.

"Good, that's good. Let's try a couple more this way."

She ran through a couple more poses, mostly focusing on Brian, but making sure to include the items she was wearing as much as possible.

"Now, we add the toys," she said.

"Toys?"

"There's an accessory package here. Things that go with the tuxedos. Um…" She pulled out a box. "Here's a top hat. The ringmaster look, I guess. Or gloves, if you want to play butler. Oh look, a whip."

She pulled out the toy whip and gave it a couple of slices through the air, making the lash whistle and even managing a little crack at the end.

"Oh fun. Lemme try?" begged Brian, anxious for anything to get his mind up out of his crotch.

He got a very respectable snap from the whip.

Adele raised her eyebrows at him. "That was pretty impressive. You look like you know your way around a whip."

Brian glanced at her, keeping his voice casual. "Yep. Whips, floggers, canes... Did a little bondage play now and again, you never know when stuff like that will come in useful."

"Well, that explains it," muttered Adele.

"Explains what, honey?"

"Umm...well...how you...er...you do such great fetish wear shoots. You're comfortable in the gear. It just comes through." Adele made a great show of laying out the accessories on a low table. "So, you still in the lifestyle, or what?"

Brian considered his words carefully.

"Now and again. I like to keep my hand in. But it's nothing I can't live without."

"Ah."

"Now what does that rather cryptic 'ah' mean?"

"It means just that. Ah. Thanks for answering my question. Now. Should we move on?"

Before I fall on my knees before you and beg you to take me any way you want as long as you end this Godawful ache inside me?

Adele's mind was spinning, desperately struggling to keep the photo shoot uppermost, but losing constantly to the rapidly deepening need for Brian that was making her wet and breathless.

His hand on her belly was torture, accompanied as it was by the whoosh of his breath.

Her nerves were screaming for him to move just a *leeeedle* bit to the side and slip his fingers under the thong. Her clit was hot and hard and waiting for him.

When he slashed the air with the whip her entire nervous system leapt to attention and a craving like she'd never known swept her from scalp to soles.

She wanted Brian. She wanted him to make her body sting, to send endorphins racing through her until she was so aroused that her cunt felt the size of the channel tunnel and only his cock ramming through it would ease her pain.

She bit her lip fiercely.

"Right. Let's try this." Mindful of the belly issue, Adele turned her back to the camera and bent over.

She couldn't help but hear Brian's gasp as her buttocks, separated by the thin black strip of silk, presented themselves to the mirror and the camera.

"Brian. Hey…Brian." She nudged him. Well, at least she was having some effect on him. His tuxedo was certainly showing signs of strain.

She glanced over her shoulder, a little imp of mischief sliding into her psyche. "Well, that's a start, but it's awfully chiaroscuro. I think we need a little color. Brian, would you mind very much smacking me on my right buttock? Right in the middle? I think a good pink handprint would be just perfect…"

And it would send me off into outer space as well.

She watched Brian's throat move as he swallowed. "You won't mind? It'll have to be fairly hard or I won't leave a print behind."

"I know. It's okay. I think it will really make the shot, myself."

"Look, Adele, perhaps we should use makeup or something…"

"Nah. Where's the fun in that? Besides, those never look real. Let's go for the best we can get, shall we?"

Adele settled her stance, gripping on to the edges of the low table, and allowing her hair to hide her face and some of her upper body. She could always amp up the volume on her hair later in postproduction.

She braced herself, cheeks thrust out, for Brian's touch.

Surprisingly, there was a little brush against her flesh.

"Right here?" he asked.

"Yep. Right there. Should be perfect." She risked a glimpse over her shoulder once more and saw Brian's face, taut and intense, as he studied her buttocks.

"All right. Here it comes."

Brian's hand smacked down on her cheek, hard, leaving a stinging sensation behind.

Adele couldn't help it. She moaned.

"Adele, babe, you okay? Did I hurt you?" Brian's worried voice penetrated her aroused fog.

"God no," she breathed. "No, you didn't hurt me."

Brian was silent for a moment. "That looks good, but perhaps we could increase the contrast a little. Can you take another one?"

"Oh yeah," she whispered.

Brian ran his hand gently over her buttock and carefully positioned himself to duplicate his previous impact.

Again, the sharp smack of flesh against flesh racketed around the studio.

"Now, Adele. Take the shots now…" Brian's voice urged her to start clicking, and without really knowing what she did, Adele's fingers pressed the remote.

The heat of his slaps was zinging her cunt, her legs were trembling and she wasn't sure how much longer she could hold still.

She'd forgotten how it felt to be spanked. Forgotten how much she loved the anticipation, not knowing when the next blow would come or where it would land. Feeling the blood rushing to her shocked flesh and striking sparks along the way.

Wishing there were more blows coming, and yet yearning for the deep penetration that would follow and bring her across that short divide and into paradise.

The flashes of the lights dazzled her, and Brian's muttered comments vaguely registered.

"Oh yeah, babe, beautiful...Let's go for it." He reached around her and grabbed something.

She jumped as she felt the whip caressing her tender flesh and then a quick sting as he lashed it out and snapped it against the top of her thigh just as another flash pumped out.

She moaned. "God, Brian, please..."

The remote fell from her hand as she lost all semblance of control. Several quick flicks and one sharp lash reduced her to a squirming pile of desire. She knew her cunt wept, could feel the moisture seeping down between her thighs.

There was no way Brian could miss it, in fact he was causing it. He'd moved now, he had to be between her and the camera, but he hadn't stopped his whipping or his occasional smack, interspersed with loving caresses and touches, and once with a swift wet lick of his hot tongue.

She knew she was moaning aloud, she couldn't hold it in anymore. It had been too long, she wanted this too much, and above all, she wanted Brian.

Within seconds her thong was ripped from her body.

The hard hand smacks continued, peppering her upper thighs, and then returning to her hot buttocks.

"Beautiful, my sweet, so beautiful." Brian's voice came from another galaxy, spiraling into her consciousness as she thrust her hips up for more.

"Brian," she groaned, letting her legs slide apart, shameless in her need for him.

She distantly heard something rip. Her top was unfastened and a pair of strong hands reached for her breasts.

She cried out with pleasure as he found her hardened nipples and pulled them, tugging them, rolling them and teasing them as the heat of his body neared her flaming buttocks.

"Brian," she sobbed again, twisting, turning, wildly and wantonly responding to his every touch.

"I know, babe..." His voice was harsh, rough, quite unlike his usual self. "Believe me I know...I can't...I have to..."

One hand left her breast and fastened onto her hips and before she knew it, one very large, very hot cock pushed its way into her cunt. Deep into her cunt. Deeper than she could ever remember anyone being before.

And as he pulled out again, he slapped her bottom.

She cried out. "Again, Brian, again..."

Brian obeyed, pumping deep, pulling out, spanking, and pumping deep again. He varied his rhythm, making her wait and then not giving her time to think between his movements.

It was incredible, it was mind-bending, and it was taking her up a path she'd thought she'd never be on again.

"Oh God," she panted, thrusting back against him as he reached beneath her and found her clit. "Please Brian, please..."

"Please what, Adele? Tell me..." He roughly pulled at her clit, making her squirm as he pummeled himself against her. His balls slapped the back of her thighs and her breath caught in her throat.

She felt her buttocks hot and trembling and the muscles in them began to tighten as her orgasm neared.

"Brian?" she screamed. "Brian..."

"Yes, Adele...yes...let it go...damn it, let it go. Give it to me..." Brian kept up his killing rhythm, refusing to let her down from her pinnacle.

Suddenly, she exploded. Her world vanished in a brilliant shattering prism of light and her body disintegrated into a million pulsating parts. Most of which were centered around the cock that pushed itself deep inside and savored every single spasm.

She vaguely heard Brian shout out her name, but could do nothing but hang in between space and time as her body came around his for what seemed like hours.

Eventually, the shudders eased.

Brian pulled gently from her soaking cunt, and she felt his hands caressing her, easing her, bringing her back down from the dizzying heights.

Boneless, she let him slide her onto the nearby Papasan chair and made no objection as he joined her.

"Dear God," she muttered, resting her head on his chest and listening as his heartbeat slowed down.

"Amen to that, babe."

"Brian. Did we just…?"

"Yep. Sure did. Oh, and I hope the manufacturer will forgive me but I used part of the product." He nimbly reached down and removed the rather normal looking condom with a practiced twist. It joined the trash in the nearby bin.

"Hmm. No tuxedo looking condoms. I'm disappointed." Adele chuckled tiredly.

"Are you?"

The question was pregnant with meaning, and Adele looked up into Brian's mesmerizing blue gaze. How should she answer? Her nature refused to let her be anything other than honest.

"No. Never. Not in this lifetime. That was the most amazing…awe-inspiring…I don't know how to describe it."

Brian smiled and snuggled her into his chest, looping her legs over his and getting comfortable.

"I'm glad. It just goes to show, doesn't it?"

"Goes to show what?"

"If you're meant for each other, eventually you'll find each other. What starts with a kiss may take some time, but sooner or later, it'll happen."

Adele looked up in surprise only to meet Brian's mouth as it descended on hers.

For the second time in her life, Adele Martin was ruthlessly kissed by Brian McMillan, and to her surprise, it was still the best kiss she'd ever had.

Chapter 5

So *this* was heaven. It looked remarkably like Adele's studio and apartment, with one exception. The lady herself was lying, sprawled, in his arms. And she was quite naked.

Except for her fifteen thousand yards of hair and a rather ridiculous little collar with a bow tie and a diamond stud on it. It was actually rather erotic, he thought.

He smiled to himself as she lazily ran her fingers down his chest. This was bliss. Exhausted, sated, best-orgasm-I-ever-had type relaxation. No need for analysis, conversation, intense and deep sharing, just an awareness on a whole bunch of different levels that the person in one's arms was special.

Beyond everything. The "one." The single other human in the world who could make bells ring, fireworks explode, and possibly launch missiles. Certainly launch his sperm into orbit.

Brian shivered again as he recalled the power with which he'd orgasmed. It was like nothing he could ever remember.

The feel of her buttocks, the flesh firm under his hand as he spanked her, made his breath shudder in his lungs. She'd responded wildly, and when he'd grabbed the whip, she'd gone insane, demanding all he had and then some.

And he'd given it to her.

He'd done scenes before, played the wicked baron, the jailer, the Dom, whatever he'd felt like at the time or his current partner had wanted.

But this? This was something new and different. This was in a whole different time zone, a place where the giving and taking of trust and pleasure and pain were all intermingled into something transcendental.

A high that needed no chemicals, an experience that defied description.

And it was all Adele. All her. All this woman who lazed in his arms and grinned at him. She was his addiction, his obsession, his love.

He knew it as sure as he knew his own name. He'd been waiting for this, aware on some subconscious plane that they were destined to be mated. His other women had been fun. Adele was so much more.

She stirred.

"I should check the cameras," she muttered, rubbing her cheek against his chest.

"In a minute," he whispered, stroking his hand slowly up and down her arm. "I'm too comfortable to move right now."

"Mmm." She agreed with a little chuckle.

"Adele? "

"Mm-hmm?"

"Will you take me to Eve's wedding with you?"

She pulled her head back and looked up at him. "She caught you, didn't she?"

He raised an eyebrow at her, pretending to misunderstand her question.

"Eve. She caught you. She's been on at me to ask you to go with me. That little scheming minx." She shook her head.

"So. Take me with you?"

"Brian. I'll be taking pictures a lot of the time, I don't know if —"

"Yes you do know. I want to go with you. I don't care if you're taking pictures. I want to be with you. I'll hold the camera. We'll go together, leave together and come home to more of this…" He slid his hand over her thigh and up to her crotch, stroking the slippery flesh. "I like it that you shave," he murmured.

"Brian, I can't think when you do that." Adele fidgeted.

"Good. Because I don't want you thinking and I'm going to be doing *that* a lot," he said, gently rubbing the soft folds of her cunt around her clit. "You're so lovely here, all pink and soft and warm. I want to taste you, Adele."

Adele jumped. "Brian, we have to talk about this," she sputtered, pulling away from his questing finger and his tongue, which was already licking over his lips in anticipation of touching her so intimately.

"No we don't," he answered.

"Yes we do," she argued, slipping off the chair and ending his fantasy of some hot oral sex and more screaming.

He sighed. "Why?"

"Why?" She fussed around, trying to find something to cover her nakedness. Brian started to get an uncomfortable feeling about where this was going.

"Adele, stop. You're fine the way you are."

"No I'm not. And that's the problem, Brian. With us. With this…" She waved her hand around. "I'm not fine. I'm an older woman and you're a younger man. This may have been one afternoon of the best sex I ever had, but it can't go anywhere. Not with us being what we are. You're talking taking me to the wedding, coming back, doing it again and again." She couldn't keep the note of longing out of her voice and Brian bit his lip against the smile.

"Yes."

"What do you mean yes?" she demanded, finally locating an old robe and pulling it around herself defensively.

"I mean yes, that's exactly what I'm talking about. Taking you to the wedding. Seeing to it that you have a good time. Bringing you back here and enjoying an evening of fucking the likes of which will rock both our worlds. Using every toy we can lay our hands on and then inventing some more. Spanking your bottom till it glows like it did today. Hell, I don't know." He ran his fingers through his hair as he stood up and stretched.

"Spending time with you, learning even more about you, loving you, Adele. That's the bottom line. Finding out if the reason you've been lurking in my soul for God knows how many years is because you're the right woman for me. Finding out what lies ahead for us. Together. Isn't that what you want too?"

Yes, yes, oh God, yes!

"I don't know, Brian. I honestly don't know." Adele shook her head, trying to clear it of the sensual haze his words had created.

She needed time to collect her thoughts, time to think about where she was and what she was doing, and time to figure out where she was going.

None of which she could do with a very naked Brian lounging in her favorite chair.

The phone rang and made them both jump, and Adele reached for it like it was a lifeline.

"Yes…he's here, just a moment…" She passed the phone to Brian. "It's for you."

"Hello? Yeah Maggie, no…that's okay…" Brian stood up, phone to his ear and stretched once more.

Adele tried not to stare at him, but failed miserably.

He was *so* beautiful. And he wanted her. All those lovely muscles, all that firm flesh, and those incredibly blue eyes, all wanted her. Adele Martin. The photographer with the saggy boobs.

She shook her head in disbelief as Brian hung up the phone.

"That was my secretary. I have to go I'm afraid, Adele. I've been waiting on a contract and it's here, ready to be signed, then it gets couriered to Hong Kong. Time, as they say, is of the essence on this one."

Adele wrinkled her brow as she followed Brian into the bedroom as he retrieved his clothes and slipped into his briefs.

Bye bye, big fella.

"You have international contracts?"

"Yeah, sure. Most financial services companies do."

"Wait a minute here. You're in financial services?"

Brian chuckled. "Honey, being a model pays quite nicely, but it's not what I do for a living. I've been lucky enough to swing a job where I can get time to model for you, but the bills are paid by McMillan and Sparks."

Adele sat down on the bed with a thump. "You? You're the McMillan in McMillan and Sparks?"

"Yep." He tugged his jeans up and carefully zipped them up, the sound of the teeth engaging dragging Adele out of her stupor.

"Shit. I had no idea." Brian had just announced he was the co-founder of one of the largest and most successful financial enterprises in the city.

His mouth curved up on one side. "I graduated with a degree in economics, you know. It does count for something."

"But I...you..." Adele was completely stunned. Great sex and now this.

"Don't worry about it, love. It doesn't matter. Not for us. We're not part of any of that. We're someplace else." He crossed to her and pushed his way between her legs, pulling her against his body.

The rasp of his clothes against her nakedness was incredibly stimulating, and she gasped as he roughly pulled the tie on her robe loose and grabbed her under the armpits.

With one swift move he had her lifted her so that she was kneeling on the side of the bed, level with his face.

"Adele, don't start trying to figure the angles on all this. This is not one of your photographs that you can pose the way you want, or control the way you want. This is us. You and me. Man and—" his hands slid to her breasts. "—woman." He squeezed.

She moaned. "Brian, I want us to talk about this," she lied, leaning into him and craving his touch.

"Yeah. Talk. We'll do a lot of that, babe, don't worry. But not right this minute, because, dammit, I have to leave." His fingers teased her nipples and his body pressed itself tight against hers.

She moved slightly, rubbing her mound against the bulge that was growing inside his jeans.

"Oh yeah, honey," he groaned, rubbing and thrusting back. "More of this. A lot more of this." He slipped a hand between them and tucked his fingers into her cunt, spreading her moisture around.

She choked in a breath, still sensitive from his loving, but feeling her arousal build anew.

He freed his fingers and slipped them further back, caressing his way up between her cheeks.

Her eyes popped open. "Jeez," she shuddered as he caressed her tight little ring of muscle tissue.

"D'you like that?"

"Oh yeah, Brian, oh yeah." She leaned against him, unconsciously spreading her legs even wider.

"Like to do even more than that? When we have the time?"

"It's been so long. But yes, I do like that," she answered, nipping his neck gently with her teeth.

"We'll do it all, babe. All of it. You and me. Saturday night, after Eve's wedding."

With a deep breath he pulled away, and placed a hard kiss on her lips. "I'll call you and set up a time for Saturday. This is one time I get to pick you up and take you out. Our first date. Be ready."

He grinned at her as he moved away. "Adele?"

She watched him, her body singing from his touch.

"Skip the underwear, why don't you?"

His eyes flashed with all the mischief she loved, and her pussy twitched in response.

The next minute he was gone.

* * * * *

The images sat on Adele's monitor. A man and a woman. Naked, engaging in strenuous sexual intercourse.

It would have been a real deal-clincher for any producer of hard-core sex toys. It also could have probably sold for at least $19.95 on the Internet.

She couldn't say what had inspired her to set up her digital camera for the shoot with Brian as well as her 35mm, but she had. And she was looking at the results.

And my God they were turning her on.

She knew that the 35mm ones would have a whole bunch of usable prints, judging by these. Which would be an excellent thing, because she wasn't sure if she could go through this again and again and again until they got the right shot. The 35mm had been positioned to get the maximum exposure of the costumes and the toys. The bodies inside them were incidental. Which was exactly the way it was supposed to be. Use the sex to sell the product.

From her digital cam, however, the view had been something else. It had caught the expression on Brian's face just before he'd slapped her buttock.

Joy, anticipation, sexual excitement, they were all there. She could crop out his face alone and have an ad campaign that would drive women wild. "How to Make Your Man Lust for You."

Then, the look on his face as he did it again. Even more tension, a deeper intensity, which had ratcheted itself up about ten notches. His face had begun to flush, his cock huge against her whiteness.

And he'd freed himself as he reached for the whip.

She admired the series of shots that showed his every muscle as he wielded the little whip with skill and accuracy. She couldn't even remember it touching her, but she was looking at the evidence that showed that it had.

Then he'd ripped her thong off and they'd lost control.

She saw her buttocks move, her legs widen.

She saw him sheathing himself.

And the final shot was of Brian, muscles rock hard and clenched, buried to the hilt in her body.

His head was thrown back, his eyes closed and he was grinning wildly.

It was primeval, pagan in a way, and she felt her juices running just looking at the still images.

God, she'd better develop the 35mm ones herself. If there were any on that roll remotely resembling these, she'd never live it down.

A nasty little whisper crept into her mind. *"They'd think you were cradle snatching, wouldn't they?"*

She looked objectively at the shots. If she hadn't known who was buried underneath the mounds of hair, there would have been no real clues that it was a young man fucking an older woman. It wasn't like there was lots of loose skin hanging around. What there was was tight and firm.

Now.

But what about years from now? What about when he turned forty, looking even more fabulous than he did today, and she was nearing the big 5-0?

Why was it that men were allowed to age gracefully and retain their sexual appeal, while women had to deal with bags, sags and wrinkles? Adele wanted to howl.

It wasn't fair. She wanted Brian, with every single cell in her body, her heart, and her very soul. But she knew she couldn't take him. Couldn't condemn him to a life with a woman who would age like that damn portrait of Dorian Gray, while Dorian himself stayed handsome, sexy, and appealing forever.

She was too old for kids. That was a given. She didn't want them, anyway. They were nice, and she was happy for other people when they had them, but somehow that maternal cuddle-gene thing that made her friends ooh and ahh over a soft bundle of gurgles had bypassed her completely.

That was another reason she had to turn away from what Brian was offering. It would be best.

For him, definitely. He deserved a wonderful life and a partner he could be proud of—for years to come. And a family. More beautiful boys with his blue eyes.

For her, because if she didn't, she'd hurt more than she could possibly imagine. And Adele knew she didn't need to be a psychic to recognize the potential for pain in this situation.

She'd managed the last forty-one years without Brian in her bed. She could manage the next forty-one.

The only decision left was whether to tell him before or after he took her up the ass and opened the gates to heaven.

Oh hell. She deserved something out of all this.

Adele turned off the monitor and went to get ready for Eve's wedding.

Chapter 6

Eve Bentley married Simon Austen quietly, beautifully and romantically, on a spring afternoon in the presence of a select group of their mutual friends.

The sun shone, the birds sang, and Adele had a really hard time taking a bad photograph of anyone, let alone the glowing bride and groom.

Trusting that their guardian angel wouldn't let them down, Eve and Simon had booked the outside gardens that backed up to the apartment building for their reception, and never had this delightful walled oasis of horticulture looked lovelier.

Simon had explained to Adele that the lot was not large enough to obtain a building permit when the original structure had been erected. That was the kind of information that architects had at their fingertips. It didn't explain why he was wearing a small tiepin in the shape of a flogger.

Adele allowed herself a little private grin over that one.

But she enjoyed the arbors and trellises that had been created over the past years by tenants of the building and other garden club members. Now the gardens were in demand for outdoor functions such as this, photographs for the garden club journal—some of which Adele herself had provided, although flowers weren't exactly her forté—and they gave the chance for apartment-bound urban types to enjoy the occasional bee.

Bees were to be enjoyed by choice, decided Adele as she swatted one away from her wedding cake. Not by necessity.

Brian was sitting next to her, idly twirling a branch of wisteria. The fragrance from the soft purple flower heads was overwhelming and she inhaled.

"God, it's incredible, isn't it?" She nodded at the flower in his hand. "I've smelt the perfumes but nothing comes close to the original."

Brian smiled at her and stroked her cheek with the blossom. "Very true. The originals are priceless. Can't be duplicated. Imitated maybe, but never duplicated." He tucked a few flowered strands into her hair.

His eyes were brilliant blue in the sunlight and Adele thought again how proud she was to be with *him*.

That annoying gremlin of self-doubt reminded her that he might not feel the same, of course, seeing as she was such an old bat and ugly to boot.

She sighed, and did her best to suppress that gremlin. Just for today.

"Adele…" He leaned forward and brushed her ear with his lips. He smelled of cologne and wine and man and she found herself salivating. "Did you leave off the underwear?"

Zingggg. Her clit jumped excitedly and her whole lower body tightened at his words.

"Ssshhh." Simon was about to say something, which was excellent because she didn't know how to answer Brian's question. To say yes was to admit that she was prepared for a long night of wild sex with him. Which sort of went against the whole *I'm a woman and therefore a mystery, figure me out* kind of thing she'd been raised to believe.

To say no, was to lie.

Simon tapped on his glass, and Brian leaned back in his chair, putting his arm around Adele and sliding it down to her waist.

The devil. He was checking for VPL. Damn him. When he didn't find any Visible Panty Lines, he'd know. And she'd know he knew, and she'd start getting real wet and real embarrassed and do something very stupid like drag him off behind the azaleas and have her way with him.

She fidgeted. The bastard grinned.

Simon spoke, although what he said went in one of Adele's ears and right out the other. Her entire focus was on Brian's hand as it gently stroked around her waist, her thigh, her hip, just an easy absent move that nobody would notice.

Nobody except her, that is.

The one who was developing such an enormously raging case of lust that she figured her earlobes were going to light up any second.

Oh. Simon and Eve were off, leaving on their honeymoon.

Adele sighed. Lucky them. What she wouldn't give for a week in the sunshine with…yeah, with Brian. Rubbing sunscreen all over her naked body. Hell, skip the sunscreen. Rubbing himself all over her naked body.

She stood, just because everyone else was.

Then Eve was in front of her, eyes filled, smile brighter than the sun. "Adele." She hugged Adele tight, sniffling a little.

"No crying, sweetie. This is the happiest day for both of you and I know there'll be lots more."

Eve grinned. "Yeah, me too. God, I'm so lucky." She leaned over to whisper to Adele. "And from the look on Brian's face, you're gonna be smiling later too."

Adele astounded herself by blushing. Then she noticed Eve's earrings. Little tiny floggers sparkled from dangling hoops.

"You two and your floggers," she giggled, flicking one of the earrings.

"Yeah," drawled Eve. "My God, Matilda's getting her exercise. Did I tell you Simon went and ordered his own? Matilda has a mate. Ed."

Adele burst out laughing. "Oh goodie. What you gonna do, breed them and get furry ticklers?"

Eve snickered. "Don't you dare laugh. If it hadn't been for you…" Her eyes filled again.

"Yeah, yeah. Go find that hubby of yours before some woman decides he's fair game and hits on him. He's way too handsome for his own good."

Brian came up to the couple with a rose in his hand. "For the beautiful bride." He smiled, passing the pink flower over to her.

"Awww, sheeeeit, Brian. You smooth talker you," grinned Eve.

"Ready babe?" Simon was there, arm around Eve, grinning even more widely than his new bride.

"Yep. We're gone, boys and girls. Don't let the food go to waste."

And with a smile, a hug, and a quickly brushed away tear, Eve and Simon left on their honeymoon, taking much of the afternoon's excitement with them.

It was less than an hour later that Brian and Adele were alone in her apartment.

Looking at each other and letting the tension build between them.

Adele felt the door behind her, cool and hard, and watched Brian in front of her. Hot and hard. His eyes had started to burn as they'd made their farewells, and although he hadn't touched her in the elevator, she could feel the waves of desire rolling off him and crashing over her.

Now, he was on fire.

And so was she.

His hands reached for his tie, pulling it loose and tossing it away from him. "Nice wedding".

Her hands pulled her shoes away from her feet and tossed them to one side. "Yeah. The best."

His jacket followed her shoes and his hands pulled his shirt free of his pants, slipping the buttons open in a single motion.

Adele reached behind her for her zip and tugged, letting the fabric of her bodice loosen around her.

Brian's shirt disappeared and his pants clung to his hips in a last ditch effort to stay up.

Adele's dress fell to the floor, leaving her standing in her lacy bra and a small half-slip.

Brian licked his lips and Adele felt their movement deep in her cunt.

"Now, Brian," she whispered, watching as he grabbed a condom from his pocket and tossed his pants aside. His briefs followed.

He threw the packet to her and without even thinking she caught it.

"Do it for me, honey, please?" The quiet demand echoed off the walls of the foyer.

"Here?" Adele wanted to make absolutely sure she got everything straight between them. Especially that wonderfully luscious cock of his.

"Right here."

"Okay." Adele swallowed, ripping the foil packet open. Brian's cock jerked at the sound, as if to make sure she knew exactly where she was supposed to be putting it.

She knew.

Carefully, tenderly, and slowly, she unrolled the latex down over Brian's rigid arousal, making sure to touch and brush and fondle every bit of him that she could on her way to completing her chore.

The occasional hitch in his breathing told her she was doing a pretty good job of keeping him on his toes. So to speak.

As she finished, his hands freed her breasts from her bra and began to caress them.

She looked up to see him watching the movement of his hands on her nipples. Seeing his vibrant blue eyes focused on her breasts as he touched her was incredibly erotic and sent a bolt of excitement shimmering through her nerve endings.

He leaned in and kissed her.

It was all over but the screaming.

Brian felt her lips soften under his and reined in his hunger. He wanted to devour her whole, starting at the top and not finishing until they were both melted puddles of desire on the hardwood flooring.

Instead, he pressed his body into hers, rubbing his chest against her breasts, his sheathed cock against the silk of her little slip.

With a muttered exclamation he reached down and pulled the slip up and away from her heat, freeing her to take his cock against her smooth mound.

She moaned into his mouth, tongue sliding and twisting within, head moving, seeking the perfect angle for their blending.

Her arms reached for him, just as he slid his hands behind her and filled them with her buttocks.

Their chests were crushed together, her breasts squished against him, nipples digging into his muscles and making his own harden as his desire rose.

He could smell her, hear her little whimpers as she wriggled in his arms, hunting for her satisfaction, her pleasure, her goal.

Him.

She lifted one leg, rubbing the soft flesh of her thigh against him. Telling him in very clear terms what she wanted.

He was more than ready to give it to her.

"Put your legs around me and hold on tight," he rasped, breath coming quickly now from lungs that seemed full of her fragrance, her warmth, and the scent of the wisteria that she still wore in her hair.

He took her weight into his hands, cupping her buttocks and raising her to the perfect position.

"Put me inside you. Let me fill you, Adele. Put my cock where it belongs, in your hot cunt." He let the words roll from his heart not his head, hoping that she'd understand the depth of his need.

Her tremble at his language told him she did. She was very wet now, slippery, and oh so hot.

She eased one hand away from his neck as he held her firmly, and reached down, finding his cock and easing it between her pussy lips.

She sighed as he lowered her a scant inch and he felt her legs tighten, urging him deeper.

"Yessss, Brian..." she hissed, eyes closed, fingers digging into his shoulders now. "More."

He gave it to her.

With one thrust he sank into her, lowering her as he rose, slamming his hardness deep into her liquid fire.

She cried out and moaned, clamping him to her with her thighs, her calves and every muscle that could hold him within her.

Brian pulled back and then slammed home again.

Adele went wild.

She moaned and shouted, panting out a choking sound with each thrust, wiggling to give him even deeper penetration, and thrusting her own hips forward to rub against him in her frenzy.

Her breasts bounced with the force of his movements, his thigh muscles started to ache, and he'd never felt the force of an orgasm creep up on him like he did right at this moment.

It was fierce and elemental, savage and loving. They mated like two animals, standing up against the wall, each claiming the pleasure the other could give as their right, their due.

Adele's slip was a twisted rope around her waist, and Brian's foot was tangled in his pants.

Her ankles were locked behind his butt and her hands had a death grip on his shoulders. He knew he was banging her into the wall, and hoped he wouldn't leave any lasting scars.

But he wasn't about to stop, and from her movements, Adele wasn't about to let him.

He felt his buttocks start to crawl with that tingly electric feeling. The base of his spine started to thrum.

"Adele, I'm damn close," he choked out, never losing his rhythm.

Adele was apparently also close to her orgasm. If her gritted teeth, strained neck muscles and grunting breaths were anything to go by.

Brian redoubled his efforts, taking her weight on one hand, pounding his cock deep and sliding the other between them so his hips slammed his fingers into her clit at the same time.

She gasped and screamed out his name. "*Brian.*"

Her cunt went into spasm around him and he held himself rigid within her, letting the clamping flesh trigger his own orgasm. He thrust more as the stars exploded behind his eyes.

He knew he was sobbing for breath, groaning and writhing his hips in a basic need to plant his seed deeper and higher than anyone else ever could.

She trembled and gasped in his arms, the last of her internal explosions fading away as his reached their peak.

She tightened her grip on him as he came, welcoming his pumping cock into her slick furnace. Sharing his every jerk and spurt even though the condom was protecting her.

It was a mutual moment of bliss, the likes of which he'd never experienced. It felt like hours before his lungs could take in air again.

Slowly her legs unwound from his waist and he eased her back onto her feet. They both shuddered in the aftermath, weak and exhausted, both physically and emotionally.

"Adele," he whispered.

"Brian," she whispered back. "The bed. Before I collapse."

Chapter 7

The room was quiet, lit only by the soft glow of Adele's night-lights, positioned low on the walls.

Clothes had been thrown on the floor again, and a trail of damp towels led from Adele's bathroom to the tumbled sheets of her bed. It was the first time Brian could remember seeing her room so delightfully messy and he took a rather male pride in the fact that he was largely responsible.

They had slept for a while after their adventures in the hallway, napping to recover their energies.

That had led to a boisterous bout of sex in the bathroom, followed by some long slow slippery loving in the shower.

Brian knew that he'd never tire of fucking this amazing woman, whose needs and wants matched his to perfection. Whose cunt seemed designed with his cock in mind, and whose body fit his with a precision that he found continually astounding.

He'd spanked her again, loving her sighs and moans of arousal as she lay across his naked thighs. He'd teased her clit, used a few toys and even slipped in some flogger play, bringing a smile to her lips as he mentioned that he'd seen Eve and Simon proudly displaying theirs.

After she'd come in great gasping moans, she'd told him about Eve and Matilda. And now Ed. And they'd laughed together.

There was no end in sight to Brian's desire, and he astonished himself with his level of arousal and his ability to continually fuck Adele. Time after wonderful time.

Give him half an hour and a whiff of her pussy and he was upstanding and ready for action. Again.

This time, it might take a little more than half an hour, he had to admit. He'd finally done what he'd been longing to do, which was bring her to orgasm with just his fingers and his mouth as he watched her face. It was damn near a religious experience seeing the profound emotions she experienced roll over her features one after another, orchestrated by his hands and his tongue.

Within minutes, she'd been all over him, hungry for his cock and seemingly unable to get enough of him. She'd used her hands and her mouth and her breasts and she'd sucked him into some other dimension where nothing existed but his need to come in her mouth and down her throat and watch her face as she took him in and let him explode.

He'd lost control. She had burrowed beneath his veneer of charm and sensitivity and found the warrior beneath, the man who wanted to imprint himself on his woman. Bite her, mark her, brand her his and parade her in chains before the world declaiming that she was his captive forever, held prisoner by their mutual desire and — their love.

Brian had realized, some time during this incredibly amazing and sensual night, that he was totally and completely in love with Adele Martin. It hadn't blindsided him with sudden enlightenment, just quietly crept up and settled into his mind.

It was as if he'd always known she would be in his heart, he just hadn't had the chance to get around to that particular place yet.

Well, he was there now.

There, where he wanted to be. Lying in the sex-scented sheets of Adele's bed, with her damp body spooned against his. His life shifted on its axis and then settled again. It was — right.

Oh Lord. I love this woman.

Adele felt Brian's skin against hers as she stretched languorously next to him. Her body felt tired but tingly, as if it was still waiting for something.

Brian's cock, that amazing piece of natural architecture that had performed so outstandingly this evening, stirred against her buttocks.

A little shiver of anticipation coursed through her body and her nipples hardened.

Conveniently as it happened, because Brian was holding one of them at the time.

"You rang?" His rich voice caressed her as his breath wafted over her bare shoulder.

She chuckled and wriggled her buttocks again. "Still awake, I see," she said, pressing back against his cock.

"Oh yeah, babe. And it seems that I made you a promise I haven't kept yet," he whispered, dropping little light nibbles over her skin.

He slid his hands down to her backside and squeezed her cheeks, then spread them apart slightly and touched her cleft with his cock.

"Brian..." Her voice was raspy with arousal. "You don't have to do that, if you don't want." She stilled beneath his touch, waiting for his answer.

"Oh I want, never doubt that I want, Adele. I want it all. Everything you have to give. Ever. You will give it to me."

It was an order, a statement, a masterful announcement of where he was and where he expected them to go.

It thrilled her and scared the hell out of her, but all those thoughts paled beside the feel of his fingers as he began caressing her secret places and opening her to his touch.

"In the drawer," she muttered, moving to give him more room.

She heard him slide the drawer open and knew he'd found the small tube of lubricant. "Good girl," he murmured.

She couldn't answer as he picked that moment to bite her neck and lick away the sting.

His cock swelled, although given his orgasms this evening she knew it wouldn't be as huge as it had been earlier. For this she was grateful. It had been a while and she wanted to be able to sit down in the near future.

She felt the cool smoothness of the lubricant as Brian worked it into her flesh, brushing his hands around and over her anus and working a sensual massage into the entire process. His touch was sure and confident and she knew in her bones that he'd done this before.

No battering ram here, just some extraordinarily good loving.

It seemed ages before he was satisfied with his lubrication, and even then he took more time. His fingers slipped to her clit, not that it needed any further stimulation, but he paid it homage just the same.

She heard wrappers tearing, God how many had they used tonight anyway? She should have bought stock in the company.

Then her rational thoughts flew out the window as Brian began a dual attack. One hand continued its teasing caresses to her clit and the other gently penetrated her anus.

Spooned against him as she was, his intrusion was barely noticeable, and she gave her body the order to relax. It wasn't hard. Their hours of loving had turned her into a mostly useless lump of human Jell-O. She figured that he could probably use a two-liter soda bottle and it wouldn't bother her.

But Brian, loving, wonderful Brian, was doing it right. Sooooo right. He'd even sheathed one finger to protect her delicate inner surfaces as he opened the way for his loving.

She felt him move his finger inside her and something shimmered through her. The muscles that would have expelled him, welcomed him instead.

She heard him sigh and withdraw and then felt his cock pressing against her.

She tensed slightly.

"Easy babe. Tell me to stop any time."

"Brian, please, I want you so much," she sighed, letting the truth of that statement ease her heart and her soul.

Her body accepted the order and opened for its mate.

The lubricant was cool, and his cock slipped inside her, past the first muscle ring and on to the second. It was as if he'd always been there, part of her, joined to her in this and a million other ways.

He filled her and she relished the almost forgotten feeling, her unused nerve endings singing at the stimulation they were receiving.

He continued his gentle play with her clit, arousing her on more levels than she had thought was possible.

"You can move if you want," she whispered, tightening and releasing her anal muscles around his hardness.

He groaned. "No need. Just keep that up."

She did. Every time her clit responded to Brian's touch, she made sure she tightened every muscle group she could control. It was an astonishing exercise and she realized that she was, in fact, contributing to her own arousal.

The feelings grew in intensity, and her need to move against Brian made her push a little, begging for more of his cock.

He let her dictate how much she took and when, just maintaining his ever vigilant stimulus of her clit. It was a slow unhurried ride for both of them, but before long her movements started his climb to the peak and his fingers teased her from warmth to explosive heat.

"Brian, I'm going to come again," she groaned.

"Go for it, honey. I'm here. I'm with you, I'll always be with you...let it come."

And she did. Rolling waves of ecstasy thundered through her pelvis, making her clit throb and her anal muscles clamp like a vise around Brian's cock. She milked him with her spasms and pulled him over the brink into another round of joy, reaching behind her and clutching him to her as he emptied his balls yet again into her welcoming body.

The feeling of his skin against hers as she orgasmed was like nothing she'd ever known, and she cried out and felt the tears fall as she came back down from her peak.

Brian gently slid from her, caressing her, loving her, and delicately wiping away the lubricant with a tissue.

"You all right, love?" he asked, settling her into his side and pulling the covers over them as her heartbeat slowed.

"Never better, Brian. *Never*, in my whole life, better than I am now."

Adele snuggled in to Brian's body and slept.

* * * * *

Brian surfaced to the land of the living in slow increments, letting his mind ramble and his body awaken in a delightfully leisurely fashion. He was surprisingly stiff in an assortment of different muscles. One of which was rooting around for its new home.

Which wasn't there.

There was no warm cunt sleepily awaiting his morning greeting. No soft bare mound rubbing up and down his cock.

No buttocks tucked neatly up against him.

There was a pillow, but it wasn't warm, sleepy, passionate, or at all interested in returning his early morning lust.

Shit. He was alone.

He sniffed deeply, inhaling some of the best scents in the entire known galaxy. Sex, Adele and coffee.

Okay. The sex he knew about, the coffee he really could use right about now, so that left Adele.

Deducing that she had probably made the coffee, Brian reluctantly pulled the last of his sleeping brain cells out of their stupor and went to find his woman. And that coffee. And a trip to the bathroom. Though not necessarily in that order.

Brian slipped into the old robe that hung behind Adele's bathroom door, and walked quietly into the kitchen to find her.

And sure enough, there she was.

She was sitting in a little patch of sunshine, wrapped in her robe, with her hair pushed into a floppy sort of knot on top of her head. Her hands cupped a steaming mug, one leg was tucked up beneath her, and the other swung free, brushing the floor with each move.

She looked — pensive.

Fabulous, incredibly sexy and amazingly fuckable, but pensive.

Brian paused and watched her as she stared into her coffee with all the intensity of a fortune-teller waiting for her crystal ball to reveal the secrets of the universe.

He wasn't quite sure if this was how she should be looking, given that last night they'd screwed themselves into a sexual dimension that he never even knew existed.

They'd touched, rubbed, loved and fucked just about every part of each other they could lay their hands on, and a few they couldn't. Brian's balls still tingled at the thought of her toes, delicately playing with them as he sucked her clit into mindless ecstasy.

Yep. It had been one hell of a night. He wanted more of it. Like a whole lifetime more.

But the woman sitting at the kitchen table didn't look like someone ready to drop her robe, spread her thighs and welcome his cock deep inside her.

Brian frowned. "You okay, love?"

She jumped. Real, honest, slop-her-coffee kind of jump. She'd been so deep into her thoughts that she clearly didn't have a clue he'd been watching her.

"Hey. Good morning. Want some coffee?" She slid from her seat and crossed to the counter, reaching for a mug.

214

Brian followed, slipping his hands around her waist and giving her a hug. "I missed you. I kind of hoped I'd wake and find you next to me. So did he..." He nudged her hip with his hard-on.

She didn't quite meet his eyes. "Sorry. I've always been a bit of an early riser. Here..." She held out the mug, forcing him to let go of her and take it.

Brian immediately pulled back, sensing her withdrawal and not wanting to make her any more uncomfortable than he felt she was already.

He pulled out a chair and sat down with a sigh. It was time for that awful experience that he, personally, loathed. It was time to "talk."

* * * * *

Adele couldn't look at him.

If she did, her eyeballs would probably roll back into her head, glare at her brain and demand to know what the fuck it thought it was doing.

She was awfully afraid that a rumpled and sleepy Brian McMillan was even more delectably edible than the regular version, and that wouldn't do at all.

Not when she was about to explain to him exactly why they couldn't do this anymore.

She'd sat with her coffee for a long time, going over and over the situation between them. Trying to come to terms with the enormous wealth of emotions he'd aroused within her, and battling the desire to curl up into his life and settle there for ever.

To rest her head on his chest and lay her burdens down along with it. To surrender to someone else the worries and difficulties that came with life as a successful business owner. To share her hopes and fears, to hold on to at night and wake up next to in the morning.

She'd gone through one pot of coffee and had started another before she'd finally accepted that it couldn't work

215

between them. No matter how great their level of entanglement, nothing overrode the fact that she was eight years older than he was.

Adele prided herself on her practicality. She'd had no choice, following her disastrous marriage. What was supposed to have been a "Happily Ever After" had turned into a "Movie of the Week" when her husband, a cool, polished, moderately successful playwright, had left her. For another man.

The marriage had been ruthlessly exposed for the sham it was, and her small-town background hadn't prepared her for the criticism that she would have to endure.

Many felt that she should have done more, *been* more, to hold the marriage together. Especially his parents. And that had hurt. She was left feeling emotionally battered, physically inadequate, and with a stubborn streak of determination germinating in her soul. Having no immediate family of her own, she was able to close down that portion of her life completely.

She had packed her clothes and her cameras and nothing else. Few friends even knew where she'd gone. She took a new name and put it on her first photographs, and thrust herself into the advertising scene with all the panache and style she could muster.

She'd never looked back. Until now.

Until the man watching her from across the table had silently asked that she step over an invisible line and take a huge chance.

Well, the answer, as always, was no. She couldn't. She'd fail. It had happened before. She'd let him down, become an embarrassment and turn into an old woman while he was still in his prime and his contemporaries would be dating nubile twenty-two year olds.

It wasn't fair, but it was real. Real life. And it sucked.

And somehow, she had to make him understand.

Chapter 8

"Nice coffee," said Brian, waving his mug at her.

"Thanks. I like it. Vanilla-mocha blend."

Brian tried again. "Domestic or imported?"

"What?"

Brian sighed. "Adele, sweetheart. I may be sleepy, but I'm not stupid. Something is buzzing in that bonnet of yours. Time to let the bee out, babe."

Adele swallowed and raised her eyes, looking at him fully for the first time that morning.

Brian wanted to howl at the pain he saw there. How could loving someone make them hurt like this? What had he done?

He reached for her without even realizing it, until she pulled back, away from his touch.

Now *he* was beginning to feel the pain.

"Brian," she began, licking her lips as if they were dryer than the desert. "I've been doing a hell of a lot of thinking this morning."

"No shit," muttered Brian into his coffee. It didn't take an Einstein to figure *that* out. "And it would probably be safe to assume that your thoughts weren't revolving around the current political situation, global warming or the Dow Jones averages," he added dryly.

She snorted a laugh. "Nope."

"So…you gonna share or make me guess?" Brian raised an eyebrow.

"I love you."

Her words tumbled out, clear but ragged. Brian's breath congealed in his lungs. "I—"

She raised a hand to forestall any interruptions. "Which is why we can't be together anymore."

Brian's thought processes got inextricably tangled up. His mental gears screeched from second into reverse without hitting neutral. The clutch that regulated his brain patterns blew out and left nothing but a whirling void of blankness behind his optic nerves.

She didn't want to see him any more because she loved him. Whoa. *Does not compute.* Error reading data. Blue screen of death appearing on eyeballs. Aaaargh. File not found.

"What the *fuck* are you talking about?"

Where the words came from he had no idea. But they did, in fact, capture his immediate sentiments.

Now that she'd gotten it out, Adele seemed a little more at ease. Well, swell.

"I love you. I'll say it again, and I want you to know that I've never said that to anyone since…since…well, for many years. We connected with a kiss a long time ago in some strange way, and recently you've become…more than just a friend. You've become important to my life and my well-being. To my happiness and my professional career. And after these last few days, I've realized that you can give me, sexually, what I've never ever found with anyone else."

She looked up at him again, her heart in her eyes.

"You give me passion. You give me love. You desire me and make me feel beautiful. You give me something so perfect there is no name for it."

Brian swallowed over the lump that had lodged itself in his throat as he listened to Adele and watched her eyes gleam with unshed tears. "Okay. I'm with you so far. So where does the 'we can't see each other anymore' bit come in?"

Her eyes dropped and she pushed her mug around on the table. "Hear me out, Brian. Let me get this off my chest."

She glanced up and he nodded, knowing that she had to clear the air before he could begin changing her mind.

"I'm a practical woman, or at least I like to think I am. I am forty-one years old. I have a fulfilling and quite successful career, and one very bad marriage behind me. A marriage whose ending forced me to take a good hard and realistic look at what I am and where I am going. It took any illusions I had and stomped on them. It killed them quite dead."

Brian winced. This was a little more blunt than he'd been anticipating.

"We are…compatible." The hand waved again. Brian tried to hold his tongue, wanting to shout at her that that was the biggest bunch of crap he'd heard this month. They were *so* much more than just "compatible."

"Well, all right. We're more than just compatible." Her lips twisted wryly.

Huh. Brian's mind flashed back to sweating bodies and the huge number of empty condom packets. *I should damn well think so.*

"But our compatibility *now*, doesn't negate what will happen *later*. It doesn't negate the fact that in nine years I will be fifty years old. I will be looking menopause in the face. I will be losing elasticity in my skin and in my body, along with calcium from my bones. My fat cells will overwhelm my thin cells and dominate them. My hormones will be going nuts and my hair will be turning gray. These are facts that women must face. We try to face them with intelligence, humor, acceptance, chemicals, medication and surgery."

Adele allowed a small grin to cross her face, in acknowledgement of her little attempt at humor.

Brian clamped his lips together, once again torn by the urge to let her finish, while he desperately wanted to negate each and every one of her arguments.

"You, on the other hand will be in your early forties. An age where a man becomes more interesting, mature, more relaxed about his life, his body, and his personality. You have, as I have learned recently, an extraordinarily successful financial career, as well as a position as an in-demand photographer's model. Your body will change as well, but nowhere near as extensively as a woman's does. The lines and wrinkles that will appear on your face will give you character, charm and a measure of wisdom."

She pursed her lips in a little pout of distaste. "You will be hailed as extraordinarily attractive with that little dash of gray at your temples. Look at Mel Gibson. Harrison Ford. Even Paul Newman and Sean Connery. Gorgeous. Desirable. Sexy. Capable of attracting just about any woman alive."

She took a ragged breath. "What I'm trying to say, Brian, is that because I love you I am facing this insurmountable issue now. Before we go too far down a path that can only lead to pain. Before I start to really let it all hang out and you find yourself stuck with someone whose breasts are flapping in the breeze like someone off the cover of a National Geographic magazine."

Brian drew a deep breath, but she wouldn't let him speak. She clearly needed to finish. *Damn* it.

"I love you too much to let you tie your life to a woman who can only embarrass you in a few years time. I love you too much to let you become entangled with someone who won't have as much energy for sex and who won't be able to keep up with you. Who is going to have skin that isn't so fine to touch, or eyes that see so clearly anymore. Who is going to need glasses and calcium supplements. Who is going to deprive you of the chance to be with the right person."

Adele turned away at this point, not letting him see her expression.

"The right person for you Brian needs to be someone who can share in your life fully. Who looks 'right' when you're out together. Who will grace your life and your career, and..." she swallowed noisily, "...and can give you a family. I can't do that either. Not now. It's too late."

She turned back, eyes sheening with tears. "Now do you understand? Do you understand that it's because I love you that I have to let you go?"

* * * * *

Brain's mind turned Adele's speech over and over, analyzing, dissecting, dismissing, and ignoring. It was his turn to rise and pace the kitchen floor, rinse out his mug, pour another cup of coffee.

Anything to quell the completely irrational anger that was building inside him.

He returned to his seat and met Adele's worried look straight on. "That's bullshit."

She flinched.

"Do you really expect me to calmly toss aside what we've discovered between us just because you have some stupid age issues?"

Adele's eyes narrowed slightly, but before she could open her mouth, Brian raised his hand, imitating her gesture.

"No. You let *me* have my say this time. You just succinctly categorized every single bad thing that is going to happen to you as you age. Well fine. Sure. Age happens. It sucks, but there it is. Age is a fact of life, along with cancer, arthritis, heart disease, snakes and a bunch of other unpleasant things."

He paused and took a sip of his coffee, fighting for control. He couldn't remember the last time he'd burned like this.

"And you know what? I didn't hear a word about how it's going to make you so mentally impaired that you won't love me anymore. All I heard was about how it was going to make you *look*. As if how you look was the only, the crucial, the be-all-and-end-all of what's between us."

Brian leaned toward her as he spoke, emphasizing his point. "What really pisses me off is that you are presuming to make a decision about our future based on the sheer superficiality of our appearances."

He narrowed his eyes. "I thought better of you, Adele. But I guess you've spent so many years peering through the lens of a camera you've forgotten that there's more to a person than what's on the outside."

Adele's brows snapped together. "That's unfair."

"Is it?" Brian lunged back in his chair, pulling away from her angry glare. "Is it really? Where's the part about how because you're going to get old you're going to stop loving me? I didn't hear that. I didn't hear how age was going to affect our lives together. Our ability to share a laugh or a joke, or just a cuddle at the end of the day. No. I didn't hear any of that."

He snorted, seething now. "I heard a lot of *shit* about how your boobs are going to sag. I heard a lot of shit about what *you* think is best for me and you're doing it because you *love* me. Well, I'm pissed, Adele. I'm good and mad. Mostly because you have presumed to make a decision about *my* feelings and what's good for me based on *your* incorrect assumptions."

Without thinking, he grabbed his clothes from the pile that he noticed on the kitchen chair and began dressing.

"I'm also seriously ticked off that your opinion of me is so low that you'd think I care about shit like that. You never asked how *I* felt about you. Did you even consider my feelings? Did you wonder if perhaps I love you too? I think I do, you know. God knows why, because you're arrogant and bigoted, and determined to pat me on the head and send me on my way to be a good boy with someone else."

He tugged his fly shut and angrily pulled his shirt together, popping a button as he did so. He cursed fluidly.

"What would happen if I walk out of here and get run over by a truck. I end up in a wheelchair. Am I supposed to say goodbye Adele, you can't possibly have any kind of a future with me because I can't use my legs?"

Adele looked uncertain. "Well, I don't think—"

"That's right. You don't think. You didn't think of anything but what's in your mirror. What's looking at you as your image stares back at you every day. You didn't think that maybe I loved the woman not the body. Oh no, Brian is too handsome to want a woman like me. Oh no, Brian just wants to fuck me now, he wouldn't want to fuck me in a few years time." He drew in another ragged breath.

"I think you're scared. Scared shitless to take a step into what could be the best thing in both our lives. Scared that because it didn't work once it certainly can't ever work again, and you're too much of a coward to take that risk."

"Brian, stop."

"No. I can't stop." Brian's breath choked him for a second or two. "I'm so mad right now I could chew steel. I find the one woman in the world I want to spend the rest of my life with and she tells me she loves me but it won't work. Simply because she's afraid she won't *look good*. How shallow is that? And what kind of fool does that make me for falling in love with her."

He pulled his jacked free and slid into it, grabbing his keys from his pocket.

"Well, Adele. I've said my piece. You know how I feel. Do you still think your hare-brained notion of why we shouldn't see each other is right? Because if you do, if you can't see what we have together is worth so much more, then at the risk of sounding like a bad soap opera, I'll walk out of here and I won't bother you again."

Adele found her lungs cramping. Her gut was twisted into a knot and she didn't have a clue whether her throat would produce sounds. Something inside her soul was screaming, a need, a hunger, a fierce urge to take what it wanted regardless of the cost.

Brian was staring at her, a mixture of anger, desire, and pain in his blue eyes. She had never loved anyone more in her whole life, and she knew she'd never love anyone like this again.

But someone had to be sensible. Someone had to face the realities of life and square their shoulders and do the right thing.

It would be best for everyone if it was her. And it would be best for everyone if it was now.

Adele rose from the table and looked him in the eyes as her life shattered silently around her and her intestines fell through the floor.

"I'm sorry, Brian."

Without a word, Brian turned on his heel and left, the apartment door slamming closed behind him as if to put the exclamation point on his departure.

Adele sat back down at the table and looked blindly at her now-cold coffee.

She could see nothing, feel nothing. She was numb, tingly, nauseous and lightheaded. Flashes danced in front of her eyes, and she realized she was bleeding where she had bitten her lip.

The pain began.

Rolling across her body in physical waves and slamming into her head and her heart with anguished sorrow.

She'd sent Brian away for good. The one man who had brought her joy, pleasure and the best sex she'd ever known. The man who had said he loved her and the man she knew she loved.

For what? Because a twist in the hand of fate had caused her life to begin years before his. It wasn't fair. It *so* wasn't fair.

A cry formed deep in her gut, erupting from her lungs like the howl of a wolf at the darkness of a barren landscape.

Desolate and alone, she folded her arms on the table, laid her head on them — and wept.

The Penthouse

Chapter 1

Simon and Eve Austen's wedding had not been the excruciatingly dull affair he'd expected. The food had been excellent, the drinks plentiful, and the company unexpectedly pleasant.

Jason Burke had, to all intents and purposes, enjoyed himself.

He'd chatted for a while with Adam Burns and his wife Laura. Something had changed the dynamics between the two of them. There was an added sparkle to Laura's smile and Adam seemed tranquil and content. Almost smug.

It probably had something to do with that night when he was hand fucking her in the elevator, grinned Jason to himself.

It helped to have a background of unusual experiences. It certainly helped him to recognize and identify certain behaviors.

Not that he needed any of his psychological insights when it came to watching Adele Martin and her extraordinarily handsome escort. Those two were shedding sexual heat like a maple tree sheds leaves in October. And if they made it back to Adele's studio without ripping each other's clothes off it would be a miracle. Jason spent a few idle moments wondering what would happen there. They seemed an unlikely couple, but very hot for each other.

And of course there was the bride and groom. Eve had finally found someone to take her mind off business.

Jason had always had a sneaking suspicion that Eve Bentley had some pretty fiery urges beneath her corporate exterior. It had been the reason he'd rather naughtily sent her that flogger so many months ago. To encourage her to explore another side to her life. He smiled, taking a measure of satisfaction in the union they'd just celebrated. Eve was one hell of a woman, and he'd bet she'd put his toy to good use.

He'd never had the urge to find out, however. His urges lay elsewhere.

It was with pleasure that he'd found a small bottle of his favorite, very expensive scotch at the wedding buffet. In fact, he was quite surprised — it had been a couple of years since he'd actually seen this brand for sale, and he'd had to content himself with bribing friends to bring him back bottles whenever they visited Europe.

Which, seeing as Jason Burke had very few friends, didn't exactly guarantee him a steady supply of Old Whillen single malt. He picked up the bottle and glanced around.

The newlyweds had left and the crowd was thinning out now, guests taking their leave. The sky darkened with the approach of night, and it was time to go home.

Jason figured no one would care if he "appropriated" this small bottle. A couple of fingers in one of his Baccarat crystal glasses would be a delightful luxury. Perhaps accompanied by some soft jazz, that great book he was halfway through, maybe a cigar...

Yes, he'd had a pleasant afternoon, and was looking forward to a fine finish to the day.

The elevator rode smoothly upwards, and his key flickered in the light as the key ring swung from the private penthouse lock button. Only a key could get a visitor to his home. And he had the *only* keys. The stairwell mandated by building codes for his personal safety was well concealed.

And why shouldn't it be? He owned the building. He could pretty much do as he pleased with it.

It was a pleasant thought that warmed him as the doors slid apart and opened out onto a richly carpeted room. No entrance or hallway necessary here — guests arrived into Jason's living space.

A huge open area held comfortable chairs and an overstuffed sofa, and fronted one wall that framed a large fireplace. Another wall was floor to ceiling windows, darkening now, as the sunlight faded from the panorama of buildings, gardens and hills in the distance.

Jason snapped the security lock on the elevator doors, and sent the elevator down with a push of the button. He was home for the night.

He crossed to the open kitchen area and tossed his jacket on the counter, loosening his silk tie with a sigh of relief and taking a heavy crystal glass from a cabinet.

Ice cubes cascaded from his steel fronted fridge with a clink and he carefully opened his small treasure, savoring the slightly smoky and peaty fragrance of the exquisite scotch.

Although the view was spectacular from his living room, this wasn't Jason's favorite place to spend his time. No, for that he had indulged his tastes for elegance, simplicity and his very own preferences.

He had designed his own library.

Backing on to the living area, Jason's library was the room created from his heart. Tall bookshelves rose nearly to the ceiling, enclosed by ornate doors and the occasional piece of leaded glass. His desk was built-in, flat wall mounted monitors glowing quietly above it. His screen saver flickered planets and galaxies across the three panels, creating a work of moving electronic art that echoed some of the more unusual paintings and statues that dotted the room.

Rich burgundy carpets softened his footsteps and a well-worn leather chair set enticingly next to a set of French doors looked very inviting.

From this side of the building, Jason could see the sea. A softly glittering mass now the sun was setting, only a few pleasure boats remained, their red and green lights beginning to twinkle as night fell.

He pulled back the soft sheer curtain and looped it over a plant stand so that he could watch the darkness lick its way over his world. With a sigh of relief he sank into the chair, flicking a remote controller as he did so and filling the room with the muted tones of his favorite jazz saxophone.

Jason Burke listened to the comforting sound of the leather cushions creak as he leaned back and savored his life. He'd learned, through many painful lessons, to enjoy each and every moment as it happened. Right now was a moment to be enjoyed.

The scotch warmed his throat as it traveled down, leaving the soft smoky taste behind on his tongue. He closed his eyes for a few moments and rested his head back, savoring the burn, the fragrance of the liquor and, although he tried to stop them, the memories its scent invoked.

He remembered the first time he'd tasted it, so many years before…

* * * * *

She hung there, arms spread wide, eyes staring at him, lips wet from her tongue passing over them.

"You're sure you're okay?"

Jason asked the question after pulling her arms high above her and fixing their restraints to the pole he'd suspended from his ceiling. He wanted to use this female subject for research, not torture.

She nodded.

"Good. I am now going to remove your clothes. " He glanced at her, seeking a confirming indication that she was allowing him to do this.

She nodded again.

Holding his breath, Jason unfastened her halter-top and slipped it down, revealing her braless body. He fiddled with buttons, trying to use fingers that had suddenly turned to jelly.

Her breasts were full, larger than he'd expected, with dark and prominent areolas surrounding hard, peaking nipples. He could feel her eyes fixed on his face as he pulled the garment free and tossed it to the floor.

Her shorts were disposed of in seconds, the elastic waist just slipping over her hips, and he pulled her panties down along with them.

She was completely naked, chained before him, and still staring at him. She had not spoken a word.

He circled her, collecting his thoughts and trying to curb his cock, which was signaling its enormous approval of the delectable dish hanging in front of it by thrusting almost painfully against his fly.

He grabbed the clipboard and re-read her questionnaire.

"You are Francesca Dalton. Twenty-one years old, junior, majoring in psych with a minor in drama. Is that correct?"

The blonde head nodded, blue-green eyes wary and still watching him, but with a hint of curiosity now showing in their tantalizing depths.

Jason struggled with his hormones. It was going to be a losing battle, but hell, he wasn't the subject here. He knew what his responses would be.

"You volunteered for this research study of your own free will?"

She nodded again, adding a brisk no-nonsense snap to emphasize her agreement.

"You also signify that you have understood what we will be exploring during these sessions. The different facets of female sexual arousal."

She dipped her head, again in assent.

"And specifically, sexual arousal through the use of what are known as bondage techniques."

She raised one eyebrow slightly. Jason's spine shivered, as if someone walked over his grave.

She was a beauty. She was hanging naked before him, breasts tipped with pebbling nipples and a soft thatch of pale, neatly trimmed pubic hair pointing the way to her cunt.

Jason could smell her. The spicy tang of her body slipped into his nostrils, wended its way through his olfactory system and imprinted itself into his brain.

He wanted to lick her, taste her, inhale her arousal. Oh, and he wanted to fuck her. Really, really, badly.

But that would be in complete and absolute violation of everything his scientific research stood for. He was a Research Associate, very close to completing his thesis on sexuality and sexual response to restraining/punishing behaviors.

In other words, he was doing a thesis on sexual bondage.

His call for volunteers had elicited mixed results. With typical student fervor, several willing women had responded. One had even read the papers he'd already published.

That one had begged to be beaten and fucked. *While* she was filling out the questionnaire. Her enthusiasm had unnerved him and he'd turned her down with polite excuses.

He thought she might well have run into Luke, Jason's housemate, and an opportunist of the first order. He'd managed to be conspicuously coming or going right around the time Jason was interviewing volunteers.

From the sound of things, he'd taken three of them out to dinner and fucked two. A 66% success ratio wasn't to be sneezed at, thought Jason wryly.

Thank God Luke had missed Francesca.

"Francesca, on your questionnaire you responded to the section on your sexual experience as—um—let me see, *varied*?" Jason raised his eyes back to the woman standing so still in front of him.

"It's okay to speak, you know. Would you please define 'varied'?"

She licked her lips with that damnably teasing tongue.

"It means just that. Varied." Her voice was low and cultured, with little trace of the local flattened dialect. He could not tell where she was from, but knew her voice would remain in his psyche forever. It whispered of hot nights, sweaty thighs, and unspeakable acts.

Damn, he was losing his train of thought again. "Please continue. I must have as much information as possible, you understand."

"Varied. Of many different types and categories. I lost my virginity at sixteen to a member of the high school football team. I became sexually active on a routine basis not long after. Most of my dates can and do lead to sex after a suitable period because I don't date people I don't find sexually attractive. However I have not orgasmed during sex with any regularity."

She was weaving a spell around him with her words and her voice, seducing him, stroking him in places he could only imagine.

"I experienced my first lesbian encounter here at college during my freshman year."

Jason exerted a heroic effort to prevent his jaw from dropping. He cleared his throat. "And?"

"And it was—pleasant. Since that time I have not ignored the possibility that lesbian sex might be fulfilling, but have not actively pursued it. My work schedule and study load has made dating difficult recently, and to be honest, I am tired of hunting for the excitement and arousal that is supposed to accompany sexual intercourse. I am here to assist in your research and also possibly find out if there is something unusual about my own response. I suppose you could say *I'm* here to research me as much as *you* are."

Jason digested her words silently for a few moments. They were pretty much what she'd written on her fact sheet. Her interest in exploring other sexual practices as a means to experiencing greater sexual satisfaction.

Clinically he was close to convinced she'd be perfect for his research. Physically he was absolutely convinced she'd be perfect for his cock. And his mouth. And his tongue. And whatever else he could think of—up to and including his ten-speed bike.

But first, he had to restrain her, arouse her, and masturbate her to orgasm while she was chained.

He sighed. The things one did for science.

Chapter 2

The melting ice in Jason's glass clinked and the sound recalled him from his vivid memories.

The sun had set, and the library was filled with soft sounds and the low light of the computer monitors. It was a moment of surreal pleasure for Jason, as he allowed the image of Francesca Dalton to stay behind his eyelids for a long minute.

He'd forbidden himself this luxury many years ago, knowing that thoughts of her would stir emotions best left alone. And they did, invariably, when she crept into his day or his night or his dreams.

He reached for the small bottle and emptied the rest of the liquor over the melting ice cubes. He swirled the glass contemplatively, watching the amber gold liquid as it conformed to the glass and the laws of centrifugal force.

She'd had a bottle just about this size in her purse.

"Do you like scotch?"

Her words had dropped like petals into the sunny silence of his room and she'd bitten her lip as if she'd broken a rule. One of her own perhaps, as he had yet to ask her to keep silent. "I'm sorry...I interrupted your train of thought. But right now, I could use a little...um...courage..."

"Yes. I understand."

"In my purse." She nodded toward her pile of belongings on the table. "I have a small bottle of a new brand I'd like to try. If it doesn't violate any of your scientific principles, I wouldn't mind a sip right now. And you're welcome to share."

Jason thought for a moment. "I guess it wouldn't hurt. I am basing my research on activities that do not include alcohol, because it's my understanding that restraint or bondage adherents tend to avoid alcohol usage. Wisely, too, probably." He allowed himself a quick grin at her. "But yeah, I do like scotch. So perhaps a little drop will be okay. Just to warm us up."

Oh yeah...like he needed warming up. He was so damned hot at this moment that he might well be responsible for his own personal sunspot. Radio interference across the globe could be traced to his door.

He crossed to the table and looked tentatively at her purse. Like most men, he viewed a woman's purse as a cross between a treasure chest and Pandora's box. There might be wonderful things inside, but one might also pay the price for looking.

"Right in the front pocket," she said.

"Got it." Jason uncapped the bottle and sniffed appreciatively. "Mmm. Nice." He poured two small shots into glasses and brought one over to her.

"Umm...you'll have to help." She smiled, moving her arms.

He closed the distance between them, uncomfortably aware of her nakedness now that it was so close to his body.

He raised the glass to her lips and watched as she allowed him to trickle the liquid between them.

Her tongue flicked out and wiped an errant drop from her mouth, and she closed her eyes on a hum. "Oh my. Yes. That's a nice one," she said quietly, savoring the taste. She accepted another swallow, her throat working so close to his hands.

Jason nearly came in his pants. Watching her, hanging naked, enjoying a fine scotch and licking her lips like that, was the most erotic thing he could ever have imagined. He wished he had sufficient control to note this event down in his journal, but he had a feeling his hands weren't working terribly well at the moment.

His cock, however, was functioning just fine.

Aware of the severe ache between his legs, Jason swallowed his scotch in one gulp and turned away.

He coughed. God, that was good. Burningly hot, but good. Yes, he was now well warmed-up. Ignoring his massive erection as best he could, he yanked his mind out of her crotch and back to business.

"Very nice, thanks." He glanced around at his selection of tools. "You are now to remain silent at all times, please. I am going to begin this experiment by applying some pressure to your sensitive tissues. You may nod if you understand."

Licking the last of the scotch from her mouth, Francesca straightened her shoulders as best she could and nodded.

Jason moved to a side table and picked up a couple of small clips. They had loose loops at the end. He inhaled, exhaled, did a few multiplication tables in his head, then turned back to her and held the loops out for her to see.

"I am going to put these on your nipples," he said, privately amazed at himself for actually being able to say that sentence to a naked woman without coming or blushing, or both. Now all he had to do was keep his hands from trembling while he tried to remember what, exactly, he was supposed to be doing with her nipples. He forcefully reminded himself that tongues and mouths were not included.

Gingerly he grasped her budded nipple and placed the clip just behind it, repeating the action on the other side.

Her skin was velvet, warm velvet, and he could feel the tiny muscles reacting to his touch as he pulled on her sensitive breasts. A quick glance at her face showed him she was watching intently, her pulse rapid at the base of her neck.

Task completed, Jason pulled slightly on the lower loops, tugging her nipples and bringing a gasp to her lips.

He watched her eyes widen and the pupils dilate as the sensation traveled through her body. There was a definite increase in her pulse rate, and the scent of her arousal grew strong.

He repeated his action, simply distending her nipples with the clips and releasing them again. Tugging with a gentle rhythm. She moaned slightly, a sound that was given strength by the movements of her body rather than the force of her throat. Her hips swayed and her chest followed his tugs, almost as if begging for more.

Jason began to sweat.

He released his grasp on the nipple clamps and lightly flicked the nipple. She sucked in a breath and gasped. He moved so that he was standing close behind her. "Did you like that, Francesca?" he whispered in her ear.

She nodded, hair flying.

Jason obeyed an instinct and lightly bit the side of her neck, licking the injury with his tongue.

Her reaction was immediate, a moan and a tilt of the head offering him more. She was responding very positively.

"Would you like to continue?"

The hair flew again with her enthusiastic nods.

He ran his hands down her spine and settled them on her buttocks. They were full and round and made for his hands to cup as he thrust into her...damn, he was in danger of losing focus again.

It was time to test his theory. Was she now sufficiently sensitized that pain would become pleasure? Or did she need more stimulation? Could women's nipples be the key to opening the flood of endorphins that would welcome additional forceful contact?

There was only one way to find out.

He pulled his arm back, aimed at the center of her luscious buttock and smacked her hard.

She jumped and cried out.

His hand left a mark that quickly reddened, contrasting vividly with the white of her flesh. Jason was beside himself as he watched the skin change color. He was harder than he'd ever been in his life.

"More," she muttered, violating her agreement of silence.

Too far lost in the moment to realize it, Jason was helpless to do anything other than follow her instructions. His hand itched to feel her again.

Another sharp slap echoed through the room, followed by a sensual groan ripped from Francesca's lungs.

The next blow fell without her encouragement, but brought a moan of pleasure and a thrust of her hips back toward him.

He couldn't have stopped himself. Her buttocks were begging, his hand was itching, his cock was about to go nova, and he realized the experiment was working.

He peppered her bottom with slaps, some hard, some soft.

Finally, she called his name, voice husky and rough. "Jason Burke."

He stilled, brain fogged with desire, eyes burning, body on autopilot.

"I don't want to be your research assistant. I quit."

"You what?" His mind roiled, trying to make some sense out of her words.

"I quit. Now fuck me."

It would have taken a far stronger and better man than he to refuse such a plea. He was weak and a dreadful person, and he wanted her.

Within seconds he was before her, hands on either side of her face. "Are you sure? You'll never be able to help in my research after this…"

"After this I won't need to," she hissed at him through teeth that were clenched as if she were holding herself together by the force of her jaw. "Dear God, Jason. Fuck me now, please, hard, I want it so bad…"

Jason pulled her sharply to him, smashing his mouth down on hers only to be met with a hunger even greater than his own.

Her arms may have been stretched to either side, but her lips and her tongue held him as firmly as if she'd been completely wrapped around him. She tasted of scotch and woman with a hint of peppermint, and Jason couldn't get enough.

Without realizing it, his hands had already stripped away his shirt, and suddenly she pressed herself against him, letting her tight nipples stab his chest and the clamps shiver against him.

His pants disappeared. It must have been magic because he sure as hell couldn't remember removing them. But they were gone, and there was nothing between him and Francesca but heat.

Boiling, steaming, off-the-scale heat.

"Are you…are you on anything?" Some semblance of sanity poked a little hole in the sexual vortex that was possessing Jason Burke.

"Yeah, the Pill," she breathed, licking his mouth and moaning as her nipples rubbed roughly against him.

"Thank God," he muttered. Slamming his body onto hers, he reached behind her and slid his hands down to her burning buttocks. They filled his hands like they'd been made with him in mind.

"Lift your leg," he urged, cock thrusting blindly for its target.

She did as he told her, twisting her hands and gripping the ropes that held her.

He bent slightly and lifted her off the ground. He was surprised by how little she weighed and how easily she found his cock with her wet and fiery folds. Her legs clamped around his hips and before he knew it he was buried balls deep inside the hottest cunt he could ever recall. She was all boiling silk and molten lava erupting around his cock, and he was stunned by the intensity of the feeling.

He'd fucked his way around and considered himself experienced, but never had anything come close to this.

She thrust herself onto him, demanding he move. With a neat bounce of his hips, he did.

And he did it again. A lot.

Until they were both soaked with sweat, bodies steaming, muscles straining and throats gasping for air. Jason knew he was hitting her clit with each thrust, he was almost positive he could feel it brushing him and stabbing his flesh as it pounded against hers.

Her breaths came in little sharp gasps and he could feel the onset of his own personal signals telling him that he was going to come.

Some kind of higher level brain function remained working, as he retained the presence of mind to free one hand and reach for Francesca's body at just the right moment...he felt the beginnings of her inner spasms...and he whipped off her nipple clamps, one after another, just as she began to come.

Her scream nearly deafened him, and her orgasm damn near squeezed his cock up into his appendix. She came in mammoth waves around him, endlessly, never slacking, never wavering, and dragging him along with her for the wild mad ride.

Within moments he was there with her, pumping, spurting, feeling his cock echo her frenzied inner gyrations. It was astonishing, mind-blowing, draining, and completely beyond anything he'd experienced in his lifetime, or probably any of the others he'd had before. If he'd had any. He didn't know, and at this moment he didn't care.

All he wanted was to fuck this woman again and again. To explore her body and her mind. To turn her inside out and find out what made her tick. To take her any and every which way there was. Then get some books and find more ways to take her.

Hell, they could probably cover the entire Kama Sutra.

His mind whirled off on its cosmic voyage while his body absorbed the aftershocks of a mammoth orgasm. Both his *and* hers.

She was still hanging from her restraints and he reached up to release her as he gingerly eased himself from her body while lowering her feet to the floor.

She sagged bonelessly into his arms as he freed her, not stirring as he lifted her and carried her over to his couch.

Gently, he tumbled them both onto the cushions, gathering her close and stroking her skin. Her body gleamed with their juices, they both smelled of hot sex and satisfaction, and she fit against him in all the right places.

My God. That had been one hell of an awesome fuck.

And he knew now that it had marked the beginning of a phase of his life that he would never be able to relegate to a distant memory. It had been too important, had shaped too many of his beliefs, his needs and his desires.

They had shared three years of pleasure, ecstasy, joy and savage pain. Sometimes all at once.

When it had ended, he had known that something very special was gone.

He hadn't realized he'd never be able to find it again.

Chapter 3

Had he really been that young? That naive? To think that the amazing time he'd spent with Francesca Dalton could be duplicated again in another place with another woman?

Jason snorted to himself in the darkness. It had been so many years ago, a different time, a different place. When the world itself had been different. Just discovering its own sexuality, to the accompaniment of flower power, psychedelic drugs, love beads and war.

When political discussions ranged from the polite to the militaristic, and everyone at college believed *they* had the answers. When free love meant just that, free love. The Pill had freed women from the risk of pregnancy, and allowed them to lead the sexual revolution. Nobody had heard of AIDS, and the worst that you could end up with was some nasty bug that would respond to a course of antibiotics and a lecture from the clinician.

Yeah, Jason shook his head, it was a different time. And he had been a different man.

And Francesca? Was she different now? She had been younger than him by several years, so she would have reached a not dissimilar point in her life, he supposed. She'd be in her late fifties. Had she married? Had children? How could he have let her slip from his life so completely? Had he had a choice?

He finished the last of the scotch in his glass, letting the sliver of ice follow it into his mouth and crunching down on it.

He shivered as he remembered other ice cubes...other times...long ago...

"I'll never get enough of you, Jason Burke."

Francesca's mouth was kissing his cock, sliding up and down, tasting him, teasing him, flicking at his most sensitive spots.

They were lying, daringly, in the sunshine, risking public exposure but not caring, just locked in their bodies' need for each other.

This little spot on the roof of the apartment where Francesca lived had become "their" place, shielded as it was from prying eyes, and yet allowing the fresh air to blow in from the ocean, stirring up goosepimples across Francesca's naked back. She'd slipped off her top, but left her long flowered skirt on, even though Jason knew she wore nothing beneath it.

The knowledge had made him hard as a rock as he followed her up the small stairs to the roof door. He had allowed her to dress him in her favorite outfit, a pseudo-maharishi sort of robe. She loved it because it required no underwear either and she adored the feel of his backside through the light cotton.

He sighed and sipped his drink, the scotch they both enjoyed.

Her hair brushed his belly and he eased the robe up away from his body even more so that he could expose more of himself to her touch. God, she felt wonderful.

Her breasts brushed against him, hard and needy, and he obeyed a wicked impulse.

As she bent to his cock, he slipped his fingers into the bag holding the ice cubes, letting the flesh cool until it was almost burning. Then he reached for her nipple.

She shrieked as his icy cold fingers caressed her, then thrust her breast into his hand with a moan, squeezing the base of his cock with her hand as he fondled her. "OhmiGod," she sputtered. "You devil. That's so — so — good…"

Jason grinned. "Oh yeah? Come here…" He pushed her down onto her back on their blanket, tugging and pulling the skirt up around her waist. She looked wanton and decadent and like every man's wet dream with her blonde hair tangled, her blue-green eyes flooding with desire and her pussy glistening with her arousal. And it was all just for him.

He picked up a slippery ice cube and ran it over one breast, loving her gasps and moans of pleasure/pain. He followed the ice with his mouth, suckling her into the warmth and feeling her squirm beneath him.

He slipped cold fingers to her clit and watched as she nearly levitated off the blanket.

"Jesus H. *Jason*..." She cursed and bucked as his fingers froze her clit and teased it, darting between her sensitive folds to play some more.

Grinning, he explored this game a little further. A larger ice cube found its way into his hand, and it took but a second to slip it into her cunt.

She made not a sound, just stared at him, eyes getting wider by the second.

"Hurt?" he asked, holding his hand tight to her pussy.

She shook her head, then nodded, then shook her head again. He chuckled.

He moved quickly between her legs and dipped, thrusting his hot tongue against the chilled flesh.

She moaned, writhing now as he teased her clit and used his cold fingers along with the melting ice cube to stir new sensations inside her. It was the work of a moment to slip an ice cube into his mouth, letting it chill his tongue and his lips, never letting his other hand cease its teasing play around her swollen and moist flesh.

He spat out the ice cube and quickly rose up, fastening his now-cold mouth around her breast.

She seemed unable to control her body as it suffered these unusual onslaughts. She moaned and tossed and bucked, and Jason realized she was so close to coming that her thighs were trembling.

What could he do? It was his fault she was so aroused. Jason prided himself on being a gentleman. So he did the gentlemanly thing.

He slid his cock into her cunt, gasping a little himself as the chilled skin brushed his hardness. The ice cube had all but melted, just leaving the tiniest spots of cold to tantalize the head of his cock.

It was wild, unexpected, amazingly pleasurable and unforgettable.

The sun burned hotly on his bare backside as he plunged himself into Francesca, time and again. She met every thrust with her hips, sobbing her pleasure, calling his name, begging him to fuck her harder, longer, to ram himself deep into her body.

He responded as he always did, silently and forcefully, slipping a hand beneath her and raising her so that he could angle his driving thrusts as deeply as humanly possible.

He lowered his head to her breasts and sucked them hard, pulling the nipples with his tongue and biting them gently, the pain from his teeth adding to her mad rush to orgasm.

They'd come together, exploding on the rooftop, high above the rest of the world. Their bodies might have been several stories up, but their minds and their souls were at a different level, one measured in astronomical units.

Jason had always believed that sex with Francesca became a galactic experience, and perhaps even resulted in the creation of life on small planets elsewhere in the cosmos.

Of course, that theory sounded better when they were sharing a couple of Luke's funny-smelling cigarettes.

Whatever the result, Jason could look back on that time with joy, fondness and pleasure. As long as he could forget the pain.

* * * * *

A soft chime from his computer roused Jason from his reminiscences. He had mail. Oh joy. At this time on a Saturday night it could only be from his agent, a man to whom the word "weekend" meant "extra hours to work."

God knew that Jason was grateful. Having his latest book top the New York Times bestseller lists for six weeks was a pleasure, and he rightfully credited Rick Jackson with the achievement.

He left the chair and wandered to his desk, his eyes registering the assortment of books that were ranged neatly to one side.

As always, a tingle of pride flittered up his spine as he read the titles and the author—JB Sims. His pseudonym. No punctuation. He did capitalize, however, not having the daring or the ability of an e e cummings to completely ignore the rules of good grammar.

His current series of six novels had pride of place on the shelf, and when "Seven Scenes, Seven Sins. Book I" had been released, the furor that had erupted over its controversial subject matter had sent sales skyrocketing.

Jason wondered if Francesca had read it. Because she was in it. She was in all his books. If it hadn't been for her, the first one might never have been written.

Oh it was fiction. Pure and utter fiction. But the story of a whore who found passion through becoming a dominatrix only to throw it all away for a chance at a straight marriage had touched chords with readers. Especially because Jason had refused his editor's suggestion to compromise and had allowed his frustrated and unhappy heroine to commit suicide at the end.

Each book had begun with a detailed scene. A scene that Jason and Francesca had either played, or discussed, or tossed around in lively conversation.

Looking back, Jason realized that their relationship defied description. Neither was submissive, and neither really dominant.

They both enjoyed the roles they assigned themselves, switching from top to bottom as their games demanded, and sometimes just going straight vanilla all the way.

If fucking your girlfriend underwater at midnight in your local swimming pool, which you had quite illegally broken into, could be considered vanilla.

Jason grinned at the memory of that one. Too much chlorine had given Francesca's hair a slightly greenish tinge for a while. She'd been royally pissed even though it had been her suggestion in the first place.

He clicked his email icon.

"JB, got the deal with the pub. SOB's didn't want to up the promo budget but I persuaded them. Book 7 is awaited with avarice and glee by all concerned. Including yours truly. Any word on when? Not that I'm nagging of course…"

Jason filed the message.

When. That was the big question. This was the final book in his series. The one that would end the adventures of Darius Malcolm through the underworld of sexual exploration. Would it bring him to the light or end his existence?

The sad thing was that Jason just didn't know.

Should he allow Darius the blessing of a quiet and fulfilling relationship which would satisfy his romantically-minded readers?

Or should he, as others insisted, have Darius pay for the hearts he'd broken and the asses he'd flogged, by sending him to some kind of literary purgatory for infinity or the run of the novel through the paperback rights, whichever came first?

Or was there a third possibility? Redemption?

His agent didn't care. It was his job to make sure Jason finished it, got it edited and then turned it over to the "machine" for presentation to a greedy public.

His readers would care, of course, bless their hearts.

They were vocal, literate, kept him on his toes and had sent him mail that would have made an interesting book all on its own.

His publishers would go for the happily-ever-after, he knew. There was safety in predictability. And also cash. Lots of it.

But could *he* live with it?

Could he write about something he wasn't sure existed? He'd created a fictional world for Darius, where women and men interacted sexually in wild and often savage ways. Darius had marched through this world, using and discarding a number of women, none of whom had managed to capture his heart.

Until now. Until Cameron McKay had crossed his path, lashed him to a St. Andrew's Cross, and beaten the crap out of him. Then fucked him.

His readers would certainly never know that he'd come close to being in Darius' position.

He could still feel the cold hardness of the wooden X as Francesca had tied his wrists to the upper supports and spread his ankles wide to lash them to the feet of the cross.

Chapter 4

It was one hell of a party. Francesca had giggled as she'd told him that they'd been invited to a Dungeon. A real, honest-to-God Dungeon.

Visions of bikers and needles had flashed through Jason's mind, then he'd yanked himself out of that fifties mentality and remembered that life had changed. It was the sixties. If Francesca said it was a dungeon, then a dungeon it was.

And she'd been right.

Of course, there were few, if any, actual dungeons dotting the New England countryside. There were, however, many small towns with big old houses, once the domicile of the local landowner, and now being repurchased, remodeled, refitted, and occasionally actually lived in.

It was to one of these that the couple had driven one stormy summer night.

The trees were tossing their branches around wildly and lightning flickered on the horizon as Jason and Francesca arrived.

"And you say these people are okay?" Jason raised a quizzical eyebrow as his eyes roamed over the assortment of vehicles parked in the overgrown driveway.

There was everything from a beat-up '57 Chevy to a state of the art Cadillac, a shiny new ragtop Mustang and a couple of Harleys.

"Sure." Francesca grabbed his hand and together they walked to the open door and into another world.

Jason considered himself an educated and informed man. He'd written knowledgeably about sex, about its psychological twists and turns, and its influence over society. He'd completed his thesis and been awarded a Ph.D. in sexual psychology, albeit quietly, as the college was proud of his achievements but even prouder of their alumni donation record which might have been threatened by the news that they were now granting degrees in what amounted to S and M.

All Jason's educational experiences, however, went completely out of his mind as he stepped from the darkness into what resembled some kind of sexual Olympiad.

Through mammoth loudspeakers The Doors were begging people to "C'mon Baby, Light My Fire," the air was thick with incense, candle smoke and distinct overtones of grass, and clothing was optional. Beads were everywhere, the long tresses of the men and women blurred into a soft haze of hair intertwined with flowers, and most everyone was fucking.

Energetically.

Francesca was unfazed. She led Jason by the hand and through the throng, even waving to one girl who was being serviced by two men at the same time. And loving it to judge by her grin.

Cries told of climaxes reached, grunts and groans of sperm being released. It was primal, heady, arousing and fascinating. Jason wished for a camera, a notebook and a quiet corner so that he and Francesca could add their moans to the soundtrack.

But she hadn't stopped, merely tugged him onward until they reached a stairway leading down.

As they descended, the ambience shifted.

The music faded, the psychedelic fuck frenzy being relegated to the floors above.

Here, all was quiet. There was a rich carpet on the bare concrete, cushioning their steps, and a small corridor running the length of the house.

The Doors were picking up the pace of their music, but only the thump of the bass made it through to this darkened domain.

Jason had a whimsical image of the interior of some great beast whose heart was pounding around them.

A blonde waif with the longest hair Jason could remember seeing outside a storybook emerged from an opening.

She held a tray in front of her with several small sugar cubes on it.

Clinically, it wasn't hard to see that she'd been sampling her own offerings. Her pupils were incredibly dilated, her focus totally gone, and how she was standing upright, let alone offering her wares, was a source of astonishment.

She was also stark naked.

Francesca leaned over and kissed her cheek, but turned down the treat. Jason breathed a sigh of relief. He'd never tripped on LSD and wasn't about to start now.

"Here, Jason. In here," she said, opening a door toward the end of the corridor.

The room was small, and pretty much empty, except for a large wooden contraption in the center of the floor. It didn't take a rocket scientist to recognize a St. Andrew's Cross.

Jason gulped. He'd seen pictures of them, of course, but never actually been face-to-face with one.

Francesca quietly closed the door behind them and sealed them into their own private space. A small window allowed flickers of lightning to dance off the chrome fittings of the cross, a tall X-shaped creation made from a soft, polished wood. There were cuffs attached to the tops of the X for the wrists, and anklets at the bottom that would secure the penitent's legs apart.

For a moment, Jason allowed himself a wry chuckle at the notion of pleasure devices emerging from the torture chambers of medieval Europe. As he so often did, he reflected on how strange the world was.

Then Francesca touched him and his thoughts ground to a halt. "What do you think?"

"I don't know, sweetheart, and that's the honest truth. Would you really want me to strap you into one of these? It's so…so…medieval."

"Oh, and we haven't gotten pretty medieval already?" she laughed back at him, blue eyes dancing.

"Point taken." Jason smiled back at her, his heart warming as he watched her walk around the cross. She had become his life, his dreams, his heart. And yet he had this continuous feeling there was something that still needed to be shared. He couldn't quite put his finger on it. He reached up and slid his hand down the smooth wood. "So you want me to spank you here or what?"

Francesca tipped her head back and grinned at him. "No, babe. This isn't for me. This is for *you*."

* * * * *

For a microsecond, Jason could swear he heard Francesca's laugh in his darkened study. Night had fallen completely, and the ocean was nothing but a black mass, broken only by the rhythmic flashing of a navigational buoy bobbing in the currents.

He ached. Literally. His heart, his chest, his lungs, his cock. Everything ached for Francesca.

It was as if the scotch had unlocked a dam within his mind that had started as a small trickle but become a flood of memories, both joyous and painful. He wanted her. More now than ever, because he'd lived so much of his life without her and he wanted to share.

His business had grown exponentially with his desire for privacy, and it had been ten years or so since he'd withdrawn from public life and started writing. His financial empire was solid, his multi-million-dollar adult toy company continued to show a profit, and he wanted for nothing.

Jason crossed the room to his computer and sat down, a germ of an idea beginning to grow in his mind.

There was nothing more in the way of material things that he wanted. He'd had it all, done it all, and sold the T-shirt at a profit. He'd been convinced that the right woman was out there and had spent considerable time and a lot of money on the process of finding out who and where she was.

There had been blind dates, courtesy dates, honest and sincere dates.

And there had been fucking. Lots of fucking. Jason Burke was handsome, wealthy, and single. He could have had his choice of women any night of the week. Several of them. Together.

In fact he had. Although he'd found himself rather confused by the mechanics of several sets of legs and breasts — rather like being confronted with an entire six-course meal all at once. Where did one start?

He opened his browser and idly observed his system welcoming him personally.

There had been several women in his life who had become important to him. A couple that would have made the very best of wives. He'd come very close to finding out. Even bought a ring.

But, inevitably, it would fail. For no particular reason other than the fact that Jason's heart wasn't in it. His mind and his body were set on a course that would have led to marriage, but always his heart had stopped it. He knew it was wrong.

That "something," that spark, that shaft of desire he'd felt around Francesca was missing. And without it, there was nothing.

His fingers trembled above the keyboard as he sat poised to do something he'd never allowed himself to do. Type her name.

* * * * *

"Whoa. You can't mean me?"

The words had popped out of his mouth as soon as Francesca had told him the St. Andrew's Cross was for him.

"I don't see anyone else in here." She crossed to him and began undoing his shirt. He must have been severely stunned because he let her undress him without a murmur.

"But…but…" Oh yes. There we go. Great conversation for a Ph.D.

"Jason, what's the problem? You've let me top you before?"

Jason took a breath. "I know, honey. And it's been fun, but this…" he nodded at the shackles, "this is really intense, you know?"

She had smiled and licked his nipple. "I know."

It was that smile that was his undoing. She could smile at him and he'd move heaven and earth for her.

He noted that her hands trembled slightly as she unbuckled his belt, and was reassured. The thunder boomed in the distance, adding a very gothic note to this night, and Jason had to chuckle. "Well, we've certainly picked the right night to explore the dungeon world. Why do I keep expecting Dr. Frankenstein to make an appearance?"

Francesca grinned. "I can assure you he won't. It's just us, Jason. You and me."

She began to fasten his wrists to the cross, turning him so that the wood touched his chest. She had to stand on tiptoe to secure the buckles, but within moments he was held naked and firm, arms out to both sides and legs splayed and restrained.

Francesca moved to stand behind the cross and stared into Jason's eyes.

Her hands went to the ties on her dress and she slowly loosened them. "Jason, this night is special. It's for both of us, but mostly for you."

Her loose peasant dress slid sensuously down her arms and dropped from her breasts, leaving them bare to his gaze.

One good thing about the device that held him was the complete freedom it gave his cock to expand. And it certainly took advantage of that freedom. Especially when she moved to a small table and slipped a pile of leather straps into her hands.

She returned to her position in front of his face and shimmied her dress off her hips to the floor, leaving her naked.

"This is sort of sleazy, but fun." She giggled, shaking the leather straps out and putting her arms through them.

It was a leather bra. Without any cups, or support, just a bunch of straps that lay across her white skin and did quite awesome things to his libido.

She followed that with a couple more straps that managed to reveal her pussy while drawing the eye downward across her belly and her groin. The outfit was completed when she laced up a pair of shiny boots. Of course, she managed to flash him a large labial display as she did so.

By the time Francesca had completed her "Kitten-with-a-Whip" look, Jason was screamingly hard. One touch, and he could swear he'd shoot his load halfway down the street.

She was not unaffected. Despite the haze of his arousal, Jason could see her pulse thumping madly at the base of her neck and her nipples, taut and beaded, framed by their leather straps.

He'd bet every dime he had that her thighs were getting slick from the juices soaking the thong that passed between them.

"Jason, you've given me so much," she said, reaching for a final tool. "I have wanted to give something back to you in return, but..." she paused, shaking out her hand and letting a multitude of lengths of suede dangle down. It was a flogger.

Jason swallowed.

"You've become very special to me, and I have never let that happen before. I don't know why it's happening now. It frightens me. But my way of saying thank you is to help you experience something. Something unique."

Jason tried to look at her, but she'd walked behind him now, out of his line of sight.

"We both know that there's a special place we can go to, a mind place that holds mysteries and marvels. Where there is nothing but sensation, heat, desire, and love. The door to this place can be opened in several ways."

He felt a brush of air pass his naked legs and heard the whoosh of the flogger as it swirled behind him.

"I don't know if you've ever really been there, Jason. Ever really lost touch with who you are."

The flogger brushed the backs of his thighs and surprised a gasp from him. The mere touch had seemed like fire against his sensitized skin.

"We've used our toys and our safe words. We've played the games and the scenes. But almost always you've been calling the shots. The responsibility has been yours. Well, tonight, it's mine."

She crossed in front of him and draped the flogger tails over his cock and around his balls with a little smile. "Mmm. Pretty. Look, Jason, don't they look pretty?"

Jason dropped his eyes and watched as she slithered the black suede over his distended and rapidly purpling cock. She tugged them quickly off and the slight abrasion of his skin over his rigid arousal made his balls tingle.

Then she slid them over her breasts.

His breath left his lungs in a whoosh. She let the tails fall to either side of each nipple, then slid them down further, flicking them between her legs, and moaning a little as she caressed her clit with the gentle thud of the suede.

Jason's mouth was dry as he watched and his head spun at the erotically sexual images he was seeing. He had a feeling they'd be burned into his memory forever.

She stalked around him again, her high heels hardening the muscles of her legs and making her look like an Amazon warrior bent on invading a nation. Hell, he was ready to surrender right this second. His hands were up, and he'd welcome the chance to be raped and pillaged, and he could even go for a bit of plundering as long as her nails were cut short.

He trembled.

"So I've decided to give you access to that special place, Jason, as my gift to you."

Jason opened his mouth to respond when the first blow fell.

Chapter 5

He slumped over his keyboard and lowered his hands to his desk. He was literally shaking as he remembered that moment.

And many other moments.

He remembered her face, her touch, the smell of her hair and the little dimple in her buttock.

It seemed as though the small trickle of memories had become a raging flood, filling every square inch of his mind with images of Francesca.

All the years he'd spent pretending to himself that he'd forgotten so much about their time together were proved to be a lie. Everything was still there, buried deep in his psyche, but still there.

And now it was out.

He gasped aloud and his cock hardened as he remembered the feel of her lips. He moaned as he saw himself sinking into her cunt, and the smile on her face as she welcomed him inside her.

His chest tightened with the image of her eyes darkening as she began to orgasm around him, never breaking contact with his gaze. She stared into him as if her cunt was her soul and he was ripping it free and claiming it as his own.

He wasn't aware of the tears falling down over his cheeks until they splashed onto his hand.

He closed his eyes and leaned back, helpless to stop this flood now that it had fully begun.

His buttocks were on fire.

She'd begun her assault with a series of regular thudding strokes, warming his flesh and distracting him from his need to come.

Alternating between his buttocks and his thighs, Francesca worked the flogger with skill and precision, sometimes hard, sometimes soft, but always there, always striking him.

She was putting her heart into it, Jason knew, because he could smell her, detect that particular fragrance of woman and musk that was distinctly hers as she became aroused and sweaty. He'd recognize it anywhere.

Then the sensation changed. It became harder, stinging his warmed flesh and making him flinch a little.

He wondered if she'd changed to a different flogger, because this one was harsher and rough, and he figured it would be leaving a definite mark as she brought it down on him without pause.

His inner thighs began to receive attention, and the more delicate skin responded to the assault very rapidly.

With quick flicks, Francesca's tool bit into his flesh, raising his skin into welts and bringing choked off cry from his throat.

"You have the safe word, Jason. Use it if you need to," reminded Francesca, sounding a little breathless herself.

Jason could only nod.

His focus was changing now, as his body received the blows so lovingly administered. His skin felt like it was hanging loosely from his body, then the next instant became so tight he gritted his teeth waiting for it to split in a million places.

The blows were harder than ever, and the pain they were causing began to numb Jason's brain. He wondered if he was bleeding profusely and images of sailors' striped backs as they were flogged before the mast danced through his brain.

Then he noticed something strange was beginning to happen. He was waiting for each blow, but with less fear and more anticipation. The touch of the flogger against him was sharp and stinging, but also arousing.

The line between pain and pleasure was blurring and becoming vague, and he began to need the next lash across his flesh.

His cock was rock hard, rigid as it had ever been, and with each stroke of the tails, it seemed to harden even more.

He wanted to come, desperately, but he didn't want the flogging to stop.

His head lolled forward as yet another barrage of lashes fell on his heated skin.

He cried out as Francesca laid a strong line of blows down the backs of his thighs.

"Let go Jason," she shouted. "Let it go, my love."

He did.

His mind wallowed and shook and then slipped from his body.

He was…he was someplace else.

There were impressions of a blue sky, bluer than he could ever remember seeing. He thought he could see himself, bound to the St. Andrew's Cross, but it was vague and insubstantial.

Words formed themselves in his brain but he seemed completely unable to voice them, nor did he find that bothersome.

He was flying. Flying in a place known only to him, that was warm, comfortable and filled with a glowing sense of peace and contentment.

He didn't want to return, just to stay there forever, and leave behind his mortal self.

He drifted, time having no meaning, nor distance a dimension.

He saw places, beautiful places he felt he knew but did not recognize. There were people sometimes, but he didn't want to speak to them. Just to watch them as he flew past.

"You must come to me, now, Jason," said a soft voice. He sensed a presence surrounding him, enfolding him in its warmth and love. It was a comforting presence, one he could attach himself to and become a part of without difficulty.

It seemed that he was sinking, dropping, lowering himself into a shell. The shell began to shake.

He opened his eyes to find himself against the cross, with Francesca unfastening his bonds.

His legs were useless, but she caught him and helped him lie down on the soft rug, cuddling him, gentling him, stroking him as his body relearned the process of functioning as a mortal being.

Her hands brought him peace and comfort as sensation returned and the ache in his buttocks made itself known. She ran her hands down his stomach and cradled his cock, which was still hard and distended.

He sighed with pleasure as she lowered her mouth to take him between her lips.

The softness of her tongue against the hardness of his arousal was extraordinary bliss for Jason. Still caught in the mental after effects of his "flight" into enlightenment, this particular experience took on surreal overtones. His balls felt like rocks and he was sure that he could feel each and every hair as it responded to her breath.

Her soft mouth and hard teeth were sharp contrasts in sensation against his skin, and her teasing flick to the little sweet spot just below the tip was a combination of pain and ecstasy. Her strokes were firm and knowing, and coupled with a fierce suckling brought him to the edge within what felt like seconds.

"Francesca," he gasped, finally finding his voice again.

She glanced up at him, eyes shining, but never stopping her movements on his cock.

He was helpless and surrendered to her with a willingness he'd never imagined.

His buttocks tightened, a shaft of electricity shot down his spine into his balls, and he began to come down her throat, spurting with a cry of pleasure that felt like it had been ripped from his lungs.

She sucked him dry, pulling every last drop of cum from the tiny eye and working his cock as he spurted everything he had, everything he was, into her.

He didn't know he was crying, until he felt her wipe the tears away.

Tears like the ones her memory invoked.

The ones he was crying now.

* * * * *

The scotch was finished and the glass sat empty, an accurate reflection of his life, thought Jason wryly.

His body still ached, as if reliving the punishment he'd received at Francesca's hands while lashed to the cross. His cock was hard, but he could deal with it.

He hadn't lived as long as he had without learning control.

Restlessly he stood, fighting against the dizziness that his emotional onslaught had produced.

A glass of ice water calmed him slightly, and he was surprised to find himself damp with sweat as well as his own tears.

Dear God, someone should rename that scotch "Old Catharsis." A couple of swallows and he'd opened up like a parched flower after a rainstorm.

And in some strange way he felt better because of it. At least he'd faced his memories and let them loose. And he was still alive.

Albeit still alone.

Sadly, he faced something he should have admitted years before.

He needed Francesca Dalton. Needed her with every fiber of his being, every particle of his existence.

And it had been his fault she'd gone and left him.

A stupid thing. A silly thing and the door had closed behind her.

Although God knew she hadn't considered it stupid. Only *he* had had that pleasure, for many years afterwards.

Stupid, stupid, stupid.

Donna had called him.

Donna his ex-fiancée.

They'd been engaged just after high school until wiser heads prevailed and encouraged them both to wait. But the sex had been hotter than hot for both of them, and although they'd gone their separate ways, they had never forgotten those stolen moments.

It had been a huge surprise for Jason to hear her voice on the phone.

"Hi hot pants," she said, bringing a smile to his face. "I'm in town for a day or so and wanted to say hello and touch base. You got any time free?"

It so happened he did, as Francesca was at a conference at a nearby college all day and into the evening. He was looking forward to introducing them, believing that everyone in the world would find Francesca as wonderful as he did.

As a matter of fact, he might well hint to Donna that he'd finally found "the one," the woman he wanted for ever and ever, 'til death did them part, etc. etc. He wondered if Donna was married.

She wasn't.

And it was pretty obvious that she remembered their time together as well. She arrived at his apartment, having suggested they meet there as she didn't want to drive all over town in traffic.

And damn, she looked wonderful.

The old Donna with the long lank hair and the beaded headband had given way to a slim sensual woman with blonde streaked and tousled hair tossed into a sexy mess. Her breasts were unconfined beneath her soft shirt and her legs revealed by a pair of very short shorts.

He could tell right away she was after more than an afternoon of reminiscing. It could have been the way she plastered herself against him when he opened the door, or perhaps it was the thrust of her hips into his groin that clued him in. Or no, wait, maybe it was the tonsillectomy she tried to administer—with her tongue.

Whatever it was, it hadn't fazed him. Much. Hey, he was a guy after all. And it was the sixties.

They'd shared a beer, or two, followed by a little tequila. They'd laughed as they remembered the first time they'd tried to master the coordinated dance between lemon and salt.

More tequila followed.

Donna politely offered to share a joint, and Jason, buzzing a little by this point, accepted.

They laughed their way through their past adventures as the shadows began to fall outside. Donna's lips grew pinker and Jason found himself fascinated by her mouth. Had she always had a lower lip that looked made for sinning?

It was the conversation about Francesca that had started the slow slide into disaster. He began to tell Donna about her. About how he felt, what he wanted, his future plans.

Donna nodded and sighed, and fiddled with her buttons, slipping a couple free.

"I'm happy for you, honey," she said, with a rather wistful smile. "I'm separated, employed, and self-sufficient. A truly modern woman. But I do miss one thing…"

She opened a couple more buttons and let Jason see that she, too, had given up wearing a bra. Damn, this new world was making it hard for men to go about their business on a daily basis without a semi-permanent hard-on.

Jason stood, a little high, a little uncomfortable and, yes, slightly aroused. Well, maybe more aroused than "slightly."

Donna had always had the most wonderful breasts.

And now he could see that they hadn't changed, since she had discarded the notion of keeping her shirt buttoned at all.

Oh look. She was pressing them against him. And my, wasn't that a nice feeling?

"Donna, honey," he said, backing up to the kitchen counter.

"God Jason, just once more, for old time's sake. Please…"

She'd pulled his T-shirt up and rubbed herself against his bare flesh sending a completely reflex shiver over him.

In a flash his jeans were unzipped and her fingers thrust inside. Since Francesca had long since convinced him that underwear was an unnecessary waste of time, his cock fell straight into Donna's waiting hands.

And she was more than ready for it.

Hobbled by his pants and numbed by the tequila and the grass, Jason could only watch in aroused confusion as she slid down his body, pressing her breasts around his cock and finally ending up with it in her mouth.

She knew all his weaknesses and used every one of them. Within seconds he was putty in her hands. Or, more accurately, her mouth.

She worked him with enthusiastic skill and he couldn't help but respond, thrusting his hips toward her and holding the back of her head as she pulled at him with her tongue.

She was moaning and caressing her breasts, as aroused as he, so it was no surprise to find that a few moments later he was on the floor, on his back, with Donna whisking herself out of her shorts.

Within seconds she was astride him, riding him, clutching him desperately with her hands and pulling his head to her breasts.

He half sat up and she wriggled until her legs were behind him, holding him deep inside her.

She sighed with pleasure. "Oh Jason, yeah, fuck me hot pants." The words tumbled from her lips, turning Jason on as much as her breasts and the feel of her cunt sliding over his cock.

He slid one hand down and found her clit, slick with her own moisture and protruding hard and ready from its hiding place within her folds.

He knew just where to touch.

She screamed and came, orgasm after orgasm shaking her body as it clasped his.

He lost control and erupted, grunting and thrusting deep inside her as her spasms pulled his seed from deep within his balls.

It was all over within moments and one thought surfaced in Jason's mind, chilling him like a bucket of cold water thrown in his face.

Francesca!

He opened his eyes. Blue eyes stared back at him.

Francesca was standing in the kitchen watching him.

She had seen it all.

The sound of the door slamming behind her was the sound of his life shattering around him, and that life would forever be changed.

He couldn't have known that *then*, but he certainly knew it *now*.

Chapter 6

The soft glow of his monitors brought a twisted smile to Jason's lips. How simple things would have been back then if he'd had the resources of the Internet at his disposal.

He could have deluged her with emails that she'd have to have accepted one way or another, instead of ignoring his letters and cards.

He could have tried her cell phone as well as her land line and left messages on her machines from here to Tuesday, instead of repeatedly being given the cold shoulder by an endless ring and finally a polite message saying the number was not in service at that time.

He could have traced her movements somehow, instead of letting her completely slip away from him like an insubstantial dream that was never real in the first place. In spite of staking out her apartment, her friends' apartments, and any other place he could think of, she'd vanished. Just poofed out of existence into thin air.

The last he'd seen of her was her blonde hair flying as she'd fled his kitchen, leaving him on the floor gazing at Donna in a horrified stupor.

It had been so stupid of him.

But was it bad enough for Francesca to walk out of his life forever?

As time passed, the pain had given way to anger. Why? Why had she just dropped him like a hot potato? Why hadn't she given him chance to explain? Or at least try to apologize, humble himself, grovel, whatever it took to keep them together? Didn't she care enough? Maybe she had someone else on the side waiting for her.

Wild and furious thoughts had stampeded through Jason's mind as he tried to pick up the trappings of his life and carry on without Francesca.

Then the offer of an appointment on the West Coast had arrived, and it was decision time. It didn't take long for Jason Burke to pack up his belongings and set out to start over as a member of a clinical practice specializing in sexual dysfunctions.

He'd never looked back, shutting the door to his memories of the years with Francesca, and rigidly prohibiting himself from wallowing in the past. And until tonight he'd kept that rule.

It had taken a small bottle of scotch to open that door again and make him face the truth, ugly though it was. He'd fallen in love and lost her, and his life had never really recovered from it.

But damn it all, it had been a wild time back then. No one talked about forever, being firmly convinced that humanity would end up being nuked out of existence.

The serene fifties were over, as was the notion of women-as-homemakers, and suddenly it was peace, love and rock and roll. Bring on the Pill, take off the bra and let's live together with fifteen other people and have lots of stoned sex.

Okay, so he'd passed on the commune scene, but the stoned sex had been great and Francesca with no bra—well, hell.

A sudden pain crushed Jason's lungs and he struggled to draw in a breath as he visualized those breasts he'd cherished for hours upon end.

In fact he'd been doing just that on the one rare occasion when she'd spoken of her past.

"I love how you do that."

Jason grunted around a mouthful of nipple. His tongue teased and twirled the bud, bringing it to a hardened peak and then laving it softly, letting it relax a little while he transferred his attentions to the other breast.

They were in bed—no surprise there—and it was a very cool night. Francesca had her period, and in a surprising display of maidenly modesty, never allowed him to touch her during those days. She said it just wasn't right.

It wouldn't have bothered him, but he respected her wishes, and merely talked her into letting him play a little while promising not to take her until she said it was okay.

So they were snuggled under a warm quilt, Jason in his usual state of nudity, Francesca with her pajama bottoms firmly in place. And Jason's mouth having fun.

She'd snuffled with pleasure as he'd suckled her, sighing and moaning her feelings into his ears as she ran her fingers through his hair. He'd rested one hand across her belly, knowing she loved the warmth of him seeping through into her pelvis and relaxing her cramps at that particular time.

"Ah, Jason, you feel so good," she murmured.

"You love to be cuddled, don't you," he answered around her flesh. "I've noticed that."

She chuckled. "Yeah, I guess I do. I remember…" She paused, and Jason's head raised up, watching her carefully.

"You remember what, sweetheart?" he encouraged.

She sighed. "I remember being cuddled when I was a little girl. My parents weren't very big on displays of affection, but my Mom did spend the afternoons with me, cuddling me as we played or read together. Then sometimes she'd let me watch a little television, but not much."

Francesca shifted a little on the bed, and Jason stretched his length beside her, still warming her stomach, but resting his head on his bent arm, listening to her. "You don't mention your parents very much," he said quietly.

"No. No, I guess I don't." She closed her eyes briefly. "My mother passed away when I was fifteen. My father…well, my father…he's another story."

"A good one or a bad one? Will you tell me?"

There was silence for a moment and Jason could see Francesca considering her words carefully.

"A little bit of both, I guess." Her lips twisted. "He loved me, that's for sure. But I guess he didn't love my Mom so much. They split when I was about nine or ten."

It was a casual comment, but coming from Francesca, Jason knew it was a very important one. "I'm so sorry, honey," he said carefully.

"I guess it was for the best. I found out later that he'd had a girlfriend on the side. She was in a nearby town and he traveled a lot—more than he needed to, it turned out. Almost like a dual life really. She was pretty."

"It sounds as though you met her?"

"I didn't actually get introduced, if that's what you mean. But I did see her. And him."

"Ah. Together, I take it."

"Yeah. Together. I couldn't understand why Dad would leave Mom and me and what they told me about not being in love with each other enough and all that stuff that parents who are splitting tell their kids—it didn't make sense to me. I had to find out for myself."

Jason tugged her closer to him, enfolding her in his warmth. Her hands were clenching and he doubted she even realized how tense she was.

"So I saved up my allowance and took the bus one afternoon during school vacation. I had written down his other address from my Mom's address book, and it wasn't hard to find." She sighed and turned her head away from Jason.

"They were there. Both of them. I saw them through the window. Then I left and came home."

"I saw them through the window."

Jason nearly jumped out of his computer chair as Francesca's words from nearly forty years ago echoed through his mind.

God damn. That was the reason she'd cut him out of her life. He'd done what her father had done. He'd bet every penny he possessed that a little ten year old had peeked through a window and seen her father loving another woman. And years later, she'd walked in and seen another man betraying her.

Could even be that the kitchen was a common theme, too.

Jason mentally smacked his hand against his forehead. How stupid could one man be? Why had he never made the connection? Oh sure, he'd drawn parallels, father leaving, shattering family, betraying their love and trust, etc. Then boyfriend fucking other woman, betraying love, and so on.

But adding the visual component into the equation made her subsequent actions much more understandable.

Jason had always considered it overly dramatic of her to just up and vanish. He'd become angry and hurt by that. And his anger and hurt and guilt had clouded his thinking and twisted his emotions. Moving away had just about capped the entire process.

Now it was a lot more understandable. Away from the heat of their passions, Jason could think clearly about it, something he'd forbidden himself for so long.

He sighed. Once again he'd been a super, flaming, idiot. Look up the word "dolt" in the dictionary and he was convinced he'd see his picture. How was it that he could amass a very tidy fortune, run a large company, write best-selling books and still, in spite of all that, act like a complete raving maniac?

He glanced down at his crotch and wondered if the feminist jokes might just be closer to the target than they realized. Sometimes men *did* let their dicks do their thinking for them. And they had one-track minds with no room for the subtleties of life.

The pain around his heart eased as he felt a rush of adrenaline flood his system. He leaned forward and hit some keys on his keyboard, activating one of his many business resources.

It was time to find Francesca.

* * * * *

It was Jason's favorite "scene."

His four-poster bed, the coverlet pulled aside, and Francesca sprawled on top of it, arms and legs tied to the corners with his specially-purchased straps.

Occasionally he would blindfold her, as he had done this particular night. Then he would take his time preparing his toys letting a few quiet sounds thread their way to her ears, which he knew would be straining to catch a hint of what he had planned.

Just restraining her was arousing in and of itself, and by the time he had her blindfold in place he was hard as a rock and then some.

This night would be one of sensory pleasure for both of them. He began by pulling a drawer open and removing the feather duster he'd found at a local five and dime.

The motherly salesclerk had smiled approvingly at his purchase, no doubt relishing the sight of such a nice man who wanted a clean house. If she only knew.

He knelt on the bed, letting it bounce with his weight and telling Francesca where he was. She was wet and glistening, her folds swelling a little as he sat there enjoying the view.

"Jason," she whispered. "What are you doing?"

"Looking at you," he answered, grinning. He knew that she was, like many women, insecure about her body. God alone knew why, because it looked damn fine to him. Especially from this angle. But she could never see the appeal, and he loved to tease her a little by doing just what he was doing. Looking at her.

Sure enough, she squirmed. "Jason." The hiss was accompanied by a blush.

Time to put her out of her misery. He leaned over and ran the feathers up the inside of her thigh, barely touching the skin.

She jumped as if he'd branded her. "Oh my God. What is that?"

Jason leaned up and kissed her firmly on the mouth. "Shhh."

She subsided, trembling a little as he flicked the duster over other sensitive parts of her sprawled body.

Within ten minutes of this she was soaking wet, shaking, moaning and begging for release.

And he'd only just begun.

He moved off the bed and heard her sigh as the springs bounced up. He dropped the duster and reached for his new toy. Finding this in a second hand store had been a real coup, and he'd been playing with it all week, using his own body as a test, making sure he knew how to handle it to cause the most pleasure and, coincidentally, the least damage.

He returned to Francesca and stood by the bed. Then he leaned down, pressed his mouth over hers, thrust his tongue inside and ran his new toy up her body from her clit to her throat.

His mouth muffled her scream.

Then he ran it around her breasts and swallowed another cry.

Lightening his pressure, he ran it around her aroused nipples, in quick, teasing strokes. She moaned and he judged it safe to stop kissing her. She was accustoming herself to his touch and probably wouldn't scream the house down now.

"What the hell…Jason…what is that?" she sputtered as he pulled back.

"Like it?"

"I—I don't know. It's prickly, but it doesn't really hurt—it kind of tingles, you know?"

He ran the small spiked wheel back down over her belly to her clit and gently rolled it around.

"Oh God, Jason…" Her thigh muscles tightened and Jason watched her carefully, noting the flush on her breasts and the shudders that racked her thighs.

She was getting very close to her orgasm, and he wasn't ready to let her have it—yet.

He backed off, and she grunted. "Please, let me—God, Jason—don't stop..." Her fractured thoughts echoed the twitchings he could see in her pussy, and he smiled to himself. This was going to be a night she'd long remember.

He kept up his play for an amazingly long time. He'd bring her to the very brink of her climax, then let her down a little, never permitting her to come but keeping her simmering, just below the threshold of no return.

Finally, she was sobbing and his cock reminded him that if he didn't want to go through the rest of his life with a petrified set of balls clanking in his trousers he'd better shoot his load damn quick.

It was time.

He tossed the little pinwheel aside and used the head of his cock this time, soothing the sticky honey of her cunt over her hot and swollen tissues. She spread her legs as wide as she could, lost in another world of sensation and need, quiet now, waiting for his intrusion into her body.

Slowly and lovingly, he claimed her body with his, sliding his cock through the ocean of her juices into the snug harbor that awaited him.

He pulled back and thrust again, more forcefully this time, and found a nipple to tease as he did so.

Restrained as she was, she could only writhe beneath him, letting him know how welcome his touch was, and how much she wanted him deep inside her.

He repeated his movements, getting faster and pushing harder against her.

Francesca's body was ready. It had been ready for quite some time now, and it strained for release.

She tensed beneath him, welcoming the pounding of his body against hers, tilting her hips, crying out as he thrust into her.

He slipped his hand between them and found her clit, rubbing it hard as he fucked her with every inch of his body. His balls were twisting themselves into knots, Francesca was crying out his name, and moments later the world ended for both of them.

With a prolonged shout, he came, buttocks rigid, teeth bared, every muscle in his body straining to push his seed deep into his woman.

She lay beneath him and throbbed. Her cunt gripped and released his cock in pulses so strong he wondered if she'd broken it.

It went on and on and Jason's mind flew along with the spurtings of his cum as he emptied his soul into her.

They were both crying, sobbing with pleasure as the sensations eased, and their heart rates dropped from redline to somewhere approaching human again.

"Jason, I flew."

Chapter 7

Francesca's voice sounded as clear to Jason at that moment as it had nearly forty years ago when he held her tightly in his arms and let them both recover from another in their long list of amazing sexual adventures.

He could see now, from the perspective of time and maturity, that the sex was simply the tip of the iceberg. It had brought them together and taken them on a wild journey, but the compatibility had run much deeper than a simple ability to come together. Their minds were in tune, their hearts happy to have found a mate, and their souls were on their way to eternal bliss.

If only it hadn't all fallen apart.

And was there any chance that he could find her again and at least say "I'm sorry?" A chance that she might look at him from those blue eyes of hers and smile and say "I forgive you?"

An idea walloped Jason around the ear, an idea for the ending of his seventh book. Darius and Cameron, together at last, redeemed by their love for each other and saved from spending their lives in darkness by the one small coincidence that would reunite them.

It hadn't happened that way for him, but he would make it happen for his characters.

Three hours later, it was done.

"The End" had been typed, Darius had had his last—and most satisfying—orgasm inside Cameron's willing body, and the readers would be left with a sigh, a smile and the possibility that at long last Darius could rest. Maybe even a child for Cameron.

He'd left the door open on that one.

As if his body recognized the moment as an epiphany, a wave of weariness swept over Jason and he slumped in his chair, waiting for the weakness to pass. There was always a "down" moment at the end of a book, but this one was quite strong.

The world was quiet beneath his windows, and hushed within his study.

Jason sat forward again, and placed his hands on his keyboard. It was time to end his saga, too.

He typed her name in his search engine.

Damn. Thousands of hits. Apparently the Progressive China Company had issued a pattern called "Francesca" some years ago. Collectors wanted it.

Hookay. Time to refine the search.

Jason's years of familiarity with the Internet paid off, and within half an hour he was down to one hundred and twenty seven hits.

Finally, he tossed in the name of her college and hit Enter.

"Francesca Dalton, Arts '68, Survived by…"

His mind blanked and the screen turned into a jumble of meaningless rubbish.

Survived by?

The humming in his ears subsided, only to be replaced by a gentle buzzing. His chest felt tight, and numbness was spreading from his toes upwards. He took a deep breath and clicked the link.

Four pop-ups and two mis-clicks later, he had it. An entry from her old collegiate newspaper.

"Survived by her aunt and cousins. Succumbed to injuries received after being involved in a multi-car collision."

The date was not too long after he'd last seen her. And not too long before he'd left for the West Coast.

She had never come back because she couldn't.

She was dead.

Jason's mind shut down. He closed his eyes and leaned back, waiting for the pain he knew would come. Trying to come to terms with the fact that his mate on this earth had been gone for all these years. He had buried her memory deep in his soul not knowing that her body had been buried so long ago.

Why had nobody told him? They may not have known and he was so busy getting ready for his trip, who could have caught him?

These things happened, he knew, but not to Francesca. Please God, not to Francesca? Did she think about him before…before…

The pain came.

Rolling in thunderous waves over Jason, he gasped at its onslaught. His breath cramped in his lungs and his arms screamed as the muscles quivered. His gut clenched against it and he bit his lip to stop himself from screaming.

She was gone. He couldn't come to terms with it. He couldn't accept it or live with it.

She was gone. Forever.

He sobbed out a cry, gasping in air to replace it and fill his starved lungs. His vision faded, the blackness creeping into his soul stealing the light from his eyes as well.

"Francesca…" To his own mind he yelled her name into the dark, but it might have been a whisper for all he knew.

He struggled to breathe, suddenly realizing that his body was betraying him. This was not grief, or pain, or loss, this was something else.

Fear warred with pain and for a few moments Jason Burke fought against his destiny.

But then the pain vanished and the light returned to his eyes.

A warm light, pulling him from his chair.

"You must come to me now, Jason."

Her words. From so long ago. Bringing him down from his flight. This time they were encouraging him to take a new one.

His heart swelled as he heard her clearly for the first time in too many years.

"I'm here, my love. Forgive me?"

"There is nothing to forgive, Jason. We just had to reach the right time. I've been waiting for you…"

And the light-that-was-Jason slowly rose from the slumped figure sitting before the computer monitors, and joined the light-that-was-Francesca.

A new journey was beginning.

Epilogue

The somber group walked through the quiet cemetery to the place where a small tent had been erected.

Simon Austen had his arm around his wife's shoulders, and Adam and Laura Burns held hands.

Adele Martin followed, chatting quietly to Maria Delgado Arrivas, who had been Jason Burke's housekeeper for many years. She was still in a certain amount of shock after learning that Jason had left the apartment building to her.

"I cannot believe it, Ms. Martin," she said, her slight accent making Adele smile. "That he should be so kind to me, when all I did was clean for him and nag him to put his socks in the hamper."

"You cared for him, Mrs. Arrivas. That would have been enough for Jason."

Eve Austen caught Adele's comment and turned, her eyes still slightly red from her tears. She had known and liked Jason Burke. She would miss him.

"Adele's right, Maria. You know Jason was a quiet man, but he was very aware of the people around him and what they were thinking and feeling. I guess that's what made him such a good writer."

There was silence for a moment as everyone struggled to come to terms with the fact that their reclusive landlord had been a best-selling author and multimillionaire.

"I have all his books, you know," said Adam Burns.

"And I'm reading them now, too," added Laura. "They're really quite amazing." She glanced at her husband and smiled. "On so many levels."

They reached the tent and seated themselves. There were few other mourners present, Jason's request for privacy having been rigidly honored by his attorney.

Only his agent, his lawyer and the few invited guests were present for this ceremony. The world would learn later that renowned author JB Sims had succumbed to a heart attack and passed away on the same night he'd finished his final book.

The appropriate words were said, and the appropriate thoughts expressed. Each of the mourners shared this acknowledgement of the fragility of life with one other, and honored the quiet man who had touched their lives in a variety of different ways.

A figure neared the group and Adele glanced over as the movement caught her eye.

She froze.

It was Brian.

Eve nudged her. "Jason told me once that he'd let a special person slide from his life long ago, and he'd regretted it ever since. I couldn't let you make the same mistake." She nodded her head toward Brian. "I called him."

Adele's throat closed and words failed her. The nature of this moment, standing near the casket of a person who had been alive such a short time before, hammered home to her the need for honesty, the need for companionship, and the need to take a risk.

Before it was too late.

She slipped away from the group and walked toward Brian.

He watched her, eyes somber and concerned.

The sun shone on him, bringing blue sparks from his eyes and making him so beautiful that Adele's heart turned over in her chest. She swallowed it back down and stopped a short distance from him.

She saw his throat move as he swallowed. She opened her mouth, but the words wouldn't come. The tears did instead.

Brian said nothing. He simply opened his arms.

With a sob, Adele ran to him, throwing herself into his embrace and almost knocking him over.

He caught her and locked his arms around her, nearly crushing her ribcage. She couldn't have cared if he'd dislocated three vertebrae while he was at it. She was where she belonged. With her man. At last.

"Well dammit, woman. Took you long enough. Why the hell did you have to wait until someone died to come to your senses?"

Adele snorted through her tears as she gazed up at his dear face. "Because I'm a fucking idiot?"

"Got that right." Brian tried a wobbly smile of his own. "Oh damn." He lowered his face to hers and kissed her gently, bringing more tears to her eyes and opening her heart to the sunshine that she felt was surrounding them.

It was a blissful moment. "I love you, Brian McMillan."

"Yes you do. I always knew that. You had to find out for yourself though, just exactly what that meant."

Adele leaned against him. God bless men with big chests. "If you are going to spend the rest of our lives together being so damnably right, I may just have to shoot you."

"I'll work on it. I promise." He hugged her close again and rubbed his chin through her hair. "But you have to make me a promise too."

She nodded, too content to move. "Anything."

Beneath her ear his chest rumbled with his laughter. "Dangerous words, my love. I might hold you to that. But what I really want is your promise that you will never, ever, even for one tiny moment, think that I only care about what I see. I want you to promise me, right this minute, that you will always believe I love you, the person, the Adele who is inside, not the Adele that the world sees every day."

"I promise, Brian. I promise." Adele said the words with her heart and her soul, knowing that she meant them. Brian loved *her*, the real her, the thoughts, feelings, desires and emotions that were uniquely Adele Martin. She'd had enough time to know that he meant what he said.

And God knew she loved him right back.

"And in return, I promise to live the rest of my life loving you. You're my other half. My soulmate. Whatever the right word is…"

"Oh those'll do very nicely," sighed Adele.

"Good. Let's say goodbye to Jason together and then go start living our new life, shall we? We've got things to do, places to go, beds to try out…"

Adele shushed him with her hand, as she led him back to the side of the grave.

The sunlight had become even brighter, reflecting the emotions on the faces of those gathered to say their final farewells.

Each took a flower from the arrangement and walked to the casket.

Eve and Simon went first, Eve with two roses, Simon with just one.

"Goodbye and Godspeed, Jason," said Eve. "I consider myself honored to have known you. As one life ends, so another begins…"

She placed one rose on the casket and touched the other to her stomach, smiling as she did so. Then she added it to the two roses resting on the shiny wood.

The others looked questioningly at both Eve and Simon.

Simon smiled. "If it's a boy, we're thinking of calling him Jason."

Both Eve and Simon were ruthlessly hugged by everyone and chaos reigned for a few moments before Adam and Laura stepped up with their flowers.

"I wish I'd known you better, Jason," said Adam. "But as it is, I have read your words and learned from them. I'm just one of many who will cherish your books. You've left a true legacy for generations to come, and in my book, that's a sign of a life well-lived."

He reverently placed his rose on the pile and stepped back, letting Laura add hers. She said nothing, just lowered her head for a moment, then glanced at Adam, waiting for his hand.

Together they turned and left.

Finally, it was Adele's turn, and Brian stood with his arms around her as she placed her rose with the tribute.

"Thank you Jason. For being wise enough to see your mistake and for indirectly stopping me for making the same one. I hope that wherever you are, you have found contentment."

She and Brian turned away, and within minutes the only sound was a soft birdsong trilling through the bright sunshine.

* * * * *

Elsewhere and elsewhen...

"Well, I think that was quite lovely," sighed the light-that-was-Francesca.

The light-that-was-Jason chuckled. "Yeah. I guess. Sort of odd, though, watching one's own funeral."

They withdrew from the quiet tableau, taking some of the brilliance of the sunlight with them as they faded from that dimensional existence.

"Well, where to this time, babe?" The light-that-was-Jason snuggled up to his mate, and tickled her with rays of brilliance in colors that defied description.

The light-that-was-Francesca giggled. "We could go to Arcturus again..."

"Oh no. I don't think so. Too many tentacles and I couldn't find your hot spots underneath that damned exoskeleton. Mind you the beaches were nice…"

"What about being human again?"

The light-that-was-Jason sighed. "I don't know. That one was rough. Especially without you. I think we should pick someplace where we stand a better chance of sharing a long life. It was so…so uncomfortable without you. Mind you, the sex was great…"

The light-that-was-Francesca flashed a twinkle at him.

"Oh wait a minute…" The light-that-was-Jason sparkled excitedly. "How about Argosy 9? I hear tell that they've just about perfected an anti-gravity unit. That might be fun…" His tone indicated that if he'd possessed something as corporeal as eyebrows, he'd be waggling them suggestively.

He received a non-corporeal elbow to his metaphorical ribs. "Can't you think of anything but fucking?"

"Like what?"

There was silence for a moment as the light-that-was-Francesca considered the question. "Good point. Argosy 9 it is. But first…"

Other lights who ventured too close quickly turned away in embarrassment. The light-that-was-Jason and the light-that-was-Francesca were doing a little non-corporeal merging. And in public too.

The flash of incredible luminescence that lit up the sky puzzled astronomers on Earth for weeks.

They couldn't have known it was two souls finding each other and two beings from another dimension loving each other.

They would never have considered that it might mark the beginning of a new journey, a new set of adventures and a new existence on a planet they hadn't even heard of yet.

They would never have guessed, not in a million light years, that it was the ethereal essence of male and female enjoying that most universal of activities.

A damn good fuck.

The End

About the author:

Born and raised in England not far from Jane Austen's home, reading historical romances came naturally to Ms. Kelly, followed by writing them under the name of Sarah Fairchilde. Previously published by Zebra/Kensington, Ms. Kelly found a new love - romanticas! Happily married for almost twenty years, Sahara is thrilled to be part of the Ellora's Cave family of talented writers. She notes that her husband and teenage son are a bit stunned at her latest endeavor, but are learning to co-exist with the rather unusual assortment of reference books and sites!

Sahara welcomes mail from readers. You can write to her c/o Ellora's Cave Publishing at 1337 Commerce Drive, Suite 13, Stow OH 44224.

Why an electronic book?

We live in the Information Age—an exciting time in the history of human civilization in which technology rules supreme and continues to progress in leaps and bounds every minute of every hour of every day. For a multitude of reasons, more and more avid literary fans are opting to purchase e-books instead of paperbacks. The question to those not yet initiated to the world of electronic reading is simply: *why?*

1. *Price.* An electronic title at Ellora's Cave Publishing runs anywhere from 40-75% less than the cover price of the <u>exact same title</u> in paperback format. Why? Cold mathematics. It is less expensive to publish an e-book than it is to publish a paperback, so the savings are passed along to the consumer.

2. *Space.* Running out of room to house your paperback books? That is one worry you will never have with electronic novels. For a low one-time cost, you can purchase a handheld computer designed specifically for e-reading purposes. Many e-readers are larger than the average handheld, giving you plenty of screen room. Better yet, hundreds of titles can be stored within your new library—a single microchip. (Please note that Ellora's Cave does not endorse any specific brands. You can check our website at www.ellorascave.com for customer

recommendations we make available to new consumers.)

3. *Mobility.* Because your new library now consists of only a microchip, your entire cache of books can be taken with you wherever you go.

4. *Personal preferences are accounted for.* Are the words you are currently reading too small? Too large? Too…**ANNOYING**? Paperback books cannot be modified according to personal preferences, but e-books can.

5. *Innovation.* The way you read a book is not the only advancement the Information Age has gifted the literary community with. There is also the factor of what you can read. Ellora's Cave Publishing will be introducing a new line of interactive titles that are available in e-book format only.

6. *Instant gratification.* Is it the middle of the night and all the bookstores are closed? Are you tired of waiting days—sometimes weeks—for online and offline bookstores to ship the novels you bought? Ellora's Cave Publishing sells instantaneous downloads 24 hours a day, 7 days a week, 365 days a year. Our e-book delivery system is 100% automated, meaning your order is filled as soon as you pay for it.

Those are a few of the top reasons why electronic novels are displacing paperbacks for many an avid reader. As always, Ellora's Cave Publishing welcomes your questions and comments. We invite you to email us at service@ellorascave.com or write to us directly at: 1337 Commerce Drive, Suite 13, Stow OH 44224.

Discover for yourself why readers can't get enough of the multiple award-winning publisher Ellora's Cave. Whether you prefer e-books or paperbacks, be sure to visit EC on the web at www.ellorascave.com for an erotic reading experience that will leave you breathless.

WWW.ELLORASCAVE.COM

Printed in the United States
31216LVS00001B/94-306

9 781419 951350